Mark: Eyewitness

Ellen Gunderson Traylor

Tyndale House
Publishers, Inc.
Wheaton, Illinois

Special Hardcover Edition for
FAMILY BOOKSHELF: 1990

Cover illustration by Corbert Gauthier

Scripture references are from the
New International Version of the Bible.

Library of Congress Catalog Card Number 89-50624
ISBN 0-8423-4102-1

1 2 3 4 5 6 7 8 94 93 92 91 90 89

To my father,
Dr. Herbert E. Gunderson,
who, like Mark,
is "useful for the ministry"

2 Timothy 4:11

Mark's story is the story of the church.
He is, therefore,
as much alive today as 2,000 years ago. . . .

CONTENTS

PROLOGUE

The Church is not a human institution. It is composed of flawed human beings, but is nevertheless a supernatural entity.

Invading the stream of history "when the fullness of time had come," it turned the world upside down and inside out. No secular historian has ever explained the phenomenon of its emergence or the incredible impact its existence has had upon society worldwide.

Believers and unbelievers alike, who live within the light and shadow of the two-thousand-year-old Church, cannot appreciate how revolutionary a force it has been.

To write of the early Church, the birth and growth of Christ's beloved, is to take on an enormous task. But when it is told as seen through the eyes of one man—one who was there, who witnessed each labor pain, each toddling step, each spurt of growth—the task becomes more manageable.

Perhaps more than any other individual in the New Testament, John Mark epitomizes the saga of the Church. For him, the reality of a movement, a force that transcended race, culture, heritage, and politics, was most pointed. And the reality of a people, who by virtue of their simple faith, overwhelmed an empire, played upon his life as upon few others.

The story of the Church is Mark's story, however, for deeper reasons than politics and human history. It is his story, and he is its story because the work of Christ transcends failure, inadequacy, pride, and compulsion. The life of the Church is meant to be a life of usefulness, power, and rest.

Mark needed to learn this, as must we all.

So his story is also the story of every Christian, the tale of every man and woman purchased by the blood of Christ.

Ellen Traylor
Spokane, Washington

"For Moses said, 'Honor your father and your mother. . . .' " Then Jesus said to them, "Give to Caesar what is Caesar's and to God what is God's." And they were amazed at him.
Mark 7:10; 12:17

PART ONE

Darkness

Why do the nations conspire
and the peoples plot in vain?

PSALM 2:1

CHAPTER

1

Date:
Autumn, A.D. 32
Place:
Cyrene, Province of Cyrenaica—North Africa

A sultry breeze, like the lisp of a soft-chanting goddess, swept over the baths of Apollo's precinct. Steam rose from the surface of the long pools, clinging to the massive Doric pillars that supported the colonnade's gabled roof.

"The breath of Cyrene," some called this evening wind, believing it to be the protective spirit of the nymph for whom their city was named. Cyrene, gem of the southern Mediterranean, was a proud place—proud of its heritage and prestigious reputation.

Tonight the temple court was robed in the purple glow of sunset. The regal hue played majestically against the patina of the columns, personifying them into rows of brooding monarchs.

Few of the spa's occupants contemplated the surroundings. To the wealthy and privileged citizens who frequented the baths, the beauty of the evening was commonplace. They may have appreciated it when in youth they had first visited the sacred baths. But now, middle-aged or older, almost all took for granted the poetry of the place, leaning their heads, eyes closed, against the poolside, as they rested their pampered bodies in the water.

Though the sea was seventeen miles north, separated from Cyrene by a dense bank of jungle forest, the town had always been associated with abundant water. Had not the oracle at Delphi, seven hundred years ago, commissioned the city's founder to search for a "place between waters"? The first Greek colonists and their leader had not been content until they located a high plateau bordered by two springs on the virgin coast of Africa. Now, centuries later, Cyrene was a legend for prosperity, philosophy, and art.

While the bathers may not have meditated upon the origins of their ancient and venerable city, nor upon the symbolic purpose of the temple pools, most considered themselves philosophers.

Here and there small groups sitting on the deck or on the low ledges beneath the water's edge engaged in animated conversation, debating the finer points of popular thought.

Names highly revered among the literate of Cyrenian society dropped from haughty lips. Heads nodded with the pleasure of analytic challenge, or shook violently in debate, as Callimachus, the poet, Carneades, the great educator, or Eratosthenes, the polyhistor, were compared, recited, and interpreted. Above all, Aristippus, pupil to the eminent Greek teacher Socrates and founder of Cyrene's philosophical school, was quoted as final authority on any contended point.

These legends of intellect had established Cyrene as an academic center, and though they had died centuries before, their spirits still lived in the Cyrenian love of mental exercise.

The young man who entered the columned porch at twilight was not a great thinker. He enjoyed spending time at the spa as a physical indulgence only. Though no women were allowed within the strictly male domain of the baths, the pools were ringed with sensuous statues to Venus, Cyrene, and Diana. These he enjoyed immensely.

But tonight he did not come to rest his athletic frame in the spa's soothing minerals, nor to linger over the artfully conceived lines of Venus's supple neck. Certainly he did not wish to join the circles of intellectual grapplers who daily exhumed the bones of dead philosophers.

Quickly he passed by the huddled scholars, his eyes scanning the evening waters.

"Marcus!" someone hailed him.

Without turning toward the caller, he raised a careless hand and flicked a greeting. "Not now, Brutus," he replied. "I have no time for taverns."

"We will see you later, then." Brutus shrugged, hoisting his huge body onto the marble deck, and wrapping a towel about his waist.

"Probably not," Marcus returned. "Not this evening."

Brutus, who had not so much as merited a glance from his friend, scowled in disappointment and gestured to a klatch of followers who rose from the pool behind.

"We will see him later," he laughed, disregarding Marcus's pronouncement.

The hefty young Romans turned toward the benches where their clothes were strewn. Quickly they donned the short-skirted tunics and wine-red capes for which their military legion was famous, and made a raucous path for the streets and the enticements of the pubs.

Marcus, single-purposed, strode across the court toward the central bath, having spied the object of his search. Argus Quintus, his father, lay poolside, stretched face down beneath the pounding fists of a masseuse, unmoving as the muscles of his lean back were kneaded and manipulated without mercy.

How magnificent he is! young Marcus thought as he hastily drew near. *If only I were half so strong!* Of course, he underestimated his own manly attributes. Youthful vigor shone forth in burnished brow and sturdy thighs. Broad shoulders and sun-bronzed arms rippled with the strength of twenty active years.

But his father was his idol. Surely, should he live to be one hundred years old, and the elder die tomorrow, he would always revere Quintus as superior to himself.

Not that his parents had failed to instill self-confidence in their son. Marcus had been taught from childhood to enjoy his doubly-rich heritage: the Roman glory of his father and the Jewish treasures of his mother.

Judeo-Roman marriages were not unusual. But where they did exist, they offered enviable privilege. Even his name, Jonah Marcus (or John Mark, as his mother called him), was a twofold endowment, speaking of great potential—*John* being Hebrew for "God's gracious gift," and *Marcus* meaning "shining" in Latin, indicative of Roman strength.

The handsome Mark, with his ebony hair and coal-black eyes, his ruddy complexion and clean-shaven face, was the pride of his parents. His mother may have overindulged him; Quintus may have promoted his self-esteem beyond the bounds of humility—but he was, after all, their only child.

"Father!" Mark called, rousing the nobleman from the low table. The masseuse stood up, rubbing his meaty, oil-smeared hands on a towel, and Quintus greeted his son with a perplexed smile.

"What brings you here at this hour?" he inquired. "You should be with your friends."

"No, Father; I have news for you from the family of Sergius," Mark explained.

Suddenly the Roman sat erect. "How does he fare?" he asked.

Mark lowered his eyes, but spoke forthrightly. "He died late this afternoon. The family mourns at Villa Ponti."

"I . . . I had not expected . . . ," Quintus stammered. "I should have been at his bedside. . . ."

"You cannot blame yourself," Mark quickly offered. "No one expected this. The physicians kept saying he would rally."

Quintus's face clouded as he stood and paced the deck. He had known Sergius Ponti, provincial governor of Cyrenaica, for ten years, serving as one of his closest legati, or lieutenants, and senior advisor.

This was not the first time he must bid adieu to an elder statesman and dear ally. More than two decades ago, after distinguishing himself in the service of Caesar's campaigns, the young sergeant had found favor in the eyes of Janius, soon-to-be governor of Palestine. He had been asked to accompany the new procurator to the province of the Jews, to serve as one of his comites, a member of the governor's suite of companions.

So capable had been the administration of his duties that when Janius passed on, Quintus received invitations from half a dozen provinces to serve in the same capacity. He had chosen to work beside Sergius, who had a reputation for discretion and honesty.

Quintus had never cared for Palestine. The peculiar rites and observations of the Jews had never appealed to him, their hatred of all things Roman alienating him from the beginning. One thing only had made leaving that province difficult. He had fallen in love with a Jewess.

When, much to his amazement, Mary Ben Haman, daughter of the wealthy merchant, Haman Ben Simeon, agreed to be his wife and to follow him wherever he went, he had chosen Cyrenaica, and the post at Sergius Ponti's service.

The handsome nobleman lifted his eyes from the floor and surveyed his son. What a match the marriage had been! Any union which would breed such a lad as Mark must have been inspired by the gods.

But now his son had questions deserving attention.

"What will this mean for the future, Father?" Mark was asking. "Will you be serving Sergius's successor? Will we be staying in Cyrene?"

Such things had not been discussed between Quintus and Sergius. As Mark had pointed out, no one had expected the governor's illness to culminate in death. Though Quintus had shouldered increased responsibility during his master's illness, his expanded duties had been considered temporary.

The Roman thought a moment before answering.

"This is not a peaceful province," he replied at last. "There are always threats of uprising among the Libyan constituents, and even," he said with a smile, "among your mother's people."

Mark nodded, appreciating his father's good-natured tolerance for the restive Cyrenian Jews. As for himself, he had never quite reconciled his two heritages and swung between pride and shame for his Palestinian ancestry. He had little interest in the politics of the local Jews, preferring to consider himself a Roman.

"I am certain the new governor will require my assistance," Quintus went on. "My decade of service in this province would be invaluable to a new ruler. What, after all, do most magistrates, fresh from Rome, know of Africans and Jews?"

With this he laughed aloud, and threw his purple toga over his naked back. Slinging an arm about his son's shoulders, he bade him accompany him from the spa.

"Perhaps we should join your friends at the pub," he offered warmly. "In memory of Sergius, of course . . ."

Mark picked up his father's careless mood, and as they entered the street, he tried to match his stride, pace for pace.

CHAPTER

2

Villa Ponti sat on the crest of Cyrene's seaward ridge, commanding a sweeping view of the nearly tropical jungle that led to the Mediterranean.

Mark accompanied his father up the hill toward the sprawling white mansion, bearing a large, cloth-wrapped fruitcake beneath one arm. The gift, prepared by his mother for the family of Sergius, was sent with her condolences, and would represent the goodwill of Quintus's household to those who mourned the governor's passing.

As they approached the villa, Mark scanned the porches and many balconies adorning the place. He had not known Sergius intimately, and though he was reluctant to admit it, anticipation of seeing the governor's daughter, Philea, outweighed heavier thoughts. The family would be keeping close within the mourning chamber, but the hope that Philea might step outside drew his gaze repeatedly to the doors.

Perhaps Quintus sensed his eagerness, in his quickened pace and preoccupied mood, for now and then his father glanced his way, a knowing twinkle in his eye.

When the butler greeted them at the gate and led them

toward the main hall, Quintus found it necessary to remind Mark of the cake he bore. Mark proffered it absently, his mind already in the parlor where Sergius lay in state.

It was not until he actually stood inside the darkened chamber, seeing the draped body upon the bier, that the aura of death affected him. Even then, it was not the sight of Sergius's lifeless form that troubled him, but Philea's sorrow.

In the blackened room, she stood at the foot of her father's casket, head bowed, holding herself with aristocratic grace. Her golden hair, where it peeked from beneath an ebony veil, reflected the glimmer of the lampstands in a halo, and her creamy skin shone like alabaster in the candleflames' warm glow.

Mark could see that tears glistened along her lashes. Despite the shadows which danced against her face, he could see the grief that lined her flawless complexion. But she did not sob and wail like others in the room. Taking after her mother, she was quiet and regal in her sadness.

Since childhood, Mark had been struck by Philea's sophistication. Often he had privately compared her to the noble women of the stage who performed in the Greek theater of Cyrene. Aloof and mysterious, she defied the mundane.

Yet Philea was a warm and gentle lady. Unlike most Cyrenian debutantes, there was no calculated coolness in her bearing. Her mystery was natural and did not overrule feminine kindness.

Quintus stepped forward when the butler introduced him and greeted Sergius's widow with a sincere embrace. As he did so, Philea glanced up, and Mark hoped that her quick survey of the doorway was in search of himself.

Indeed, when her large blue eyes fell upon him, he was certain she trembled. And he longed to rush to her side, to embrace her, even now, as his father did her mother.

But such a gesture would not have been proper.

It was against tradition for a widow to leave the bier of her deceased husband. But Vesta, Sergius's wife of forty years, must speak with Quintus. Taking him by the arm, she quietly excused herself, guiding him to the garden court.

Mark hesitated to follow, not wishing to leave Philea. But when his father bade him come along, he followed close behind.

The aroma of roses filled the small arbor, and sunshine smote the widow's dark-accustomed eyes.

"Sergius loved this place," she said, her voice bearing remarkable control.

"I know," Quintus replied.

"He never let the servants tend it . . . not even the gardeners," Vesta recalled.

"Indeed." Quintus nodded. "It was his favorite pastime. . . ."

Suddenly, Vesta's composure dissolved. As if she had resolutely waited for Quintus to arrive before she revealed her sorrow, she turned to him, burying her wrinkled brow upon his shoulder. She evinced no sound as she wept, but Mark watched uncomfortably as her aged body convulsed in his father's arms.

Never had he seen Quintus cry. Even now, the nobleman displayed no tears. But a stubborn flush rose to his cheeks, and his lower lip quivered.

For a long moment he held the grieving widow, until she regained herself, wiping her eyes with the kerchief tucked in her sleeve.

With a sigh, she gazed again into the face of her husband's closest friend.

"He told me to tell you . . . ," she began, "he wished for you to know that he sent word to Rome . . . he requested that you be commissioned to remain . . ."

Quintus listened patiently as the distraught woman struggled for words. "Remain?" he spurred her.

"Yes, Quintus. Sergius desired that you remain at your post . . . in service to his successor."

The Roman studied her carefully, framing his reply with great respect.

"It would be an honor to fulfill his wishes," he said. "I shall serve such an assignment as though I still served your husband . . . with loyalty and allegiance to his memory."

Vesta heaved another sigh and grasped Quintus's hand to her lips.

"My lord will rest better, knowing that you manage Cyrene."

The nobleman shook his head. "Manage Cyrene?" he shrugged. "Why, I am but an advisor, nothing more."

The widow objected with a smile. "I may know little about my husband's work, Quintus. But you and I both realize that your experience cannot be matched by any magistrate."

The nobleman did not reply, for she spoke the truth. But he had given little thought to what she was saying.

"It could be months before Rome appoints a new governor," she reminded him. "Sergius said as much. Then, once he is appointed, it will be yet longer before he arrives. You, Quintus, must serve as interim."

When he scrutinized her in surprise, she nodded matter-of-factly. "Sergius has said it must be so."

Mark, registering as much amazement as Quintus, studied his father with pride. They would be remaining in Cyrene. The prospect pleased him.

A movement at the edge of the court drew his attention toward the door where they had entered. Philea stood there now. How long she had been present, he did not know. But it seemed she had overhead the conversation.

And, if Mark interpreted her expression correctly, she was as pleased as he that he would be staying here.

CHAPTER

3

It was love and not neglect that convinced Mark's mother, Mary, to delay paying a call on the widow Ponti. After the rush of statesmen's visits and the formal mourning that would occupy the villa for the next few days, she would offer her assistance and her time. She knew it would be more welcome then, when Vesta would be alone in her grief.

Today Mary had her own guests to entertain. And though the occasion of their visit was a happy one, it brought its own measure of poignant emotion.

Upon low pillows in the parlor of her tasteful home, three black men sat, Simon and his sons, Rufus and Alexander, recently returned from a business trip to Cyprus. Simon, a Cyrenian shoe merchant, though Libyan by ancestry, was a close friend of this Roman family, having ties with Mary's elder brother, a Cypriot leather exporter.

The connection with Mary's kin was broader, however, than business affairs. Simon was a Jewish proselyte, one of the few black Africans who had adopted the Hebrew faith. It was this that he and Joses Ben Haman, Mary's brother, had in common. And listening to Simon speak of their mutual beliefs, Mary's fondest feelings were aroused.

The lovely woman's dark eyes were wide and wistful as the merchant told of visits to the Cypriot synagogue with Joses. Though she frequented the Jewish meeting hall in Cyrene, her husband and son rarely accompanied her. She longed for the days when she had worshiped with family.

"Your brother had just returned from a trip to Jerusalem when I saw him," Simon related.

"Ah, yes. He wrote that he had been there," Mary sighed. "How I would love to see the Holy City again!"

Memories of her father's house in Jerusalem, temple-crowned site of her nativity, and recollections of the fine home which graced one of the town's major thoroughfares, never failed to warm her heart. Rarely since she had left with Quintus had she been privileged to return. But Jerusalem's streets and byways were emblazoned on her soul.

"He spoke of very strange things," Simon was saying.

"Strange things?" Mary asked, emerging from her reverie.

"Yes." The black man nodded. "Perhaps you have heard of the peculiar rabbi from Nazareth who has created such a stir in Palestine."

"Vaguely," Mary replied. "But there are always those who claim to be miracle workers wandering the countryside."

"So I have been told," Simon acknowledged. "But Joses says he has, with his own eyes, seen this one perform great feats in the Holy City itself."

Mary listened respectfully. "I admire no one more than I admire my brother," she assured him. "But even he could be duped. . . ."

"Well," Simon said shrugging, "I have no stake in the matter either way. I only know that Joses speaks of this fellow constantly."

"Constantly?" Mary marveled. "I have never known my brother to be obsessed over anything. He is the most moderate of men."

"I agree," Rufus now chimed in. "I would describe him so. But the Nazarene has captivated him."

Alexander nodded his turbaned head, pondering the phenomenon with great wonder. "It is an oddity, madam. I have visited Joses often with Father. Never have I heard him go on as he does about this."

Mary raised her eyebrows, bewildered. But, shrugging calmly, she reached for a plate of candied apricots and passed them to her guests. Pouring them a third cup of spiced tea, she tried to change the subject.

"Other than this, he is himself?" she inquired.

"Never better," Simon assured her. "He implores you to come to Jerusalem for Passover this year. He says he will open up the estate, have it cleaned and outfitted with servants for the holiday, if only you will join him there."

Since the death of their father many years ago, Mary and Joses had rarely stayed at the same time in the old residence. The Cypriot had done his best to keep the place up in their absence. But Mary feared it had been a difficult task.

"Did my brother say he had seen the house?" she asked. "Is it in good condition?"

"He did not speak of it, my lady," Simon replied. "But I am certain he would spare no expense to renovate it, if you were to reside there, even for a short while."

Mary knew this was no exaggeration. Her brother was famed for his generous spirit. "I should like nothing more than to be with Joses at Passover. You know this, Simon. But as much as Quintus respects my faith . . ."

She need not explain further. Simon and his sons knew that her marriage to the Roman had not been spiritually nurturing.

As she finished speaking, Mark appeared in the chamber doorway, pleasantly surprised to find the old acquaintances in the room.

Mary rose and ushered him toward the guests. "We have visitors, Mark," she said excitedly.

"So I see!" The young man greeted them.

"*Heis ho Theos!*" Simon responded, quoting his favorite maxim and bowing where he sat. "God is One!"

Mark smiled awkwardly and shook the man's outstretched hand. He had never been comfortable with Simon's ready reference to God.

"Do you bring word from my uncle?" he asked.

Though Mark had met Joses only a few times, the Cypriot merchant was one of his favorite people.

"He is well," Simon said, clasping Mark's friendly hand. "But we understand you have just come from a house where there is great sadness this day."

"There is mourning at Villa Ponti," Mark confirmed. "However," he said, turning to his mother, "matters have gone well for Quintus this hour. He will be interim governor until a new administration is established! I left him at the villa to discuss such matters with officials quartered there."

The young matron was speechless, pride in her husband's achievement overriding regret sometimes experienced in her marriage. But when Mark made yet another pronouncement, she was overwhelmed with self-doubt.

"And, my dear woman," he reported, "this means you will be first lady of Cyrene for the next few months!"

"What?" Mary stammered. "Why, I have no preparation for such a task!"

Simon shook his head. "Nonsense, madam!" he objected. "Hospitality is your hallmark. And no quality could serve a governor's lady better."

Mary bowed graciously, humbled by the compliment, and then asked her son to sit with them awhile.

As Simon settled down upon his pillow for further conversation, he surveyed Mark carefully.

"I must be going in a moment," he said. "But before I do, I have something to say."

Gazing intently at the young Roman, he began, "Your uncle impressed upon me his earnest desire that your mother attend the Jerusalem Passover next spring. I have passed his message along to her, but she seems to think such a journey is out of the question."

Mark considered the matter with a vacant expression, wondering why Simon should bring it to his attention. As silence followed, however, and Mary did not offer a word, he sensed he was being urged to intervene.

Studying the woman, he shrugged. "I see no problem. My mother knows she is free to pursue her religion. Quintus has never interfered. If she wants to go to Jerusalem, no one would stop her."

Mary did not look up from the floor, but fidgeted with her tasseled sleeve. It was out of place for a woman to interrupt men's conversation, but even though Simon had invaded private territory, she was glad to let him speak.

"Your father is a tolerant and beneficent husband," Simon quickly agreed. "I hope you will take no offense at my intrusion into family affairs. But I know I have your indulgence, as I am dear to your uncle."

Mark nodded, still perplexed as to why Simon should involve him in an issue that properly belonged between Quintus and Mary.

When the merchant risked further boldness Mark was even more puzzled.

"I dare say, Mark, that your mother would be more likely to fulfill her brother's wishes if some member of her household were to accompany her to Palestine."

The lad pondered this, then shook his head.

"I perceive that you refer to me," he guessed.

Simon sat back, his grin broader than ever, and slapped his knees with determination.

"Indeed!" he applauded. "Surely Quintus would be disinclined to make such a journey . . . given his new duties, of course."

Mark cleared his throat. "What makes you think I would be more prone than my father to go to Jerusalem?"

From the corner of one eye he saw Mary flinch. But, too proud to apologize, he only looked at her lamely.

Still Simon would not be deterred.

"The answer should be obvious," he replied. "You are more Jewish than Roman."

Mark, taken aback, almost laughed. But, sensitive this time to Mary's feelings, he chose his response with care.

"How so?" he asked. "How is the son of a Roman statesman equally a Jew?"

Simon pressed him to the heart. "I did not say 'equally.' I said you are *more* Jewish than Roman."

Mark bit his tongue, listening in amazement as Simon defended his ludicrous position.

"The Hebrews teach that a man's lineage is traced primarily through the mother. If he has a Jewish father, he is a Jew by law alone. But if he has a Gentile father and Jewish mother, he is a Jew, in every way, by law and race."

The proud son of Quintus stifled a sneer. He wished his father were here. The strong-minded Roman could set matters straight.

But Simon and his sons were rising now. Mary was seeing them to the door, chatting amiably and inviting them to come again.

As the sound of their departing footsteps faded, Mark rolled his eyes and covered a yawn with his hand. He did not see his mother glance at him as she returned past the chamber, having bid her guests good-bye. Had his eyes met hers, he would have detected the glimmer of tears.

CHAPTER

4

The days of mourning had passed at Villa Ponti. But ever since Simon's visit, Mark had experienced inexplicable heaviness.

Since he had turned eighteen, having completed his education in Cyrene's public schools, Mark had spent his days studying government under Quintus's direction. Though his best friends had entered the Roman military, it had always been assumed that Mark would follow in his father's footsteps, acquiring an elementary post in service to the state, with glamorous potential for advancement.

The temporary fear that, with Sergius's death, the Quintus family might be called away from Cyrene had been assuaged with news that his father would be retained here. And the interim position into which Quintus had been catapulted could only mean greater opportunity for Mark's future.

But none of that satisfied his restlessness this evening.

It was sunset as he walked alone on the flat at the mouth of the sacred Fount of Apollo, the exuberant spring that was the focal point of Cyrenian history. Winding its way through a three-hundred-meter channel, it emerged beneath an ornate portico from an artificially enlarged tunnel, along which were inscriptions and graffiti left by a thousand visitors.

Many generations ago, Battus, bidden by the Delphic oracle to found a city upon this African highland, had been led by Libyan barbarians to this very site. Through the years, prayers to the gods, dedications to good fortune, wishes for happiness and prosperity had been carved into the walls and niches of this cavern. Even on the decorative portico itself could be read a hundred pleas for personal blessings, success in business, in love, and in war.

Mark had never whittled anything on the fountain's chamber. He had little faith in the gods of Greece and Rome. Quintus gave lip service to any deity who might exist, and since he had no reason to believe the gods were fables, he gave cursory honor to 'them all. Mark, following his father's lead, had never questioned such practice. The fact that little heart was put into Quintus's devotions did not trouble him. To both men, religion was an expedient only, and no stone was left unturned if it might supply a blessing.

The same vague reverence was paid to the God of the Hebrews, although Mary had often warned her husband and son that such duplicity was blasphemous, that Jehovah would not countenance it forever.

Mark leaned over the railing that enclosed the tumbling fount, trying to numb his mind in the ear-shattering din of the white waters. The very walls of the cave thundered about him, but the pounding vibrations only echoed a drumming heart.

Stepping out from the large alcove, he peered up the westward hill that cradled the raging flume to view the city's enormous Acropolis. Fronted by the main entrance to Cyrene, it had been the scene of countless sacred processions to Apollo, the town's tutelary deity, and to his closest cohorts: Zeus, Athena, Artemis, Pluto, and others.

Mark had never begrudged homage to these beings. Their festivals and holy days had provided many hours of revelry and celebration. But tonight he bristled at the realization that their service was quite meaningless, that his heart had never been stirred by anything but the merriment of a good time.

"Get hold of yourself!" he whispered through gritted teeth. "Are you a Rufus or an Alexander to take such things so seriously?"

He had never been close to the sons of Simon. Though he had known them since childhood, they always seemed overly exercised in matters of duty and tradition. As fellow students in the public schools, they had studied Greek and Latin alongside Mark. But after hours, when he spent time playing with the rowdier boys of the neighborhood, they stayed home to pursue Hebrew and Aramaic, languages of their father's adopted faith.

Mark had never fit with them, but tonight he felt out of stride with himself as well.

"Straighten your shoulders, Marcus! Lift your chin! Surely you are no philosopher," he chided, recalling the huddled thinkers who debated in the marketplace and muttered in the spa. But it was no use. He only grasped at casual indifference.

Russet shades of evening were giving way to the silver black of a Mediterranean night. Few carts or pedestrians passed this way; few voices broke the growing silence.

When, at last, he turned for home, however, a pair of the city's most renowned scholars approached the fountain, one hoary-headed gentleman and one dark-haired youth, so engrossed in conversation that they did not notice him lingering in the shadows. In fact they bore the same posture for which he had just criticized himself, and his curiosity was drawn to them.

Never before had he heeded the joustings of philosophers. But since they spoke of the pursuit of happiness, he could not resist eavesdropping.

Coming to the edge of the fount, they stopped against the railing where Mark had stood only moments before, and they discussed the ancients as though they had not died aeons before.

"Did not Socrates hold that virtue is the only human good?" the elder asked the younger.

"Of course, Brother," the younger quipped, "but he did acknowledge that happiness is at least a subsidiary end of moral action."

"Indeed," the first responded, "but Aristippus and his followers seized upon this, making it the prime factor of existence and denying that virtue has any intrinsic value. Why," he said with a shudder, "I blush to think that his school of thought is named for our beloved city."

The younger chafed at this and defensively inquired, "So, would you deny that happiness as a goal is a noble pursuit?"

"Indeed not!" the older one objected. "It is the Cyrenaic definition of happiness that appalls me. Why, Aristippus claimed that logic and physical science are useless, that feeling is the only possible criterion of knowledge and conduct. This I cannot accept."

"I suppose he did teach such a thing," the youth conceded. " 'Our modes of being affected alone are knowable,' " he said with a hesitant tone, quoting the venerable Aristippus, founder of the Cyrenaic tradition.

"Aha!" his challenger said, nodding. "And he did not stop there, but claimed that the single universal aim of all men is pleasure. Nor did he admit to any distinction among the various pleasures that can be experienced, except in degrees of intensity. In fact, he went so far as to teach that bodily pleasures are superior to intellectual ones! And he even claimed in his baser conclusions that momentary pleasure, especially of the carnal kind, is the only good for man!"

The younger philosopher sighed deeply now, drawing his robes tight to his chest and mentally filing through points of defense until he recalled with some relief that Aristippus did not always hold such an extreme view.

"Brother," he said with a catlike grin, "our great teacher admitted that some actions that give immediate pleasure entail more than their equivalent of pain. In fact, he taught that this is the basis of conventional distinctions between right and

wrong, and therefore regard should be paid to law and custom."

" 'Cyrenaic hedonism,' " the elder spat, "a mere contortion
of morality to gratify the flesh!"

"So you see it." His antagonist nodded. "But do not forget
that our mentor insisted the truly wise man must abstain from
that which is wrong or unjust. 'True pleasure belongs only to
him who is self-controlled and master of himself,' " he countered, quoting the ancient sage.

The elder scholar controlled a blustering red countenance.
But he quickly rallied, and, feigning a concession, admitted,
"It seems the lauded Aristippus mellowed in the direction of
morality in his old age. From claiming that the highest good
was carnal pleasure to acknowledging that virtue is the greatest value, he returned to Socrates's original truth."

The youth was silent, bowing a little from the waist in
deference to the elder's sound reasoning. But he was not
prepared for the coup de grâce which was to come.

"It is simply unfortunate that Aristippus's followers did not
support his more temperate conclusions." The older debater
sighed, and as though his reference was clear to his opponent,
he peered off into the sky.

The young one awaited an explanation, curiosity consum-
ing him.

"Of what do you speak, sir?" he inquired, his tone marked
with a respect absent earlier in the dialogue.

"Why," the skilled logician said with a shrug, "it is com-
mendable that later Cyrenaics accepted self-control as essen-
tial, that passing pleasure may be a delusion, and further that
permanent tranquility is a truer end of conduct. But, they
went so far as to deny the possibility of real pleasure entirely,
advocating suicide as the only insurance against pain!"

Now the novice blushed violently. Lowering his head, he
stammered, "Certainly there were those who carried the master's teachings to an extreme, as always there are those unrea-
sonable wretches who cannot be moderate. But surely there
are no such thinkers in Cyrene today!"

"I agree." The old one nodded, a triumphant smile crinkling his cheeks. "But I made the reference to show that Aristippus's original teachings are prone to disastrous outcome. Therefore, I maintain that the entire philosophy is rooted on shaky ground."

The student bowed again, acknowledging the elder's superior logic. For a long while he said nothing, gazing into the tumbling fount just as Mark had done moments before.

Then suddenly his eyes lit with some ultimate insight, and straightening his shoulders, he confronted his wiser friend. "Perhaps," he whispered, punctuating each syllable with a pointed finger, "perhaps true pleasure consists primarily in identification with others' pleasure."

The veteran contemplated this a moment, and then shaking his head, placed an arm around the lad and began leading him from the portico. "Such a thing is not logical," he insisted, "for then there would be no possibility for independent pleasure. . . ."

As their voices were lost in the distance beyond the fount, Mark stepped away from the shadows. Now he remembered why he had never enjoyed philosophy. From carnal pleasure, to altruism, to suicide and back, the conclusions of great thinkers led a merry chase.

He wondered what Quintus would make of all their palaver, of these seekers who never found. But as he considered his father's response, a chill crossed his shoulders.

Quintus, in an unvarnished way, was as empty as these vain debaters. He had no god and no high thought. Quintus would have nothing to offer but a laugh.

CHAPTER

5

Mark had always lived in his father's shadow, following the road of statesmanship to come as close as possible to his father's example.

One aspect of Quintus's experience, however, had been denied him. Trained for government, he had never been a soldier.

Since childhood he had thrilled to tales his father told of battles in Caesar's campaigns. Quintus had fought under Tiberius, Augustus's coregent, in Gaul and Germany, had killed many enemies, and had distinguished himself as a brave and able soldier. When Mark was but a child, his father had donned the purple cloak of a legate and had passed on to his son the Roman-red cape that was the symbol of his military legion. The retired garment was Mark's favorite possession, but though he wore it proudly, he often wondered if manhood could fully flower in one who had not known adventure.

Such doubts troubled him, especially when he was around Brutus, his lifelong friend, one of many companions who had made career commitments to Rome's armed forces. Brutus, in fact, belonged to the same fine corps Quintus had served.

Today Mark oversaw the servants who moved Quintus's furniture and supplies from the legate chamber of Cyrene's assembly house to the governor's quarters in the same building. Winter sun poured through the open window grates high in the vaulted hallway that led past the senate meeting room. But a seasonal chill descended the marble walls, draping the corridor's mammoth columns and casting an unfriendly pall across the floor.

Mark spurred the burden-laden workers with sharp commands, and hunched his shoulders beneath his scarlet mantle. Eager to be inside the fire-warmed chamber which would be his father's new office, he looked above to the exposed sky and barked, "Why was the grate not closed? Hurry now, Demas, and mount the ladder!"

An unwilling servant laid down his load of scrolled legal briefs and, taking a long pole from the wall, scurried up the oak rungs. When he was at a precarious height, he clung to the ladder with one hand and with the other guided the pole's hook through the heavy grate, forcing a shutter to fall with a clap.

Sunlight was obliterated, but not the cold.

Mark stamped his numb, sandaled feet on the tiled pavement and made his way to the governor's headquarters at the far end of the hall. As he did so, the tramping of soldiers could be heard near the corridor's entrance.

"Marcus!" a familiar voice rang out.

The son of Quintus need not turn around to know it was Brutus who called. Apparently just getting off duty where he had stood guard at the assembly house, the husky sergeant sought sanctuary against the wind outside. With him were other friends of Mark who served the same post.

"A cup of ale would warm the bones on such a day as this," Brutus announced, slapping Mark on the back as he drew near. "Can you get away?"

Mark glanced down the hall where the servants carted the last of Quintus's crates into Sergius's old chamber.

"I think I can." He smiled broadly. Massaging his blue

knuckles, he hailed a straggling workman to take charge and joined his companions.

The dusky warmth of the taverns would ease the winter chill, and in those gathering places where drink sparked felicity, he always felt kinship with those who had followed a different path.

The immense white stone grounds of Cyrene's government sector were brilliant beneath the stark sky. Flashing sunlight bounced off the enormous bronze eagles that spread their wings atop wreathed pedestals in the compound's four corners. Each gigantic bird held in its clinched talons a cluster of golden spears, and the sun's noon rays glinted off the shafts like fiery arrows.

When Mark had been a lad he had believed the mighty eagles were alive, encased only temporarily in metal armor. One day their gilded pinions would shake free and their Herculean wings would lift them arcing into the Mediterranean sky. That would be Rome's greatest moment, he believed, and Cyrene's finest hour.

Now he knew that was childish fantasy. But never could he glimpse the birds without recalling it.

Today, as he strode across the terra-cotta pavement, his closest friends on either side, he felt very Roman indeed, and some of the heaviness that had haunted him since Simon's visit lifted.

When he and Brutus came to the compound gate, ready to make their way through the pub-lined streets, they halted to allow passage to an ornate vehicle. Mark did not register its identity until Brutus placed a hand on his arm and leaned close.

"The carriage of Sergius . . . ," he whispered. "It is the widow and her daughter."

Instantly, Mark caught the tone of admiration in Brutus's voice, and as he sought a glimpse of Philea in the quick-moving conveyance, his pulse raced.

Here was a fantasy more glorious than bronze eagles on soaring wings.

While Vesta still wore black, as was common for widows months after a death, the daughter was radiant. In a gown of pale yellow, light as the winter sun, she was oblivious to her admirers. As her chauffeur, standing haughty in the driver's spur, whipped the white horses through the gate, she lifted a slender hand to brush blonde locks from her shoulder. Mark's eyes traveled down the curve of her throat revealed by the open neckline.

"She is a beauty, that one," Brutus was saying. "I intend some day to court her."

Suddenly Mark's full focus was on his friend. As the carriage disappeared toward the assembly house, on some family errand, he contemplated the announcement and studied Brutus in silence.

"I didn't know you admired her," he stammered.

"Who could not?" Brutus laughed. "A fairer damsel has never graced the courts."

Mark followed the sergeant's lead down the city viaduct, his ears burning.

"Next year she comes out," Brutus went on, referring to the annual review of debutantes which young Cyrenian males always enjoyed. "I'll take my stand then. No young girl can resist a soldier."

The son of Quintus noted the confident cock of Brutus's head and surveyed his proud bearing with dismay.

Though Mark wore his father's military cape and bore a government insignia on his breast, it seemed when he walked with Brutus that his own manhood was vicarious.

He wondered how Philea would compare them and feared to know the answer.

CHAPTER

6

The stark brilliance of daytime translated into a vivid night, lit by a full moon over the house of Quintus.

Mark could not sleep, though all the servants had retired. As he passed down the gallery from his chamber, taking in the open air of the court, he could overhear his parents' low talking as they readied themselves for bed.

He had not meant to pause so near their quarters, but the light caught his eye, and he saw through a crack of the door that Mary sat before her dressing table, drawing a heavy brush through her hair. Behind her stood Quintus, an appreciative look in his eye.

When the man moved forward, placing a gentle hand on her shoulder, Mark stepped quietly down the stairs to the patio.

He ached for Philea. Indeed, she had not been off his mind since he had seen her in the carriage at midday.

With a sigh he sat on the fountain bench and aimlessly traced his finger over its mother-of-pearl mosaic.

Suddenly his sad reveries were interrupted by a knock at the front door. Then the knock became a banging, and he could hear someone shouting for Quintus.

Rushing for the entryway, he opened the peephole shutter and peered through the latticed slit. Outside stood Simon, the black merchant, his face full of urgency.

"Open, please!" he cried, his voice harsh against the door though he looked this way and that for fear of being followed.

Mark lifted the heavy bar which secured the entrance and Simon forced his way inside.

"Heis ho Theos!" the merchant whispered anxiously, bowing as he rushed into the house. "Where is your father?"

"I am here," Quintus replied, having come to the gallery. "What is it?"

"The Libyans!" Simon cried breathlessly. "They plan revolution!"

Quintus descended the stairs, as his personal servant, roused by the clamor, rushed to fetch the master's cape.

"How do you know this?" the governor demanded, throwing his mantle over his shoulders.

"I was at a merchants' meeting and overheard the plot being whispered among my brethren. Because of my ancestry, the Libyans assume I would support an endeavor to overthrow Rome's provincial regime. But, sir," he said with another bow, "you must know that I could not sanction such treachery. Rome has been good to me and mine, and I am your friend."

Quintus clapped Simon's shoulder. "I believe this," he assured him. "Tell me, now, quickly . . . what did you hear?"

"Tonight . . . midnight . . . the assembly hall . . . fire . . ."

Rapidly the story was told, as Simon unfolded the Libyan plan to destroy the Senate chambers and the governor's headquarters.

"I fear for your safety, sir, and for that of Sergius's family," Simon continued, rubbing his hands nervously together. "There were those who claimed they would storm Villa Ponti as well as the government compound."

The elder statesman grasped Simon by the arm. "Please,

friend, take my wife and servants to your home!"

"Certainly," he said with a bow. "I am under no suspicion. Your family is safe with me."

Mary, who had by now descended the stairs, wasted no time in gathering what she might need, and Mark stepped hastily forward. "Father," he implored, "someone needs to warn the Pontis."

Quintus easily read his son's desire and nodded. "Of course, Son. Go!"

Mark departed, hoping he was not already too late. The governor called for a carriage to take him to the compound. There he would call out the troops and prepare for the worst.

Mark's horse pounded the moonlit path to Villa Ponti. Nostrils flared, the horse climbed the steep incline with dexterous speed.

As the rider reached the white wall of the estate, he was relieved to see no sign of mayhem. But he shuddered as he approached the front gate. The great doors stood open, no guard in sight, a sure sign that something was amiss.

Adrenaline coursed through him, chasing Mark beyond fear. Philea's safety was his first priority.

Spurring his frothing charger up yet another incline, he at last reached the house's veranda and, leaping to the ground, ran toward the entry.

He saw no sign of the intruders, and seeking none, he pounded on the door, calling for the widow and her daughter.

Cries of terror suddenly resounded from the interior, then a rush of footsteps. Mark wrenched the door open and embraced the two hysterical women.

"Libyans are here, Marcus!" the widow gasped. "In the servants' quarters!"

More shouts came from the back hall where the invaders had entered. Mark, knowing he could do nothing more useful than take the women away, left the hapless servants to their own devices and led Philea and her mother outside.

Mounting his steed, he pulled them up behind him and sped toward the undefended gate.

As the mistresses of the mansion peered over their shoulders at the retreating villa, it was suddenly lit by an orange glow. Flames leapt from the sprawling back wing where the Libyans captured their first victims.

Though the widow had not wept aloud at her husband's wake, she wept sorely now. And Philea entwined her arms around Mark's waist, burying a tearful face in his red cape.

CHAPTER

7

Had Mark been near government headquarters at midnight, and not just arriving at Simon's house with his fragile cargo, he would have seen the same ominous orange glow about the assembly house that cloaked the silhouette of Villa Ponti.

True to their plans, the Libyans had invaded the provincial headquarters, looting, vandalizing, and setting the precinct ablaze. Though the troops had been put on alert, some of the revolutionaries had crept into the council chambers during working hours and had been preparing for the ouster since sunset. The arrival of a Roman brigade was nothing more than the signal to put a match to dry tinder. Though the Libyans would never know who had informed on them, they had been able to carry off their plot from the inside.

This was not the first time restive Africans had challenged Rome. Since the founding of Cyrene, when Greek colonists had employed Libyan aid in locating the two highland founts, Egyptian and Libyan nationals had sought to dissuade European settlers from sinking roots on African soil. And when the mighty Roman Empire had taken over where Greece left off, territorial competition had sometimes manifested violence.

There were provincial subjects, other than the Libyan constituents, who would applaud the night's activities. Many Cyrenian Jews would commend any move against Rome.

Mary Ben Haman Quintus was not among them. Long
ago, she had taken her place at the side of a Roman, and if her
loyalty was divided, it was toward her old homeland, not
with any great allegiance to Cyrenaica.

When Mark entered Simon's house, delivering his charges
into the care of his mother, Mary took the task gladly, guiding
them into the parlor, where Simon's servants waited to serve
the guests. Never had such notables graced this home, and
though it was a sumptuous establishment, used to finery and
the granting of commodious hospitality, Roman officials had
little reason to frequent the residence.

Simon, seeing that the newcomers were comfortable,
turned to Mark who was still breathing hard from his chase.
"Come," he whispered, leading him by the arm to the home's
wide porch. "See there," he said, pointing to the sky which
loomed red and glowering over the government compound.

"Fire!" Mark cried, pushing away. "I must go to Father!"

But as he headed for the entry, Simon called him to a halt.
"Not so fast!" he demanded. "What can you do? Your father
has the forces of Rome with him. Your mother needs you
more!"

Mark would not listen. Rushing to the street and mounting
his still-sweating steed, he disappeared into the frantic night.

Mark got no farther than the Senate precinct's main gate
before the insurrection reached its climax.

Though the rebels had done considerable damage, they
were a small band, about one hundred in all. As the son of
Quintus charged toward the compound, the troops were already emerging from the looted assembly hall, having round-
ed up and herded the guerrillas into a queue of ankle chains.

The strand of black faces, perspiration-streaked and glow-
ing in the flame-inspired night, leered at the governor's son as
he rode up, triumphant despite their short-lived sabotage.

Mark tried to ignore their obscenities, desperately scanning the scene for a glimpse of his father.

A special contingent was just returning from Villa Ponti, the mansion's invaders in tow. But Quintus was nowhere to be seen.

Leaping from his horse, Mark dashed to the torched assembly hall, throwing off his cloak as he approached the inferno.

Flames darted between marble pillars, licking at oak abutments and charring the ornate doorposts. Interior alcoves smoked with the remnants of fine tapestries, and cushioned lounges sat like charcoal figures against the walls.

"Father!" Mark shouted, as he ran heedlessly down the corridor.

Suddenly, a strong hand grabbed him from behind, and he was wrestled to the floor. Peering over his shoulder, he found Brutus's rugged face looming at his back.

"Marcus! You fool!" the sergeant whispered. "Get out of here!"

"Where is Quintus?" Mark demanded. "What have they done with Father?"

Struggling beneath the weight of Brutus's body, he tried to crawl toward the door of the magistrate's chamber.

"Friend . . . ," his captor persisted, "the governor is not there. . . ."

Something in Brutus's voice sent a chill through Mark.

Defying his instincts, he cursed vehemently and pulled yet harder to be free.

At last, his strength spent, he fell prostrate, burying his face on his arms.

Brutus knelt beside him.

"The son of a Roman does not weep . . . not even when that Roman dies," the soldier whispered.

Mark stared numbly into his friend's eyes. The unspeakable had been spoken. The impossible had happened.

Quintus was dead, and Mark's soul was consumed with darkness.

CHAPTER

8

Now, as Simon had said, Mary would need Mark more than Quintus needed him.

It seemed only days ago that the governor's son had stood at the wake of Sergius, watching as the widow, Vesta, and her daughter mourned the death of the magistrate. Now his successor lay in state, a man who had never sought the office and who would have shunned the pomp which accompanied its glory.

Quintus had not been an overly modest man. He had been confident enough to rise high in provincial ranks. But neither had he been overly ambitious. He would have been content to serve in an advisory position for a lifetime.

After all, Mark recalled, his father had wisely seen that it was the advisor, and not the magistrate fresh from Rome, who wielded more influence.

Now, Quintus's widow was obliged to see her way through the rituals and ceremonies attending the death of a governor. And it was Vesta's turn to minister to Mary.

Mary performed her duties with grace and dignity, Mark at

her elbow through it all. Then came the day when she must look to her future.

When Mark began to suspect that her thoughts were turning increasingly toward Israel, concern compounded his grief.

Again it was Simon who pressed him to consider Mary's welfare.

"You must accompany her, you know," the merchant said one day.

Mark was busy with his father's horses in the stable behind the family home, brushing them as Quintus used to do.

The elder Roman had never left this chore to stable boys. He had loved his animals, just as Sergius had loved the private garden of Villa Ponti. Tending them had been a diversion, an act of love which reminded him of his summers in Caesar's campaigns.

Today, as Mark groomed the horses, his brow was furrowed and his hand moved the brush perhaps too aggressively over the horse's tender flank.

"Had you not brought Quintus word of the uprising and then taken in my mother and friends, I should believe all black men to be my natural enemies!" he swore, cursing the Libyans beneath his breath. "Do not push our friendship, Simon, by advising me yet again."

The merchant, too wise to be offended by Mark's remonstrance, stepped close.

"I am no advisor, Mark," he conceded. "I could never fill your father's shoes. But I am one who loves your family."

Mark peered at him, his eyes narrow slits. Still Simon persisted.

"I do not suggest you stay in Israel. Your future may well be charted in Cyrene. But your mother needs your encouragement. She wishes to return home," Simon insisted. "If you will not take her there, I will!"

This last pronouncement stung Mark to the quick. Simon, who was not even related to Mary, was committing himself to a journey of several weeks, and to an interruption of his affairs for the sake of another man's widow.

Suddenly Mark's selfishness was a knifepoint of guilt. Stepping back from his work, he let his hand fall to his side and tossed the brush to the hay-strewn floor.

"Must she go so far away?" he pleaded. "Does she find nothing to keep her here?"

"She would stay for your sake," Simon acknowledged, sensitive to the abandonment which even a grown man can feel if his mother withdraws. "But . . . for your sake only. She feels herself an alien in this land."

Mark studied the man uncertainly. "Tell me," he challenged, "how do you know such things? One would think you were closer to my mother than her own son."

Simon shook his head. "It does not take a very perceptive observer or a very sincere listener to read Mary's heart. Just how close have you been to her, lad?"

Mark looked at the floor again, his face reddening. But then, lifting his chin, he asserted, Roman-like, "I was my father's child."

"Very well," Simon said with a nod, "but perhaps there are even deeper kinships to explore."

It was not customary for a woman to travel alone. Even if she possessed servants, it was not proper for a lady to go abroad without a companion of her own class.

Therefore, when Mary learned that Mark was willing to accompany her to Jerusalem "until she established herself," she was overjoyed.

Already, without Mark's knowledge, she had received word from her brother, Joses, that he would meet her there, though it was not yet Passover. Learning of her husband's death, and surmising that she would be ever more lonely in Cyrene, he offered eager assistance.

"The house will be made suitable to your liking," he had written, "whatever the cost. Only let me know when you will arrive, and I will count the days."

It was clear that Mary was also counting them. Grief for Quintus was somewhat ameliorated as she kept busy arranging passage, overseeing the packing of crates and bundles, and preparing her maids and butlers for the journey.

Dreams of Jerusalem and of reunion with childhood friends added pleasant anticipation to the days.

The nights were still very hard. Vesta knew this would be so. Therefore, the elder widow often came to visit when darkness fell.

This evening, Vesta brought Philea and the two of them made their way laughing through aisles of boxes and bags strewn about Mary's courtyard.

Mark, who planned to live alone and to occupy only a section of the house when he returned from Israel, watched like an awkward stranger as the two guests carefully stepped through the stacks.

How well they bear up! he thought. The Pontis' home had not yet recovered from its losses. Two long-time menservants were killed the night the intruders broke into their quarters. And the villa itself was yet a shambles, where vandals had looted and burned. Even with the generous care Rome bestowed upon a statesman's widow, it could take the women years to refurbish the residence and replace the valuables that represented a lifetime of acquisition.

Yet, their spirits were courageous.

And so was Mary's.

Today, Mark observed her in a new way, seeing her for the first time as a woman, and not just his mother. Perhaps the fact that she was now alone, not dwelling in the shadow of Quintus, cast her in a different light.

It struck Mark that she was truly beautiful, her form graceful and slender, her long hair made exotic by silver glints among the dark locks.

She will do well, he projected, realizing that some day some man would doubtless come courting.

He pushed the thought aside, not relishing the idea. To him, she must remain, for a while at least, his father's devoted wife. It did not occur to him that he would have little power to release or to bind her as time unfolded.

Something in her ability to survive Quintus's demise troubled him, and it was not without resentment that he turned from the courtyard, leaving the three women to themselves.

Suddenly life was quite frightening. Until now, Mark's purpose on earth had been certain, his mission predictable. He would emulate his father, take a seat in Cyrenian government, and pursue things that would merit Quintus's approval.

Now, within days, a new magistrate would be arriving to take control. The empire would not hesitate this time to focus attention on the strife-torn province. And Mark's certain link to a career with Rome could no longer be taken for granted.

Not only this, but he faced life without family. For once, he could empathize with his mother's loneliness since leaving Israel.

Suddenly, many things were becoming clear—his self-centeredness most of all.

Glancing skyward from the wide veranda that fronted the Roman home, Mark could see gables of the forum buildings some blocks away. Recalling once again the orange night when he had spied the firelit heavens, and remembering the pyre of the assembly hall, he shuddered.

"I should have been with him . . . ," Mark whispered.

"I, too, have lost a father," a tender voice came from the archway.

Wheeling about, Mark discovered Philea had joined him, and as she stepped near, she placed a consoling hand on his arm.

"But there was nothing you could do to stop Sergius's death," Mark objected. "I . . . I should have been fighting beside my father. . . ."

Again he looked at the sky, and Philea detected a trickling tear upon his cheek.

"Yet, instead, you came to save me and my mother," she reminded him.

Mark knew not how to respond, his head a muddle of guilt and pride. "Yes . . . ," he said, smiling, "that was no mistake. Quintus would have done as much."

Philea, drawing closer, brushed a tear from his face. "But, it was *Marcus* who saved us, and not Quintus. Can you not see the good in yourself?"

As she spoke, the familiar longing for her charged Mark's being with its own brand of fire. How he yearned to enfold her in his arms, to crush her small body to his heart!

"Dear lady," he sighed, drawing away, "I . . . I go to Israel, you know."

"I know," Philea replied, gazing at the floor.

Mark, seeing her disappointment, steadied himself.

"I shall speedily return, my lady," he replied. "I cannot leave . . . business in Cyrene . . . for very long."

Both he and Philea knew he now had little to occupy him here. He had not set foot in the assembly hall since the insurrection.

But the falsehood sufficed to ease the tension of the moment. With a nervous laugh, he assured her, "Besides, I want to be home before the maidens come out next spring."

Philea glanced at him, a twinkle in her eye, knowing he referred to her scheduled emergence with the other debutantes.

Looking away shyly, she whispered, "For you, I have already come out."

The revelation rang in Mark's ears, infusing him with irresistible energy.

Reaching for her, he pulled her close and lifted her chin with his hand.

As their lips touched, there was light in the shadow of his soul.

PART TWO

Conception

I tell you the truth,
unless a kernel of wheat falls
to the ground and dies,
it remains only a single seed.
But if it dies,
it produces many seeds.

JOHN 12:24

CHAPTER

1

It was a brilliant dawn when Mark first glimpsed the Holy Land of the Jews. Four weeks at sea had brought him and his mother to one beautiful palm-lined port after another, from Catabathmus to Pharos and finally to Israel's only maritime colony, Joppa.

Each stop-off had broadened Mark's appreciation of the world. Though he possessed a cosmopolitan spirit, he had never been beyond his own province. And until he entered Joppa harbor, he could not have imagined any shore more glorious than North Africa's.

Here was splendor unrivaled by anything he had seen. Like stairsteps, pink in the dawn, the city rose along the hillside, pristine, compact behind walls which hugged the beach.

As he and Mary awaited the caravan that would take them from the coast to Jerusalem, the capital, they browsed through the quaint streets and shops of Solomon's ancient port.

Though Joppa was a bustling city, touched by elements from all corners of the Roman Empire, Mark marveled at the care with which Jewish citizens maintained their environment. The inlet, harboring a hundred ships under every national banner, was unpolluted and the busy avenues were litter free.

"It is the Law," Mary explained, reading his amazement. "And the Jewish way. Moses taught us cleanliness, as well as righteousness."

Mark had learned of Moses at Mary's knee when he was but a small boy. He had not thought about his early training for years, having been released to Quintus's apprenticeship when old enough to enter Cyrene's schools. Now, as he gave her his undivided attention, more of his mother's teachings came to memory.

"Who was the warrior who made the sun stand still?" he asked as they climbed one of Joppa's white-walled hills. "I liked that story."

"That was Joshua," Mary replied, her eyes bright. "I am surprised you remember the story."

Mark pondered her comment. "Quintus often told me stories of the gods and goddesses of Greece and Rome. He never took them seriously; neither did I. But I remember your stories were always told with sincerity, and the tales themselves, though full of adventure, were somehow . . ."

". . . believable?" Mary responded.

"Yes, Mother. How was that?"

"They are the truth, my son. That is how."

"And Quintus's were not?"

Mary hesitated to give an opinion, honoring her husband's memory.

"Oh, well." Mark shrugged. "Not even Father believed them. Still, I was always . . . touched by your tales."

The two were quiet a long moment. Finally Mark queried, "I was very young when you stopped telling me Jewish lore. Why did you stop, Mother?"

Mary looked up at her handsome son, wondering at the one borne of her love for a Gentile. The tenderness in his voice moved the mother's heart with compassion and hope. "The question should be," she replied, " 'Why did you stop listening?' "

CHAPTER

2

The sun was just setting over Joppa, three days to the west, when Mary and her party drew near the rise leading to Jerusalem.

The caravan would set up camp one more night beneath a copper sky, and the next morning would wend past the Herodian Towers separating the Holy City from the rest of the world.

As the little train drew within sight of the capital's cradling hills, Mary grew unusually quiet. Mark, who walked beside her, wondered if she were troubled, and leaning close, took her hand.

"I am all right, Son," she whispered with a smile. "It is just that I have longed for so many years to gaze again upon these slopes. . . ."

The young man put an arm around her shoulders and inquired, "We are so close to our destination. Why does the caravan stop again this evening?"

"The master is a devout Jew, Mark. I believe he wishes to enter the city at sunrise, rather than at dark."

"Why is that?" Mark puzzled.

"When you see Jerusalem in the dawn, you will understand."

If Mark had been dazzled by the beauty of Joppa, he was even more smitten by Jerusalem's glory.

The instant the sprawling city was revealed at daybreak, and as Mary and her people passed through the towered gate, a sheen of flashing gold met their gaze.

The mammoth dome of Herod's Temple, completely covered with the yellow metal, dominated the valley. Beneath this gleaming crown the city lay in descending terraces, the resplendent levels spread to every side like prostrate worshipers.

Every part of the walled metropolis led the eye templeward. In the brilliantly waking morning, Mark understood why the caravan had waited through night to enter.

The caravan master and his crew stopped once the train was inside the walls. Mark observed in silent wonder as the elderly gentleman raised his mantle over his head and fell to his knees. Behind him, all the men did likewise, covering their heads with their hands.

The master began to bow repeatedly, his forehead touching the ground again and again as he stretched his hands toward the temple.

"If I forget you, O Jerusalem," he chanted, "let my right hand forget her cunning . . . if I prefer not Jerusalem above my chief joy."

Over and over the words swelled as the crew, then the entire party, joined the hymn.

Mark studied his mother's upturned face and radiant expression as she, too, spoke the refrain.

He had not recited a Jewish prayer since childhood. Now he found the impulse hard to resist, and yielding to the emotion of the moment, blended his voice with the others.

"If I forget you, O Jerusalem . . . ," he said hesitantly. But he faltered over the next words.

Mark had long ago forgotten Jerusalem and the teachings

of his youth. As he chanted the applicable curse, he drew his right hand to his bosom, enfolding it protectively in his cloak.

There were not many black faces in the teeming crowds that occupied Jerusalem. Except for this, the populace resembled Cyrene's. The common citizens dressed much like the folk of any marketplace. And the outdoor bazaars sold goods familiar throughout the Roman Empire.

There were notable differences, however, and Mark was reminded of Quintus's frequent, though good-natured, assertion: "The Jews are a peculiar people."

Not only was there an abundance of men in the orthodox black gowns that marked certain Jewish sects, but they drew considerable reverence from those who passed in the streets. Mark had seen such folk in his hometown, exclusive and austere members of the synagogue's strictest constituency. In Cyrene they drew curious stares, even outright ridicule, from the Roman populace. Here, they commanded authority, and Mark wondered about their doctrine.

Conspicuous for their rarity were the fashionable Greco-Roman women who adorned Cyrene society. Because he missed Philea, he was aware that few women here approached her beauty.

This was not to say there were no charming ladies in Jerusalem. On the contrary, something in the modest attire and quiet grace of many Jewesses strongly appealed to him.

In fact, the occasional Romanesque woman who did traverse the avenues in handsome chariot or canopied cab looked out of place, resembling a gaudy flower against Palestine's more demure background.

Philea did not fit either theme. She was neither gaudy nor understated, her style neither flashy nor retiring. She would have circulated as easily here as at home.

Mark tried to suppress the memory of their parting kiss as he and his mother walked the crowded streets, skirting the central squares.

Like Cyrene, Jerusalem's public district was occupied by sprawling governmental and religious buildings. But something was missing. Gazing up the temple's terraced mount, Mark realized no statues or other likenesses dedicated to heroes, gods, goddesses, or even creatures adorned this hallowed place.

Yet the courts and palaces that loomed behind iron gates were elaborately conceived. The wealth of Israel was evident in lavish ornamentation, carving and gilding on every gable, column, and lintel.

Mark remembered, as he was remembering many things, that Orthodox Jews considered facsimiles of humans and animals to be idolatry and did not allow their artists to duplicate such parts of creation, except in tapestries, personal portraits, or small works for private enjoyment. They were banned in religious use or in publicly sponsored art.

The Ark of the Covenant, which rested in the innermost chamber of the temple, was said to bear upon its lid the likenesses of great angelic beings. But this sacred furnishing abided in God's own dwelling place and was part of the invocation of the Deity himself.

Whatever the reason for the stipulations, Mark found the lack of statuary disturbing. As he walked past the temple compound, his mind was drawn upward, toward the House of Holiness. And this was something new to him, for the precincts of Apollo and Zeus appealed to another spectrum of urges.

Never before had he thought of these urges as low. Only now did they seem so.

As Mark followed his mother through the shadow of the temple district, he tried to shake the sense of awe.

But it was persistent—much like Simon's haunting challenges.

CHAPTER

3

Joses was waiting at the family estate when Mary and her son arrived.

Mark had not seen his uncle since entering his teen years. The elder had aged, but Mark found him more distinguished, his hair marked silver at the temples, and his neatly groomed beard streaked white.

The nephew warmed instantly to Joses's fervent greeting, receiving the man's embrace and a kiss upon each cheek as though he were used to such gestures.

Mark had often heard of the home where his mother lived before meeting Quintus. He was not, however, prepared for its grandeur.

He knew that the Ben Haman wealth came from a long line of priestly heritage. Mary's father had been descended from the tribe of Levi, from whom the Levites, or priests of Israel, took their name.

It was the function of the Levite male to carry out the work of the priesthood, to tend holy things of worship in tabernacle and temple, and to teach the Law. Through the years this ministry had been ignored by the majority of Levite families.

Not even Joses, firstborn of Haman, had been groomed for the task.

The tradition was still given lip service in Israel. Priests within the temple were of Levite ancestry. But the custom was largely overlooked, as were many Mosaic injunctions.

Nonetheless, wealth had devolved to Joses through his ancestral connection. No Orthodox Levite would own property, but the family of Haman had long ago forgotten this.

Joses and Mary were, however, devout worshipers of Jehovah. If they did not follow the original stipulations to the letter, it was due to the influence of society, which gave only casual respect to the old ways.

Mark could not have imagined a more principled or honorable man than his uncle. Certainly, the son of Quintus, more schooled in Roman materialism than in the spirit of Judaism, took no offense at Joses's wealth. He was happy that the accommodations afforded his mother were so luxurious.

The home's spacious courtyard was ringed not only by a gallery, but by a mezzanine, the building rising three full stories from the street. As Mark looked toward the roof's richly carved balustrade, he recalled Mary's references to the chambers, the parlor and even a small patio that actually occupied that level. In addition, there was an extra house, or apartment, across the back alley, though this had rarely been used since Haman's death.

The household had been famous, in its heyday, for hospitality, entertaining an unusual number of guests throughout the year.

Haman and, in turn, Joses had always taken seriously the injunction that Jerusalem's citizens should make their homes available to pilgrims during festivals and holy weeks. At such times their house became an inn, though they never charged a penny for their services.

The roof had its own private entrance from a flight of stairs ascending the outer wall. One of its chambers was even designated for bathing, so that no guest would need to intrude upon the household.

Not that the family avoided mingling with those who stayed at their home. On the contrary, the Haman residence was famous for sumptuous dinners, and guests were welcome to dine with the family. Should they prefer privacy they were served meals in the rooftop parlor, a chamber large enough for a small banquet.

As Mark saw Mary's accounts of her childhood home confirmed in rich appointments of furniture, fountains, and flowering plants, he understood her yearning to return.

As for himself, he had planned to leave within a few days of delivering his mother here and seeing that she was provided for, both missions now accomplished.

But when Joses reminded his sister, with much enthusiasm, that Passover was only six weeks away, Mark wondered what such a time must be like in Jerusalem, especially in this house.

"Of course, we shall fill the rooms with guests once again!" the uncle insisted. "These old walls ache to embrace strangers."

"Oh, Joses!" Mary picked up his excitement. "Wouldn't that be wonderful? It has been so many years!"

Mark observed their magnanimous spirit with admiration, and with a prick of conscience. He was a cosmopolitan Roman, one filled with imperial pride. But he had never been so open to the world as were these folk.

CHAPTER

4

During the next few days Mark was more impressed than ever with the elegance and finery of the House Ben Haman. In addition to unusually adequate guest accommodations, it had five bedrooms for family and several more for servants. Each of these had a small fireplace, and the largest had private garden courts.

Since the house had been shut up for a long time, most of these rooms had fallen into disrepair. It would require much work and money to restore their original state.

When he first heard of Mary's bereavement, Joses sent orders from Cyprus to have the family quarters and some servants' rooms refurbished.

Now that Mary had arrived and Passover drew near, carpenters and tile masons kept up a clatter every day, reconditioning the guest chambers and finishing the rest of the house.

Not only would strangers occupy the roof hostel, but once family friends learned that the old retreat was being revived, they would be arriving from different parts of the world to

spend the holidays with Joses and Mary. Third story apart-
ments, more luxurious than those on the roof, were reserved
for such folk as these.

The days were hot. Mark missed the cooling breezes that
blew across Cyrene each evening. He was not used to living
so far inland, and compared to the temperate coast of his
homeland, Jerusalem was uncomfortably dry.

He rested his feet this evening in a damp towel layered
with mint leaves. As he reclined upon an upholstered chaise in
Joses's courtyard, he breathed in the herb's soothing fragrance
with appreciation.

A patio fountain spilled in descending stages over alabaster
lily pads, and formed miniature waterfalls, pleasing eye and
ear.

Mary sat beside her brother, a swatch of needlepoint draping her lap, as she worked a pattern of wild roses in tiny
stitches. It did not escape her son that the lines of grief and
loneliness that had etched her forehead only weeks before
were diminished, her nearly youthful countenance full of
peace.

"Uncle," he broke the silence, "I have been in Israel a short
time, yet everywhere I see kindness and tranquility. Where is
the discontent rumored of this province? I have always heard
that Jews are fiercely guarded and exclusive."

Joses sat back, smiling thoughtfully. "You are right to question whether there beats another heart beneath the quiet exte-
rior of this nation. Where I live, in Cyprus, the Jews are more
exclusive than in the homeland, as is often true in Gentile
regions. Some of the rumors are justified. A man is more
hospitable when he is secure, and the land represents security
to devout Jews and nominal alike.

"But even here there is, as you say, 'discontent,'" Joses
added. "Were you to walk our streets in the red cape that your
father gave you, you would not receive a friendly glance."

Mark nodded. "Of this I am aware," he said. And then
with wry humor, "I threw the cape in my satchel the moment
I entered town."

In anxious silence, Mary absorbed Mark's sarcasm, all too reminiscent of Quintus.

"Is it not true," Mark proceeded, "that Israel has been allowed to retain its own legal structure and religious practices to a greater degree than other provinces? I have seen very little of Roman art and architecture, such as dominates Cyrenaica. It seems to me that Rome has been most liberal with the Jews."

Suddenly Joses's gentle demeanor betrayed a zeal with which Mark was not familiar.

"You speak of Rome *allowing* Israel its heritage, as if the empire had a choice. Do you now know that Jehovah only *allows* Rome a foothold in our land to chasten us? Israel is the Lord's and not Rome's. Nothing happens to the Jews apart from the will of God. Rome has no power to strip us of our worship or our laws!"

Mark had not expected such a firm rebuttal. How like Simon this man was!

"You . . . you speak of Jehovah as though he were a . . . father," Mark marvelled.

Joses was silent, considering the observation a long while.

"So I do . . . ," he pondered, "just as the young Rabbi speaks of him. . . ."

"Rabbi?" Mark queried.

"Have I not mentioned the Teacher from Galilee? Jesus is his name. He speaks of God as Father, even claiming to be his Son. Our leaders wish to silence him, but so far have had no success."

Mary attended even more closely, now that the conversation had taken this unexpected twist.

"Simon spoke of this Rabbi when he returned from Cyprus," she recalled. "Is he as controversial as we hear?"

"Indeed." Joses nodded. "In fact, agitation in Israel arises as much, of late, over his teachings and miraculous signs, as over the oppressions of Rome."

Leaning forward, his hands on his knees, the Levite peered intently at his listeners. "Have you not heard reports of his spectacular healings? Even his small group of disciples, mostly simple fisherman, have wrought wonders. It is said that Jesus raised a man from the dead! One who had been buried four days!"

Mary stared at Mark, who silently studied his uncle.

"Since then, many have turned to Jesus, heralding him as Messiah," Joses went on, "and the Pharisees have put forth an order that anyone knowing his whereabouts must report him to the authorities!"

Sinking back into his chair, the speaker seemed caught away again, his face bearing a somber aspect. "Jesus claims to be a light for our darkness, but there are those who wish to snuff him out."

CHAPTER

5

"A light for our darkness . . ."

Mark pondered the meaning of those words, and being of a Roman frame of mind, was curious about the political implications.

Healings and miracles were not prominent in Roman thought. But Mark had heard of the hoped-for Messiah, the one the Jews had for centuries awaited, as Savior from all their troubles.

If it was true that this Nazarene Rabbi was creating such ferment as Joses claimed, Mark knew that Israel's Roman overseers had taken note of him. Always on guard against insurrection, provincial magistrates would be watching him carefully and likely would know who his enemies were among the Jews.

It was Sunday, the first day of Passover week, and five days until Passover itself. Mark walked among the shops of Jerusalem's bazaars, his uncle at his side. Mary was busy at home, working with her servants on the family quarters, establishing herself in the house she meant to keep for years to come.

"Will you be staying for Passover?" Joses asked, as they drew near the sacred grounds of the temple mount. "It is less than a week hence."

Mark had known the question would be asked sooner or later, and his brow knit, though a smile lit his eyes.

"I promised a friend I would return to Cyrene for the coming out of the maidens," he admitted. "To get there in time, I must leave before your holiday."

Joses understood why his nephew referred to Passover as if it did not pertain to himself. He could not resist the impulse, however, to use Mark's own words to advantage.

"It is intriguing to me that the Romans celebrate a 'coming out' just as do the Jews."

Such bait was hard to ignore. "You see a comparison between a debutantes' review and Passover?" Mark said with a chuckle.

"It is not difficult. Did the Israelites not have their own 'coming out' from Egyptian bondage on that day?"

Mark was speechless. Then laughing, he shook his head. "Surely you jest, Uncle. Jehovah would not appreciate the analogy."

"I think he would," Joses insisted. "Spring is a time of emergence, a time of leaving the restrictions of the past and embracing a future of fulfillment. I think the two celebrations are remarkably similar!"

Mark silently contemplated the argument. And Joses drew the net tighter.

"I also find it curious and perhaps portentous that four years ago this season, the Rabbi Jesus had his first great 'coming out' before the public. It was during Passover that he first drew the attention of friend and foe alike by wielding a whip in the temple."

"He what?" Mark exclaimed. "Tell me more!"

Reading the young man's sudden interest, Joses smiled. "This is no ordinary rabbi."

"Truly! He is a violent man, then? An insurrectionist?" Mark's Roman eyes snapped.

"If he were, would you loathe him or admire him?" Joses laughed.

Mark drew back, hesitation answering for him.

Joses did not press the point, seeing better use for his nephew's vulnerability.

"No, son," he suggested. "I do not think he is violent. And he preaches no politics whatever."

At this, Mark was disappointed, despite Roman allegiance.

"What then does he preach?" he inquired.

Joses recalled the temple incident vividly. "That day, he drove the moneychangers from the House of God, where for centuries they have robbed the public of all nations who come to worship. He overturned their tables, tore open the cages of the doves and pigeons kept for sacrifice, and set free the tethered sheep and rams.

" 'Make not my Father's house a house of merchandise!' " Joses repeated Jesus' proclamation.

There it was again, the reference to God as Father.

Mark studied his uncle's upturned face and widespread arms, riveted by his convincing portrayal.

"Do you think Jesus will come to Jerusalem again this Passover?" he asked, awe in his tone.

"Why don't you stay with us and see?" Joses suggested, his eyes atwinkle.

Mark sensed the triumph in the Cypriot's voice. But he did not resist it.

Joses and Mark were not the only ones in Jerusalem questioning whether the notorious Rabbi would attend the festival.

Daily in the temple, folk discussed the possibility, poised for any hint of his arrival.

If four Passovers before he had been so bold as to upset the moneychangers' tables, what might he do now, were he to enter the holy place under much publicity?

It was early afternoon when Joses and his nephew headed home. As they proceeded up the boulevard, they found the street unusually overpopulated.

Thousands stood along the viaduct, as though anticipating a

parade, their heads turned expectantly toward the Mount of Olives and the road that descended toward the city.

A huzza filled the air, newcomers asking the reason for the crowd.

"The Rabbi is coming!" folks said. "He approaches from Bethany."

No one need ask which Rabbi. Jesus of Nazareth was the obvious subject of such reference.

Suddenly, as Mark and Joses stood beside the road, their eagerness for the Nazarene's appearance keenly piqued, a great shout arose from the vicinity of Olivet. The two men stood on tiptoe, but their view was blocked by a rush of enthusiastic worshipers waving palm branches and spreading cloaks on the road before the Rabbi and his entourage.

"Hosanna! Hosanna!" the people cried. "Blessed is he who comes in the name of the Lord!" Over and over the crowd chanted the refrain.

Mark had seen the victory parades of Roman warriors. He was used to the emotion which the passage of drum and stallion, shield and scarlet banner could evoke.

But there was no such glitter here—no blast of trumpet, no flash of chariot. No armed forces accompanied the Nazarene. The Master could not, in fact, be seen by many of his ardent devotees.

Surely, however, there must be something spectacular pushing through town. Mark waited with strained patience for the Rabbi's party to draw near, determined to catch a glimpse.

What he saw, at last, was neither spectacular nor unusual. In fact, Mark could not believe that such a common-looking character could provoke adoration.

Dressed in homespun and dusty sandals, the Nazarene proceeded down the compressed path, sitting atop the lowliest of beasts, a donkey. His hair and beard, the color of Israel's pale-earthed hills, framed a face which in itself was not distinctive.

But then, there were the Rabbi's eyes.

It was when the Master's gaze fell upon Mark, that the young Roman—the young Jew—sensed the unfathomable mystery of the man, the spiritual presence that could, indeed, captivate a nation.

For only a moment did those eyes lock upon Mark's soul, mirroring back to him his own neediness and the heart hunger he had only recently experienced. But in that short encounter, the shouts of the crowd faded from Mark's ears, the jostling of the masses made no impact. It was as if, for that brief span of seconds, he and the Rabbi were face to face, alone.

When the Master's party had passed and the Nazarene was beyond view, Mark still felt the impact of that knowing look.

As if it had seared a brand upon his heart, he would find it a sensation not easily shaken.

CHAPTER

6

As Passover drew near, the House Ben Haman was filled with guests and friends. The third-floor bedchambers were taken— all but one. This was reserved for Simon the Cyrenian, who had recently sent word of his intention to visit Jerusalem. He would be tending to business affairs in Alexandria and would not arrive for Passover, but would hasten to spend time with Joses and Mary directly after.

Mark hoped that Simon would bring word from Philea, a message that she eagerly awaited his return for the spring rites. But he knew he would never make it home for the event. He had become more involved in the Jerusalem scene than he intended.

He could not understand himself these days. When news spread that Jesus of Nazareth had again entered the temple, re-enacting the hour when he had driven the bankers from their coffers and sent the wares of the merchants flying, Mark's soul again stirred with curiosity.

He loved Philea, but he could not tear himself away from Jerusalem just yet.

As for Mary, when news came of Simon's pending visit, her spirits were more elevated than ever. She was the happiest Mark had seen her since the death of Quintus.

Hospitality was her chief joy, and she was able to practice it grandly in her native land.

Mary never shunned the chance to work beside her servants. As the widow of a Roman statesman, and with her own portion of her family's inheritance, she was a lady of means. She was not bound to house and hearth or to the toil of the lower classes.

But Mary took pleasure in scrubbing the linens for the guest chambers. She saw to it that the washbowls were fresh each morning and that the water was scented with mint and blossom oil. She took delight in calling her visitors to supper. She planned the menu, selected the produce and the meats, inspired the spice cake recipes and the cinnamon sauce that glazed the sweetdough rolls.

She even saw to it that the roof rooms, equipped for strangers, were almost as sumptuous as those occupied by close friends.

As the hour drew near that Passover would be commemorated, Mary enlisted the assistance of the men in carrying out to the last detail the gracious nuances for which her home would become famous.

It was, at last, the day of the feast, and Mark found himself involved in woman's work. Had Quintus been here, he would not have allowed this indignity. But Mary saw it as a necessity. Joses only winked at Mark's scowling face as the young man left the house with a waterpot on his shoulder.

Women usually drew water in the early morning or at evening, avoiding the heat of the day. It was noon when Mark went to the nearest plaza and expected to be alone. But it was a holiday demanding much preparation and the well was busy throughout the day. So Mark arrived to the sideways glances and covert snickers of a dozen servant girls.

His face red, he waited in line, the empty pot strangely

heavy on his arm. He hoped he was only imagining that men who passed by spoke of him beneath their breath. As he placed the pot on the well's lip, attaching the rope that would lower it into the fountain's cool depths, he was certain that at least two fellows had found his presence here worthy of scrutiny.

Quickly he let the weighted rope plummet through his hands, sending the vessel to a hollow splash. As the container grew heavier, he knew they discussed him. Drawing the pot upward, he hoisted it again to his shoulder. As he passed through the crowd, a glimpse back told him that he was being followed.

He walked as fast as possible toward the house. The men were now virtually at his heels and he wondered if they were spoiling for a fight. Two against one were not odds he wished to tackle.

Not until he reached the door did he turn to confront them.

"If it's trouble you want, step across this threshold!" he demanded.

The men were of sturdy build, one husky as a bear, tall and dark; the other, not quite so large, but clearly a strapping youth, with light hair and swarthy complexion.

They appeared to be transients, road-weary and windblown. From their demeanor, they might be men of an outdoor vocation, durable, accustomed to hard ways.

Nonetheless, despite the fact that they had brought the confrontation on themselves, they seemed taken aback by it.

"Sir," the larger one said, surprisingly apologetic, "we mean no harm. We would speak with the goodman of the house."

Beyond this they gave no explanation. After an awkward silence, Mark set the pot on the porch and wiped his hands on his cloak.

"Uncle Joses!" he called into the courtyard. "Two men wish to speak with you."

Joses emerged from the parlor and poked his head through

the portal. He was used to strangers approaching his door this time of year.

"Do you seek lodging?" he asked amicably.

Mark marveled at his congeniality. He had expected foreigners and dusty travelers to descend upon the home, but these fellows were beneath the quality of this gracious hostel.

Still, the men were strangely tight-lipped, surveying Joses as scrupulously as he surveyed them.

Now it was the blond man who spoke.

"The Master says to you, 'My time is at hand. Where is my guest room where I may eat the Passover with my disciples?' "

Such peculiar words! Surely these men were up to no good.

But Joses seemed to see things differently. Mark was speechless as his uncle studied them briefly, his face conveying awe.

"Yes . . . yes!" he said nodding, throwing open the door and leading them into the hall.

"Up this way," he said, hastening toward the stairway that ascended from the court. "Follow me!"

Mark trailed behind, incredulous, as his uncle directed the men past the second and third levels, to the rooftop banquet room.

"See," Joses said breathlessly, pointing to the clean, linen-spread tables and flower-decked balustrade. "It is furnished and ready. You may prepare your meal here!"

The men quickly examined the chamber and nodded approval.

"We will be back shortly," they said as they turned to go.

Down the stairs again they exited, leaving Joses behind, where he bowed anxiously to their backs.

Mark, bewildered, hesitantly tapped his uncle on the shoulder.

"Sir," he whispered, "what are they up to?"

"At first I did not recognize them," Joses explained. "But when they spoke, I remembered. I saw them with Jesus of Nazareth the day he entered the city. They are his disciples!"

Mark glanced over the roof rail toward the door where they had just departed.

"The Rabbi will dine here tonight?" he asked in amazement.

"This very evening," Joses replied.

CHAPTER

7

It was not merely the Rabbi's prominence, nor his miraculous acts, that kept Mark's attention focused on the entryway to Joses's home.

At any moment Jesus and his companions would be arriving. Energy ran high, not only because the family had made its own preparation for the feast, but because everyone who lodged here knew the home was about to be graced by Israel's most popular yet most despised celebrity.

It was more than Jesus's fame, however, which caused Mark's hands to tremble as he carried the bowl of matzoh balls from the kitchen. It was more than the controversy surrounding the Rabbi which made him spill a dab of wine upon the tablecloth as he poured it into silver goblets.

His eyes, like those of Joses, Mary, and every other member of the house, wandered repeatedly to the doorway as he worked. But it was a spiritual awe that overwhelmed him, not simply the giddiness of one who would entertain a star.

The impact of the Rabbi's penetrating gaze still haunted

him. The realization that the one who had seared his soul
with a glance would be dining here caused him no end of
uneasiness.

He wondered if anyone else felt the same way. Had Joses
been as transfixed as he the day they watched the Rabbi's
entrance into town? Had any servant or guest received such a
heart searching?

When close to mealtime a knock was heard at the door, his
heart leaped. At the entry stood the two men who had earlier
approved the upper room.

The burly one, who had first spoken to Mark when they
came to the house, carried beneath his arm a burlap-covered
package, doubtless the carcass of lamb that the company
would roast upon the upstairs spit. Behind them came others
of the Master's men, each bearing some portion of the meal to
be prepared on the rooftop.

The Rabbi himself entered with his disciples, not leading
them, but accompanying them as though he were only one
more guest. He stood head and shoulders taller than most of
his companions, and in his bearing was that indefinable maj-
esty that had first spurred Mark's heart to wonder.

Mark stood at the table where he had been arranging seats
when the company arrived. He watched as Joses welcomed
the Rabbi and his men. He would wish, later, that he had
raced forward in greeting. But he was paralyzed with fascination.

There was a rush of servants to accommodate the strangers,
and his mother sent several of her maids ahead to light the
rooftop lamps.

Mark was unmoving, studying the Teacher as he ascended
the stairs and disappeared with his followers behind the balustrade.

In the company there was nothing noteworthy except their
commonness. No one stood out save one fellow dressed in
Judean garb a bit finer than the rest and lagging behind the
others as they traversed the mezzanine and gallery.

Mark wondered what his story might be. And he wondered

what it was about him—the closed expression or bent head—that sent a chill to his heart.

Mark had never experienced a traditional Passover meal. Annually since childhood his mother had prepared dinner for this night unlike any other fare served in the Quintus household.

But Mary had been stifled by the Gentile atmosphere of her Roman home, and though she had done her best to produce a mood of reverence and uniqueness for Passover evening, the feast had never been fully commemorated.

The son of Quintus was familiar with bitter herb salad, charoseth sauce, unleavened bread, and lamb, the main dishes. He was used to donning traveling garb and sandals and was accustomed to keeping a staff beside his chair throughout the dinner in remembrance of the Israelites' escape from Egypt. But the historical explanations that accompanied the feast, the spoken introductions, and the hymn sung with each cup were unfamiliar.

It was therefore with the enthusiasm and awkwardness of a foreigner that he observed his uncle's administration of each portion and partook of the rites and songs.

Joses was highly adept at fulfilling Passover customs. Mark had never admired him more than he did tonight as he watched his uncle, his mantle-covered head bowed in reverence while he blessed the the lamb and raised four toasts in keeping with tradition.

The nephew's thoughts, however, were not fully on the feast. Over and over he glanced at the rooftop.

There was no reason for him to visit the banquet hall above. Any excuse to do so would have been seen for what it was—the desire to eavesdrop.

The Master had kindly rejected Mary's offer of servants to assist with his meal. It had been apparent that he wished privacy. There would not even be a maid or butler to question as to what happened in the rooftop sanctuary.

The servants who waited on Mary's commands were kept

busy. As they dished up the third course, Mark's mother asked him to request another pitcher of wine.

Rising, he went to the kitchen arch and whispered to the waiter in charge that the cups were going dry. Quickly the servant fetched a jug, and Mark was about to join the table again when a movement at the pantry window caught his eye.

Mark stepped to the latticed opening and drew the shutter back. Just in time, he caught a glimpse of someone passing down the dark alleyway. It was a hunched and miserable looking character who skirted the house, bent, it appeared, on some terrible mission.

As Mark studied his furtive departure through the black corridor, he recognized him as the peculiar fellow who had trailed at the edge of the Master's company.

Surely the Rabbi's feast was not yet over. No other disciples slipped through the alley with this one.

Mark watched, filled with uneasiness, as the shadowy figure cast a desperate glance over his shoulder and disappeared into the night.

A full moon shone through a cloudless sky over Jerusalem's streets. Mark wondered if he should follow the man.

Thinking better of it, he returned to the table and his kindred, drawing the curtain across the kitchen arch.

But the memory of the fellow's dark and slinking passage provoked an eeriness which would not be dismissed.

CHAPTER

8

Mark found it difficult to sleep that night. His room on the mezzanine was flooded with the light of the full moon. He could have closed the blinds across the chamber's narrow window, but it would have done no good. He could not shut out the memory of the character whose suspicious behavior he had witnessed earlier.

He wondered if he ought to tell Joses of the incident. But, due to the command of the authorities that Jesus' where-abouts should be reported, his mother was already nervous enough about the rooftop residents. With no evidence of foul play, he hesitated to create further anxiety.

Besides, it was almost midnight. His uncle was sound asleep, and even though the guests in the uppermost room had gotten a late start on their supper preparations, they likely rested in slumber by now.

Almost he had persuaded himself that he only imagined the worst, and was ready to go to sleep, when a sound, low and enchanting, roused him.

Sitting up in bed, he strained to hear. The outer wall of his room backed onto the stairway leading toward the roof, and coming from the rooftop room he heard the minor chords of a hymn.

He was certain the song was the same one with which Joses had closed the family feast this evening. Though he could not make out the words, he recognized the somber tune and knew it was the final hymn of Passover, traditionally sung by all who celebrated the holiday.

Could it be that the Rabbi and his men were only now completing their feast? Surely they would turn in now, each man to his own comfortable pallet.

As he drifted once more toward slumber, he was again awakened—this time by the sound of footsteps on the outer stairs and by the flash of lantern light spilling across his window.

Leaping to his feet, he stood beside the opening, keeping out of view, but peering carefully toward the steep descent.

Jesus and his men were leaving the roof, still garbed in the clothes appropriate to the feast, as though for a journey. Each wore heavy sandals, carried a drawstring bag upon his belt or a satchel, and most bore a staff in hand. Mark even noted the shining hilt of a sword here and there.

They were very quiet, not so much as though they feared detection but as though deep in thought.

In the light of the lanterns which a few carried, Mark could count twelve men—the Master and eleven disciples.

Twelve companions had entered the house with Jesus, so Mark knew that the one who had earlier departed had never returned.

The young Roman's heart tripped with urgency. Surely something evil was afoot.

Retreating into the shadows of his room, he did not stop to grab the cloak he had thrown across his bed, nor even to pull on his sandals. Wearing only a linen wrap about his loins, he raced for the chamber door and onto the moonlit mezzanine.

For a fleeting second he considered waking Joses. But casting the idea aside, he descended the court stairs and fled for the entryway.

If he hurried, he could follow the Rabbi's party and see for himself what was to happen.

And if he kept a careful distance between himself and the Galileans, they would never know of his presence.

Mark's pulse throbbed as he pursued the distant company through the shadow-patched streets of Jerusalem.

A fickle moon darted now between straggly clouds, alternately drenching the rough cobblestones in azure light or dismal blackness.

Everything about the night was eerie. Trying to keep a safe space between himself and the huddled group ahead, he sometimes found it necessary to slow his pace, to dip into some dreary corner where he knew not what might lie in wait.

When at last the Rabbi's little band reached one of the city gates and disappeared down a slope toward the foot of Mount Olivet, he breathed easier. At least here were open spaces and not the dangerous alleys of the city.

He wished he had a cloak about his shoulders. The warm temperatures of the day were giving way to a cool breeze, and Mark's flesh stood in gooseprickles.

Clasping his arms across his chest and rubbing his shoulders with both hands, he fought nervous anxiety.

It was becoming nearly as difficult to follow the Rabbi's trail in the "open" as it had been in the twisting streets of town. Clumps of oak and cypress now filled large tracts of ground, and though the Galileans seemed to know exactly where they were headed, Mark was completely unfamiliar with the landscape. Occasionally even the lanternlight that betrayed their location was obliterated by intruding vegetation.

Nor did the company make much noise as it wound its way through the maze of Palestinian undergrowth. Though Mark had earlier found it imperative to keep a safe distance from the group, he now needed to follow more closely than he wished for fear of losing them altogether.

A disturbing wind tossed the treetops like sacks of black wool. Sinewy branches reached for the young trespasser as he slunk criminal-like through the slapping shadows. Mark wondered why he had risked such an ordeal.

Now joining the rush of the breeze was the sound of gurgling water. Peering past the limbs of a wild olive tree, Mark saw the moon reflected in a small stream, across which spanned a narrow bridge leading to a garden.

As the men slowed, filing two by two across the bridge, Mark hid in the bushes bordering the rivulet.

Not knowing what the night might hold, he was determined to proceed no farther. Were the Rabbi's enemies to come seeking the Nazarene, it would be safer to be this side of the stream, not trapped within the cloistered garden.

Settling upon his haunches, Mark parted the leaves of a bush to observe whatever might transpire.

The Rabbi left all but three of his disciples stationed at the edge of the grove. He took the three men with him to the center of the garden, where almost immediately he seemed overtaken with great anxiety, his face lifted to the sky in terrible sadness. Mark could not hear his words, but it seemed he told his companions to wait where they were while he went yet farther into the little grotto.

To Mark's amazement, the Rabbi knelt on the ground, falling on his face, and for a long time appeared to be praying in some kind of torment, writhing and lifting his fists in a beseeching manner to the heavens.

Because this interlude was so lengthy, Mark, like the Rabbi's followers, found drowsiness nearly overpowering. He was awake enough to observe when the Rabbi returned from his prayers, and finding his disciples sleeping, rebuked their leader, the large, burly stranger who had first approached Joses's house.

But at last, his own eyelids growing irresistibly heavy, Mark also succumbed to slumber, resting his head upon his knees.

It would not be until a great tramping sound and a shaking

of the ground filled the vale that Mark would rouse again. Jerking fully alert, he hunched into the bushes and shielded his face from the glare of a dozen torches.

From the direction of the city a crowd had approached through the wilderness patch, descending into the grove and crossing the little footbridge, just as the disciples had done. Momentarily disoriented by the noise and the dizzying light, Mark could not instantly interpret the scene. But it was evident that these intruders were on no friendly mission.

Mark rose on his knees and cautiously peered over the wild hedge. It did not require military training to know that a commission had been sent to seize the Rabbi. The soldiers were not of Caesar or any Roman magistrate; they wore no uniform familiar to him. They must be a Jewish force, perhaps temple guards, he determined. And they were accompanied by several elder men wearing what appeared to be the frocks and tasseled mantles of the religious hierarchy.

Reflecting torch and lanternlight, swords spiked the air and clubs cast long, threatening shadows across the ground.

More hair-raising still was the sight of the man who led the throng—the culprit whom Mark had seen sneaking through the alley this evening.

As Mark studied the sunken eyes and gaunt face of the traitor, hideously haloed in yellow lamplight, his skin crawled. And when the evil one stepped forward, indicating which of the Galileans was to be targeted, Mark was filled with revulsion. For it was with a brotherly kiss upon the Rabbi's cheek that the betrayer made his sign.

"Judas, do you betray the Son of Man with a kiss?" Jesus asked, speaking the first words of the night which Mark could clearly hear.

Rather than resist the treachery, Jesus seemed ready to volunteer for the arrest. Stepping toward his would-be captors, he asked, "Whom do you seek?"

His enemies, surprised at his undefended posture, hesitated, then answered, "Jesus of Nazareth!"

"I am he," Jesus simply declared.

Instantly, a most peculiar thing occurred. As Mark and the disciples looked on, the crowd, including Judas, drew backward, and, as though smitten by some irresistible force, fell to the ground.

"Whom do you seek?" Jesus asked again, standing over them with an authoritative expression.

This time the answer was given in a stammer. "Jesus of Nazareth. . . ."

"I told you that I am he," he asserted. "If you seek me, let these go their way," he demanded, gesturing to his disciples.

By now the soldiers, who lay in disarray at the Rabbi's feet, had gathered their weapons and were shakily standing up. Determined to fulfill their mission, they lunged at the Master, seizing him.

"Lord, shall we strike with the sword?" one of the disciples cried, raising a glistening blade.

As a body, the Rabbi's followers attempted to intervene between him and his captors. The group's leader, the large fellow who always seemed to head things, drew another sword and, with a careening slash, struck one of the enemies on the side of the head.

Mark winced as the hapless fellow slumped to the ground, screaming and holding his gushing wound. In the lamplight, at the Master's feet, lay his severed ear.

Surely mayhem would have broken forth had the Rabbi not performed yet another incredible feat.

Bending over, he placed a hand on the bleeding man's shoulder, and then reached for the grisly piece of flesh lying in the dust.

"Permit this!" he commanded. Touching the man's ear to the side of his head, he restored it, the skin new as a baby's, the blood disappearing in the blink of an eye.

"Peter," he said, turning to his weapon-wielding follower, "put up your sword! All who take the sword will perish by the sword! Do you think that I cannot now call to my Father and he will furnish me more than twelve legions of angels? But how then would the Scriptures be fulfilled, that it must be so?

The cup which the Father has given me . . . shall I not drink
it?"

At the sound of these words, Mark was flooded with the
same strange sensation that had overwhelmed him the day he
first saw the Rabbi. Surely, this one who referred to the Deity
as Father was no mere mortal!

Still, the Nazarene was speaking, this time to his awestruck
antagonists.

As though he would not be satisfied until they took him, he
proffered himself.

"Have you come out as against a robber, with swords and
clubs, to seize me?" he inquired. "Daily I sat with you, teaching in the temple, and you did not arrest me, nor did you
stretch forth hands against me. But, this has all come to pass
that the Scriptures may be fulfilled. This is your hour," he said
with a sigh, "and the power of darkness."

Suddenly, as the disciples saw that he was determined to
comply with his enemies, there was a rustling within their
group. One by one, and then in mass, they fled beyond the
farthest reaches of the garden, disappearing upstream, where
they would hide themselves in the undergrowth.

Horrified, Mark crouched beneath the hedge, afraid to
move until he saw the Rabbi being bound, his hands tied
behind his back, his arms strapped against his body. At the
sight of this brutality, the spectator reflexively stood up, forgetting himself as his breath came hot and fast.

His foolhardy move would not go undetected. In an instant, the guards were crashing through the brush toward
him, ready to haul him away with the Rabbi.

But he was an athletic youth, speedy and agile. The soldiers
could only grasp at his garment, tearing from his loins his
flimsy nightcloth. He was well on his way through the city
gate and into the dark byways of Jerusalem before he realized
his disgraceful condition.

Naked and terrified, he sought the sanctuary of Joses's
house, wondering why he had ever left Cyrene.

CHAPTER

9

Though there was nothing Mark could have done against so many of the Rabbi's enemies, he felt guilty for not warning the Nazarene of the brewing betrayal. Surely he had suspected it when he saw the hunched form slink through the alley.

Terror and humiliation stalked him as he groped his way through the streets, tears of frustration streaking his cheeks at every blind turn.

"No way for a Roman to behave," he could hear his father's voice. "Walk like a man, my son."

But the best he could do was hunch, shielding his nakedness with his hands and peering behind him at every shadow, every sound.

His heart drummed thunder-like as he paused long enough to pull a light tarpaulin off a neighbor's tethered hay cart. Wrapping it around his chilled body, he ran for the house which loomed miraculously ahead upon a mist-cloaked corner.

In his haste to follow the Rabbi earlier that night, Mark had given no thought to the possibility that the great door of the residence would be barred when he returned.

When he arrived, beating feverishly on the entry, he received a most bemused greeting from the servant girl who admitted him.

Gritting his teeth, he tried not to show his embarrassment. But he wished it had been someone other than this young woman who had come to the door!

Most of his uncle's servants were intelligent folk whom Mark respected. But this girl was an irritant. Rhoda was her name, "Rose," befitting a much more graceful damsel than this addle-pated thing. She did not take orders well and needed to be told two or three times how to do the most simple tasks. Also, to his consternation, Mark had sensed that the girl was smitten with him—her eyes following him whenever he entered a room, her lisping speech turning to a giggle whenever he spoke to her.

Stumbling past her, he wrapped the tarp closer to his waist and tried not to make eye contact. As he raced up the stairs to the gallery, he could not help but catch a glimpse of the wide-eyed maiden, her hand raised to her mouth, stifling a snicker.

Madly he tore to his room, donned his clothes, and emerged again, running to Joses's chamber.

"Uncle!" he cried. "Uncle! Wake up! The Rabbi has been arrested!"

Quickly the story was told, again and again, as the family, guests, and servants gathered along the gallery and mezzanine.

"Betrayed . . . ," he said, swallowing hard on the word. "The Rabbi has been betrayed by one of his friends!"

As he spoke, a servant boy called out from the kitchen, "They are returning now! Up the outside stairs!"

In mass, the household, guests and all, rushed to the rooftop. Mark, pressing through to the front of the crowd, reached the upper chamber just as several bedraggled characters opened the outside door.

Surveying the refugees, he saw that the leader who had first reserved the upper room was not among them, nor was his blond companion.

"Where is Peter?" he demanded, using the name by which the Rabbi had addressed the impetuous disciple during the garden ordeal.

The weary Galileans, seeing the company that filled their quarters, turned fearfully to flee again. But Mark called out once more, "Where is Peter?"

They stopped and studied him suspiciously. "How do you know our brother?" they asked, surprised to hear him called by the nickname that only the Rabbi's followers recognized.

Mark, feigning an authoritative stance, drew back his shoulders. "I know many things about you," he proclaimed.

The disciples looked at one another uneasily and surveyed Mark again, up and down. By his peculiar accent, they knew he was neither Judean nor Galilean. And when he introduced himself, they began to move back through the door.

"I am Marcus Quintus, relative of the owner," he said, enjoying the suspense he created.

"A Roman," he heard someone whisper, making him an enemy both of Israel and their Teacher.

"Your presence here only endangers my family," Mark asserted. "Though we respect your Master, we cannot risk giving you lodging another night."

Now Joses, who had also pressed toward the front, hurried to Mark's side.

"Nephew!" he demanded. "Enough of this! These are our guests, and their troubles are our own. No Israelite will cast out a stranger taken into his home." Then, beckoning the men, he led them into the chamber. "You are welcome to stay as long as necessary," he announced. "Come, friends," he gestured to the onlookers, "let us return to our own rooms. There are yet many hours before morning."

One by one, the group filed back down the stairs to the gallery and mezzanine, whispering to one another and shaking their heads in bewilderment.

The young Roman who had intimidated the disciples only seconds before was silent and perplexed as his uncle took him away.

Neither did Mary say a word as she followed her son from the roof, clinging to his sturdy arm, and wondering at the peculiar events that had accompanied her long-awaited Passover.

CHAPTER

10

During the hours that followed the garden scene, the plot against Jesus' life escalated.

Though it was the middle of the night, the unassuming Rabbi was hauled from the High Priest to the Roman Procurator for trial, as the Jews sought first to have him indicted under their own code, and then under the laws of Caesar.

The elders and priests who accosted the Nazarene hoped to achieve a sentence before dawn—before the people could intervene. They knew the Rabbi's popularity could spark revolution should word leak out of their intentions.

Such a thing could not be kept secret, however. When Jesus was led through the court of High Priest Caiaphas, he was seen by servants lingering near the patio fire. The hearing before Pilate, the Roman governor, further aborted his enemies' hopes. The governor, not wishing to judge what he considered a local case, sent Jesus to Herod, ruler of the Rabbi's province, who was present in Jerusalem for the feast. This inquisition pushed a decision into morning. And by the time Herod sent Jesus back to Pilate, having passed no judgment, the entire city was abuzz with the matter.

It seemed that every few moments since dawn, some new development in the case was heralded through the streets and was often brought directly into the house of Joses and Mary as their many guests came and went.

When word spread that the Teacher had been sent a second time to Pilate, and that an angry mob was outside provincial headquarters, Mark was determined to attend.

Joses, likewise, wanted to witness the proceedings. Together the two trekked through the crowded streets as hundreds made their way to the procurator's palace.

The mood of the city was a desperate one. Mark was not surprised that the frantic tone seemed to be in support of the Nazarene. The people's love for Jesus had not diminished since his triumphal entry into the city only a few days previous. The same men who had thrown their cloaks on the pavement before his humble donkey-steed, and the same women who had waved palm fronds in rhythm to songs of praise, had not changed their opinion of the miracle worker. Had they possessed power to crown him king, they would have done so. And the evil which their religious leaders plotted against the Teacher only piqued their zeal.

This was to be expected. What was not anticipated was the dramatic turnabout of the throng upon reaching the governor's mansion.

In the interim between the hearing before Herod and the appearance of Pilate in his public courtyard, the elders, priests, and temple soldiers circulated among the waiting crowd. As more and more citizens converged upon the yard, flocking against the open fence, they were greeted by people strangely confused in their opinion. Gradually the Jewish leaders were turning many of the Rabbi's supporters into skeptics.

Taking advantage of the mob spirit, and cleverly manipulating the people's high emotion, the elders planted numerous accusations, then watched them fester into rapid bloom.

"He says he will destroy the temple," they whispered. "He claims to be God's Son! Blasphemy! Blasphemy!" they shouted.

Posing at their pious best, they bore down upon the ignorant populace, intimidating them with knowledge and authority. In a less frenzied moment, the people might have seen through their badgering—they might have interpreted the evil in their piercing eyes and sinister smiles. As it was, it took only a few falling to their deception to sway the multitude.

Shortly before Pilate emerged, accusations shifted from the religious to the political. With crafty timing, the elders stirred up the throng not only to turn against their beloved Teacher, but to defend Rome, their mortal and spiritual foe.

"He calls himself a king!" they insisted. "He forbids tribute to Caesar!"

"There is no king but Caesar!" they cried, setting up a chant.

By the time Mark and Joses reached the scene, it was a bloodthirsty, hostile mob that surrounded the court. They were shouting for the death of Jesus.

When Pilate appeared, it was to the cheers and not the hisses of the crowd.

Mark turned to Joses, speechless, and the uncle shook his head. "Satan has filled their ears with lies!" he whispered.

"Uncle . . . ," Mark gasped, "you speak of the priests of Israel!"

"Indeed!" Joses nodded.

Mark surveyed the scene with wonder—the fickle masses clinging to the fences, shaking their fists and shouting hate-filled epithets against the Nazarene.

Pilate carried himself with typical Roman aloofness, his chin raised, as though he felt only haughty indifference.

Mark read more than coolness in the governor's bearing as the man fidgeted with the hem of his purple cape. Suddenly, Mark's eyes fell on the flashing pendant hung about the governor's neck. Quintus had worn such an insignia when he was interim ruler of Cyrenaica. Mark knew well the dangers that came with the office.

The olive wreath interwoven with Pilate's tightly curled hair was indicative of peace, but there was no peace in this confrontation. As Pilate surveyed the crowd, he looked confident, but he must have wondered how to handle such an emotion-ridden case.

Snapping his fingers, he called for the defendant. Two guards emerged from the palace, Jesus between them.

The sight of the Rabbi aroused another chorus of hisses and spit from the railing crowd—the same people who only days before had hailed Jesus as Messiah. Mark ached for the humble Galilean, yearning for a show of force on the Nazarene's part.

But the Teacher only stared quietly at the pavement, his hands bound at his back.

"You brought me this man as one stirring up subversion!" Pilate began. "But upon examining him I find nothing worthy of accusation."

"Guilty!" the crowd cried, primed by their leaders. "Blasphemy! Treason!"

"Not even Herod, one of your own rulers, could accuse him," Pilate objected. "Nothing worthy of death has been done by him."

More shouts and curses filled the court, and Pilate's face evinced fear. Raising his hands, he tried to calm them.

"You have a custom . . . ," he shouted above the mob, "you have a custom that I release to you one prisoner at Passover. I will chastise him," he offered, "and then release him."

If the crowd did not accept his suggestion, he dreaded the consequences.

There was a lull in the din as the people considered this. Mark saw the elders circulating once more, whispering here and there. As they did, a peculiar name began to be chanted, over and over.

"Barabbas! Barabbas! Give us Barabbas!"

Joses flinched, grasping Mark by the arm. "They cry out for Israel's most notorious criminal! They would rather see an insurrectionist and murderer released than the Rabbi!"

"Who is the man?" Mark asked.

"He has been incarcerated for months, awaiting death. Strange, isn't it, that the Nazarene's case should be so speedily decided?"

Mark shook his head. "Barabbas must be very popular."

"A b_____ of the streets." Joses smirked. "A no-name! They would trade this rabble for a miracle worker!" The uncle hung his head in shame. "Almost I wish myself a Gentile . . . and not a Jew."

"What then shall I do with Jesus?" Pilate was asking, his voice cracking with anxiety.

Again the crowd was quiet, as the dreaded verdict hung in their hearts. "Let him be crucified!" someone cried at last. And the people agreed, echoing, "Crucify! Crucify him!"

"Why?" Pilate shuddered, his tone heavy with frustration. "What evil has he done? I find in him no guilt deserving death." Finally, with a look of authority, he asserted, "I will chastise him, and I will release him!"

Snapping his fingers, he directed the guards to escort Jesus from the courtyard. The throng, watching his departure, went wild. Leaping upon the fence, young men pounded their bodies against the poles, shaking the thin wall with a vengeance. And women shrieked unladylike curses at the governor.

The Rabbi was not held in the palace for long. As Mark and Joses waited fearfully among the crazed spectators, Pilate announced the entrance once more of the Nazarene.

"Behold the man!" his voice rang across the yard in Latin syllables.

Mark and his uncle stood on tiptoe to glimpse the one who had emerged from the palace's dark interior. And as a hush fell over the crowd, tears blurred Mark's vision.

If the mood of the throng were to change, it would surely do so now, for the gashes and bruises of a Roman whipping showed upon Jesus's back. He was covered with a gaudy purple robe, and on his head was a thorny crown, blood trickling from fresh wounds where some cruel soldier had driven spikes into his brow. Beyond this obscene garb, he wore nothing but a loin cloth, and he stood quiet, his eyes expressionless.

Suddenly the telling stillness was followed by more curses and shouts, as the multitude spurned the pathetic figure of the once-adored Teacher.

As in the garden, every muscle in Mark's body screamed for revenge. But again he could do nothing against so many and stood helpless, while the Galilean, whom he was beginning to love, remained silent before his captors.

He could slay them all with a glance! Mark thought, remembering the Rabbi's show of power last night. *Reveal yourself!* he longed to cry out. *Smite your enemies!*

But Jesus only gazed at the ground, as even the procurator tried in vain to spare him.

"Crucify him!" the chief priests demanded. "Crucify! Crucify!" the officers echoed.

"*You* take and crucify him," Pilate snarled, "for I find no guilt in him!"

At this, the chief elder raised a daring fist. "We have a law, and by our law he ought to die," he lied, "because he proclaimed himself the Son of God!"

Pilate shook his head, speechless before this alien logic. Suddenly he turned again for the palace and without explanation led the prisoner and his guards inside.

Mark and Joses clung to one another as the jostling crowd grew wilder. At any moment the fence would be wrenched from its posts, so violent was the press of the throng.

When Pilate emerged for the final time from his palace, he shook visibly before the threatening mob. Yet once more he tried to redeem justice.

"I have spoken with the man again!" he cried, sparring weakly with the din of the masses. "He has been chastened. I shall release him!"

The clusters of priests and elders huddled hyena-like, conferring against the governor. At last the primary leader stepped forward, warning brazenly, "If you release this man, you are no friend of Caesar! Anyone making himself out to be a king is speaking against Caesar!"

Upon hearing this, Pilate's face went ashen. As he studied his challengers, his shoulders slumped, and the shadow of his chin clouded the gleam of his pendant.

Raising a palsied hand, he gestured for the prisoner to be brought from the palace. And as Jesus stood before him, he surveyed the Rabbi sadly for a long moment. With a helpless sigh he turned toward the judgment seat, which sat like a throne above the court, and he took his station.

Sunlight, only two hours old, reflected gold and topaz off the mosaic pavement. Tears glistened in Pilate's eyes, and he raised a finger but did not wipe them away.

Lifting his chin, his voice husky, he called to the crowd, "Behold your King!"

"Away with him! Away with him! Crucify!" they howled.

"Shall I crucify your King?" Pilate cried hoarsely.

"We have no king but Caesar!" the priests replied, and as the multitude took up the chorus, repeating the incredible claim again and again, Pilate imagined the mob breaking across his pavement and devastating his palace.

At last, the governor hailed a servant, who came running toward him with a bowl of clear water. Rolling his gold-embroidered sleeves up to his elbows, Pilate dipped first one hand and then the other into the liquid. Though Mark had been reared in the customs of Rome, he had never seen such a ritual performed in a public court. The symbolism was obvious as Pilate displayed his wet hands to the crowd.

"I am innocent of the blood of this righteous man!" he declared. "You will bear witness to it!"

"His blood be on us! And on our children!" the multitude shrieked.

Mark trembled. Were these indeed the kindred of his loving mother? The nation of his gentle uncle?

He was glad that he was Roman, cruel as Rome might be.

As the Nazarene was led away Mark steeled himself against the public mania.

Hate such as he had never known filled his heart. And as he studied the crazed people all about, he wondered how they could be God's chosen.

CHAPTER

11

Because the mob moved, Mark and Joses moved. There was little else to do but be carried along with the surging masses as they passed from the Praetorium, the Roman hall of judgment, toward the bare hill outside the city where the Master would be executed.

Mark and his uncle would have preferred to go home and spare themselves the ghoulish prospect of observing the Nazarene's torment. All along the route they attempted escape down numerous byways that could lead them circuitously back to the Ben Haman residence. But they were in the thick of the mob, and so great was the momentum that it was impossible to do anything but follow.

To make matters worse, they were in the segment of the crowd that could most clearly witness the Rabbi's arduous trek. He carried upon his bloody back a crude Roman cross, hastily constructed by the men who had beaten and mocked him in Pilate's house. He stumbled often beneath its weight, but the guards would allow no one to assist him.

By this point in the journey, strangers who had not seen the trial, and who had not been prejudiced against Jesus by the hounding elders, were joining the parade of spectators. There were men and women, including Mark and Joses, who cried out for the Nazarene to be spared this unnecessary burden. But they were pushed aside at spearpoint.

The disciples who had accompanied Jesus at Passover were nowhere to be seen. Joses thought he caught a glimpse of the blond-haired fellow who had inquired about the upper room the day of the feast, but in this dense company it was impossible to say for sure that it was he. And certainly Peter, the leader of the group, was not present.

Mark ran a hand across his perspiring brow and cursed the mob which closed in on every side. Ahead, he could see Jesus tumbling beneath the cruel load of his cross, and because the guards once more denied him help, Mark cursed them as well.

His vision blurred with the heat of the half-mounted sun. It would be noon in a short while, but already, in this compacted mob, the temperature was exhausting. A sleepless night and an angry heart strained Mark's nerves, giving rise to murderous thoughts.

He could not love his mother's people who sadistically mocked the hunched and battered Nazarene. But suddenly even Rome, the empire that Quintus had adored, was detestable. As Mark witnessed Caesar's steel-eyed soldiers carelessly push the Teacher beyond endurance, he wondered if any nation or god were worthy of allegiance.

The mob was drawing near the city gate. Beyond lay half a dozen barren hills. Upon several were the silhouettes of yesterday's crosses, now vacant of bodies that had been buried unceremoniously in a criminals' pit. Mark had seen such hills outside Cyrene in his father's province. As a child, such sights had troubled him. But Roman practicality had not tolerated squeamishness, and compassion toward enemies of the empire had early been squelched.

Today, however, the horizon of deadly spires splintered his eyes. He could not turn. Not only did the crowd spur him on, but now, as the Nazarene collapsed in helplessness, his wooden load crushing him to the ground, Mark knew he had to stay nearby.

"Help him!" he cried.

Nor was he alone in his sentiments. Joses likewise demanded mercy, as did countless voices in the crowd—even those who had earlier called for the Rabbi's death.

When the throng began to press the guards for a change of heart, they, like Pilate, looked to their own safety. It would be easy to choose one of the badgering spectators to assist Jesus. But none of them, though they demanded his relief, relished the task.

The mob was passing beneath the fortified gate. Ahead was the highway skirting Golgotha, the Place of the Skull, where the empty crucifixes loomed. A few people, coming to the city from distant parts of the province or from regions of the coast were traveling on the road, innocent to the approaching drama.

The soldiers raised their hands, calling the crowd to a halt. As two of the guards rushed forward to lift the cross from the fallen Nazarene, another hailed a pedestrian, pulling him aside.

The bewildered newcomer, awestruck at the sight of the frenzied crowd and their pathetic subject, trembled at the sudden arrest.

"You! Man!" the unrefined soldier shouted. "Bear this cross up yonder hill!"

Jerking the poor fellow into the middle of the road, he cast him to the ground beside the Nazarene. The stranger knelt shakily, staring into the bruised face of the miracle-worker.

He could not know this was Jesus. He had heard tales of the Galilean but had never seen him.

Standing, he brushed the road dirt from his cloak and straightened his turban. As the shadow of the brutal cross fell across his back, he reached forth shaking hands and, with a heave, hoisted the cross upright. The foot of the wooden instrument settled into the dust, and he slid his hands up the neck letting the crossbar nestle on his shoulder.

The stranger was not a large man. But strong muscles rippled at his collarline, and his arms supported the burden with relative ease. In his appearance there was nothing remarkable, except that he was black, atypical of this predominantly Semitic crowd.

As Joses peered around the people who stood between him and the traveler, he suddenly clutched his nephew's arm.

"Mark," he whispered, "is that not Simon, our friend from Cyrene?"

The son of Quintus craned his neck for an unobstructed view. When he saw the unfortunate one assigned to bear the cross, he drew a sharp breath.

It *was* Simon, only now arriving to spend the holidays with Mary and her brother.

The guards gave a shout, and the crowd surged forward. As Mark watched his fellow Cyrenian struggle up the incline to Golgotha, an eeriness enveloped him.

The Nazarene was coming too close to home, settling omenlike over everything Mark knew and loved. Unbidden, the Galilean was invading, and Mark was powerless against him.

PART THREE

Birth

And I tell you that you are Peter,
and on this rock
I will build my church,
and the gates of Hades
will not overcome it.

MATTHEW 16:18

CHAPTER

1

The scorching heat of morning had given way to unearthly gloom by midafternoon. A morbid wind swept black sleet across Jerusalem's streets, and the city was dreadfully still.

Mark staggered toward the House Ben Haman, his clothes drenched with rain, hot tears mingling with the icy moisture on his face. It might have been night, so dark was the sky, but he and those who followed him were oblivious to time.

Behind him traipsed a small huddled group, several women weeping and three men attempting to console them. Joses, Simon the Cyrenian, and the blond disciple who had reserved the upper chamber embraced the women, speaking now and then to them but having little credible comfort to offer.

Jesus was dead. Mark and his companions had been among a meager handful of spectators who had stood by the six-hour ordeal of execution. By the time the Master's cross had been reared heavenward, the Rabbi's pain-wracked body suspended on it, most of the crowd who had trekked to Golgotha were weary and had gone home.

But Joses had insisted on staying, and Simon, having learned the identity of the one whose cross he bore, remained with him. Mark likewise felt constrained to abide by the cross, though he did not understand how the Galilean's career had led to such an end.

There were others nearby whom he did not know—one or two men in Pharisaical garb who appeared to side with the Master, and the mourning women who now walked with Mark through the streets. When Joses saw that the blond fellow had come with the crowd to Golgotha, and that he was the only disciple present, he joined him.

Mark had been sufficiently exposed to his uncle's hospitality to know this guest of the House Ben Haman would merit their loyalty. And when the fellow, whose name was John Bar Zebedee, was invited to bring the women home, Mark was not surprised.

As the small entourage wended its way through town, he pondered the events of the day and night previous. Of all the scenes emblazoned upon his memory, the image of the Teacher's grisly death was the most haunting.

Mark had never witnessed a crucifixion close up. He had passed by countless criminals as they writhed upon their crosses outside the walls of Cyrene. But always he had been in a chariot, or had been occupied with business and friendly conversation, so that he felt no compassion for their situation.

Certainly he had never stood at the foot of a Roman tree observing a man die. He had known the method of execution was torturous. But he had never cared.

Today he had cared deeply. Today he had wept.

The house was dark when they arrived home. Even Rhoda was subdued and thoughtful as she opened the door, admitting Mark and his uncle.

"Fetch my sister," Joses said softly, and the servant girl hastened to obey.

Mary Ben Haman emerged from the dimly lit parlor and ran across the court to her brother's side. Embracing him, she trembled.

"Joses," she whispered, as though to speak aloud were dangerous, "I have been so afraid! Most of the guests have departed, fearing the Sanhedrin. And the streets have been so noisy or so quiet, I have feared to go seeking you!"

Her brother cupped her hands tenderly in his and led her toward the entry. When she saw through the streetlight that he and Mark had brought folks with them, she trembled again.

"Do not be afraid, Sister," Joses soothed her. "Do you not recognize Simon?"

At the sight of her beloved friend, Mary began to weep, and grasping the Cyrenian's turbaned head to her shoulder, she hugged him fondly.

"Come, come!" she cried. "We have been awaiting your arrival! But where have you been? Did you travel through the rain? You are damp to the bone, my dear man!" With renewed warmth, she guided him into the court and called for dry clothes.

"And who are these with you?" she asked, her smile broader than her trepidations. "Have they come from Cyrene?"

Simon, still overwhelmed by the things he had witnessed this day, could not answer, and Mark intervened.

"Mother," he explained, gesturing toward the blond disciple, "you recall John Bar Zebedee, one of the Rabbi's men . . . and these are some of the women who followed the Teacher."

Mary studied the ladies carefully, noting their mournful countenances and stooped postures. One in particular troubled her, and she turned anxious eyes to her son.

"This one . . . she sorrows so. . . . What has happened, Mark?"

"This is the Rabbi's mother," Mark explained. But seeing that his own mother still did not understand the woman's grief, he shook his head. "Has no one told you?" he asked in astonishment. "Do you not know that the Rabbi has been . . . crucified?"

At this, Mary's face went pale, and she shook her head incredulously.

"Oh, dear women!" she cried, embracing the Nazarene

lady. "No, my son," she replied, "I knew nothing. I have been alone. The guests departed early, and the Master's men have been locked within their chamber all day."

"They have been hiding?" Joses asked, his usually gentle tone tinged with anger.

When Mary assured him it was so, Joses clenched his fist. And Mark was outraged. Staring at the rooftop balustrade, his breath came thick and hot.

Memories of the slinking culprit who had betrayed the Master flashed to mind. And recalling how the Rabbi's men had fled the garden the night of his arrest, he was spurred to action.

"Traitors!" he cried. "Traitors are they all!"

Racing for the court stairs he leapt them two at a time, ignoring his uncle's pleas to reconsider.

He reached the upper chamber before anyone could detain him and, kicking against the door, demanded entrance.

Moments passed with no more than the sound of shuffling feet coming from the room. He was about to knock the door down when a hesitant hand moved the latch and one leery eye peered through the open crack.

Mark pushed open the unbolted door.

"Where is Peter?" he demanded. And recalling the name by which Jesus had addressed the traitor in the garden, he shouted, "Where is Judas, who betrayed your Teacher?"

The room was dark. Mark's eyes were still adjusting to the lack of light as the men inside surveyed his hostile countenance and fight-ready stance.

No one responded to his question, and when he ventured across the room, stumbling over legs and feet, no one said a word. A small candle stood on a shelf at the far side of the chamber. He grasped it in one hand, and holding it up, began to search the disciples' faces.

At last he found him, the leader of the group. He would not have recognized him, except that he sat with his face buried in his hands, his giant frame slumped shamefully in a corner.

Grasping him by the shoulders, Mark snarled, "Look at me, man! Are you Peter?"

The Galilean only peered fearfully at the young Roman.

"I have just come from the hill where your Master died!" Mark grilled him. "Where were *you*?"

He had not expected an answer. When none came, he stood up and spat on the floor. Wheeling about, he surveyed the other fugitives and laughed derisively.

"Do you hide the betrayer in your midst? Judas?" he cried, a fury in his fist. "Where is Judas?"

Suddenly light spilled from the doorway across the room, and the huddled disciples shielded their eyes. Joses had come to intervene, and with him stood John, Peter's fair-haired friend.

"Come out, Mark!" Joses called. "We have no business here!"

"This is your home, Uncle!" Mark objected. "Can you tolerate traitors on your roof?"

Bar Zebedee stepped forward, ready to speak for his friends. Mark raised a hand to halt him. "Do not lower yourself, John," he quipped. "You are too good a fellow to mix with these cowards!"

Then, mocking, Mark railed, "I seek Judas, loyal follower of the Nazarene! He deserves a medal for valor!"

The disciples murmured now, wondering where the traitor might be.

"Do not ask these men where Judas has gone," John spoke at last. "They have not seen him."

"And you have?" Mark spat.

"I was with the Sanhedrin when word came of his death."

At this the men stirred, more fearful yet.

Even Peter sat up, gazing at John in disbelief.

"Judas is dead?" he stammered.

"At his own hand," John acknowledged. "Hung by his own sash, upon a tree . . . just as Jesus was nailed to one."

CHAPTER

2

A spirit of gloom, like the darkness that had descended on Jerusalem the day of the crucifixion, had settled over the House Ben Haman, and for two days it had not lifted.

Though Joses did not approve of the disciples' cowardice, he could not bear to evict them. And part of him knew that their fears were well-founded, that indeed they were in danger should the elders and priests discover their whereabouts.

The fact that anyone harboring friends of "The King of the Jews" was in equal danger did not dissuade him from traditional responsibility as their host.

And so the house was full of foreboding quiet, interrupted only by the weeping of the women who had come to abide under Mary's loving care.

There were, among those who had accompanied John, two other Marys: Mary Bar Joseph, the mother of Jesus, and Mary of Magdala. Had there been much interaction between the people of the house, this might have given rise to confusion, but generally folk kept to themselves.

Until the morning of the third day.

From that point on, the tenor of the home began to

change. And Mark did not know whether the change was for the better or the worse.

It started when Mary the Magdalene, having visited Jesus' tomb early Sunday morning, came running back to the house with strange news. Bolting upstairs, she summoned Peter and John, insisting that the grave had been broken into, that the body of the Master had been stolen.

Peter and John, checking out her story, found that, indeed, the tomb was empty. And the disciples were gripped with even greater fear. If the enemies of Jesus could stoop to such vindictiveness, of what else might they be capable?

This was only the beginning. The woman of Magdala, who followed Peter and John to the tomb, remained there after they departed. And when later in the morning she returned with a more fantastic tale, the disciples were full of consternation.

"He lives!" the Magdalene asserted. "I saw Jesus with my own eyes, and he called me by name!"

Simply the ravings of a grief-stricken female, the men concluded. But could they overlook a similar story told by the Rabbi's mother?

When Mary Bar Joseph and her companions confirmed the Magdalene's encounter with a report of their own separate meeting with the Master, the men were troubled. Nevertheless, they rejected the stories as idle tales. It was not until Peter himself claimed firsthand witness of the living Nazarene that the disciples began to take heed.

Mark and his family spent the next week cloistered within the house, quiet and unobtrusive. Whatever transpired among their guests was, as Joses would say, private information.

They listened to the rumors with even more skepticism than the Rabbi's followers. But it was difficult to ignore the transformation that colored the mood of the men upstairs.

The same night that Peter announced an encounter with Jesus, two others claimed to have walked, spoken, and even to have eaten with the Master. Then, to hear the entire group tell it, he appeared to them all within the upper room!

Mary and Joses had endured much for the sake of these Galileans. Now for the first time they considered asking their guests to find other accommodations.

Joses had respected the Rabbi's ministry. A large part of him yearned to embrace everything he taught, to believe all the miracles attributed to Jesus.

But . . . the Master was dead. To have the group claiming that Jesus had been seen within this very house . . . why, even Joses's trust could be strained.

Joses discussed the situation with his sister, with Mark, and with their old friend, Simon. A consensus was reached. They would allow the Galileans to stay one more week in the House Ben Haman. "Seven is the number of completion," Joses reasoned. "Surely they will not need lodging in Jerusalem for more than an additional seven days."

So it was that Mark ventured up to the roof the following Sunday, a full week after the first reported sighting of the risen Rabbi. The disciples had been given notice of the departure date and had told Joses they would be returning to Galilee. The goodman, having waited through the afternoon with no sign of their leaving the premises, sent Mark upstairs to spur them.

"It is nearing sunset," Joses observed, "but if they hurry, they can be well beyond the city gates and on the road north by dark." Then rubbing his hands together, his brow etched with concern, he glanced at the roof and sighed, "Be gentle with them, Nephew. They have been through much."

"I will," Mark assented, privately puzzled again at his uncle's magnanimity but relieved to know that the peculiar folk would be gone once and for all.

He had said nothing to his mother of his intention to depart for Cyrene once matters were brought back to normal in her home. But as he bounded up the stairs, he envisioned the shores of his native land with eager anticipation. He would see the intruders out the door, then pack his bags.

Energetically he knocked on the chamber door. "Peter!" he called. "It is Marcus Quintus!"

He enjoyed using his Roman name when he wanted to don an aura of authority. Let the Galileans resent him. He had ignored his imperial heritage ever since setting foot in Israel, and today he cared not for humility.

Still, no reply. Tense with impatience, Mark again called through the portal. When at least James Bar Zebedee, John's brother, opened the door, he saw that the men were just beginning to arrange their satchels for a trip.

"The hour grows late," Mark warned, as James shut the door behind him. "We will need to begin charging you if you stay longer."

They knew that he knew they had little money. Peter glanced at him narrowly but said not a word as he drew the knapsack string tight, shook the contents to a settled lump, and sat down to wait for his friends.

John, whose bag already rested on his back, replied simply, "We are on our way. Tell your uncle we are grateful for his hospitality."

At this, most of the disciples murmured appreciation. Mark stepped away from the door, waiting for them to leave.

But Peter was in no hurry.

"The Master would have blessed this house," he announced. "We should not depart until we have invoked his spirit on our hosts and on our journey."

Mark questioned his sincerity, but quickly bowed his head as the big fisherman said a benediction.

When Peter's voice trailed off and another added, "Peace to you," Mark opened his eyes, assuming the prayer was ended. But the salutation was not an amen. A hushed silence had overcome the group, and here and there men had slumped to their knees, transfixed with awe.

Following their gaze, Mark realized a newcomer had entered the chamber. When he recognized him, a chill passed down his spine.

In a thousand years he could never have mistaken the face of the Nazarene. It had been chiseled by soul-fire upon his memory. And he knew . . . this was Jesus!

Not a sound nor a movement broke the tension in the room. For a long while, the men gazed upon their Lord.

Then the weeping began. Grown men started to sob, reaching toward the Nazarene like little children.

He allowed them to touch him, and they did so reverently with their fingertips, one by one.

At last, a shuffle at the back of the room parted the ranks, and Matthew Bar Alpheus, a former tax collector from Capernaum, led a fellow Galilean to the center of the room.

Bowing cautiously before the Master, he presented his friend and explained, "Thomas was not here, Lord, when you appeared to us a week ago. And he has not believed us."

"Yes," someone else confirmed. "He told us that unless he sees the imprint of the nails in your hands, and feels the mark of the spear in your side, he will not believe!"

Mark studied the shamefaced Thomas and wondered how his friends could expose him to ridicule. Their jibes seemed good natured, however, and a ripple of nervous laughter sparked through the somber air.

An apologetic smile worked at Thomas's lips, and shaking his head, he began to slink back into the crowd.

But Jesus surveyed him for a long moment, evincing nothing but compassion for the poor man's frailty.

Turning to the men, Jesus told them with a single look that he knew how prone each had been to unbelief. Then he called Thomas forward.

"Put forth your finger," he told him, "and feel the print of the nails in my hands. Thrust here your hand and feel the place of the spear in my side."

Thomas choked back tears. The Master, however, would make a probing example of him. Tenderly grasping his arm he pressed Thomas's fingers to his scarred wrists.

The disciple trembled, nearly sinking to the floor, but Jesus held him up, and opening the waist of his cloak, he thrust Thomas's hand against his wounded side.

"Be not unbelieving," Jesus commanded. "Believe!"

"My Lord and my God!" Thomas cried, slumping before

him and nestling his forehead on the Master's feet.

At this, the men were overcome with emotion, and half-laughing, half-weeping, they surrounded the Rabbi, embracing him and shedding tears on his neck.

Jesus wept with them. But then, extricating himself from their grasp, he reached down and lifted Thomas to his feet, peering intently into his eyes.

"Because you have seen me, Thomas, you have believed. Blessed are those," he said, "who have not seen and yet have believed."

The lesson was fitly spoken. No man stood faultless before the Master's exposing gaze.

Mark chafed. Though his mind resisted, his heart could not deny what he witnessed.

The shield of Roman practicality, which he had to this day borne, suddenly slipped from his grasp. And he might never again retrieve it.

CHAPTER

3

Joses and his family were alone in the House Ben Haman. Though the Rabbi's disciples had been gone for several days, having ventured north into Galilee, Mark had not yet told his uncle what he had seen in the upper room.

Perhaps Joses would think him mad. Perhaps, he, himself, would think so.

But as days passed, and yet more rumors of the Lord's appearing spread up and down Palestine, Mark's agitation to tell his story festered.

The desire to return to Cyrene had all but disappeared. When memories of Philea pricked him, they were repeatedly overshadowed by the excitement that grew daily in Israel.

The rumors perplexed the entire household. Joses, who always tried to do the honorable thing, now wondered if he should have asked the disciples to leave his home. If it were indeed true that Jesus had been resurrected—that he was . . . the Son of God . . .

The goodman feared to think that he had shown an inhospitable spirit to the Master's followers.

When it was reported, nearly forty days after the crucifixion, that Jesus had appeared to five hundred people at once, upon a mountain in Galilee, the kindly Levite was greatly distressed.

That day Mark met his uncle in the courtyard as he spoke with Simon near the central fountain. The householder gazed sadly up at the flowering baskets suspended from beams above his patio, and the sun, filtering through the greenery, accentuated the bewilderment in his middle-aged face.

It was apparent that Joses and his friend had been deep in conversation, and Mark would have slipped away quietly had Simon not beckoned to him.

The young Roman sat beside his elders and listened in awe as they spoke of the most recent and most publicly acclaimed witness.

"How could five hundred people be wrong?" Joses sighed. "Even if there were a conspiracy to promote the belief that Jesus lives, five hundred would not confirm it."

Simon nodded sympathy as Joses expressed his quandary. And at last he too sighed. "I have never told you," he began, "just what I experienced the day I bore the Rabbi's cross up Golgotha."

Mark had often wondered how that event had affected the Cyrenian, but out of respect he had never inquired. He and Joses studied the black man's wistful countenance in silence, for, from his tone, they knew he was about to touch on a sensitive subject.

"As you know," Simon said, "I had heard tales of the Nazarene but had never seen him for myself." Here his eyes took on a faraway look, and his face lit with wonder. "When I knelt beside Jesus to take his cross upon my back, his gaze caught mine, and for an instant . . ."

He shook his head, finding the description inexpressible.

Mark's chest grew tight, remembering how he, too, had been moved by the Master's probing glance the day he entered Jerusalem.

Joses leaned forward and placed a hand on Simon's knee. "I think we understand," he whispered. "No one could witness his death, as we did, and ever be the same again."

At this, the two joined in reminiscence, full of undisguised ardor. "I shall never forget his words as he hung upon the cross . . . 'Father, forgive them, for they know not what they do. . . .' "

The Levite's voice cracked over the divine syllables, and tears filled his eyes.

Mark observed his companions uneasily. He knew it was time to speak of his experience in the upper room, but he feared to verbalize it.

At last, taking a deep breath, he began to tell his story.

"Sirs," he said shakily, "I too have a story to tell. Perhaps, now, we can all believe it."

The two elders listened in awe as Mark described the evening when Jesus stood before the men in the rooftop chamber. As one word followed another, he gained courage, and as he finished, his whole body quaked.

" 'Blessed are those who have not seen, and yet have believed,' the Master said. Oh, how that command has troubled me!" Mark shuddered.

For a long while his listeners said nothing. When Joses leapt to his feet and began pacing the court, Mark wondered if he was angry.

"I would give anything to undo what I have done!" his uncle declared, wringing his hands in despair.

"What do you mean?" Simon asked.

"I should never have sent the Lord's followers from this house!" he sighed. "I would give anything to have them back!"

His words still pierced the air when a knock came at the front door. Rhoda, scurrying from the kitchen, unlatched the peephole, and turned in wonder to her employer.

"It is John, the Rabbi's disciple," she called.

Joses, stunned, gawked at the girl as though she were mad. But then, shaking himself, he cried, "It is all right, Rhoda! Let him in!"

The door opened to a wary and apologetic Galilean. When

he was greeted by unexpected enthusiasm, he hesitated beneath the portal. "May I speak with you, Joses?" he inquired.

"Come in! Come in!" the goodman insisted, leading him by the arm toward the fountain. "Hurry, Rhoda!" he ordered. "Bring tea for our friend!"

When Joses energetically took his cloak, John was bewildered. "I know that my friends and I caused much trouble for you when we resided here," he began. "I had hoped, however, that I might prevail upon you one more time."

"Anything, anything!" Joses assured him. "When did you return to Jerusalem?"

"A few days ago," John explained. "We have stayed at a hostel, but . . . we have no privacy."

Joses knew he referred to the disciples' need for anonymity. He did not presume to ask why they had come back to the capital. But he knew the Holy City was not a safe place for any follower of Jesus.

"Please," he exclaimed, "bring your people here again! They may have the upper room. It is waiting for them!"

John was incredulous. "I had not expected . . . Sir, your generosity is beyond . . ."

"Nonsense!" Joses asserted. "I shall be offended if you do not lodge here!"

"You are too kind," the disciple said with a bow. "However, there is more I must explain. We are now many in number. More than before . . . And we do not know exactly how long we would be staying. . . ."

"My house is yours!" Joses declared. And raising John's right hand to his lips, he kissed it fervently, bowing repeatedly as though the Galilean and not he, himself, were the host.

CHAPTER

4

Mark had not counted them, but there must have been one hundred and fifty people residing in the Ben Haman house.

During the days since John and Peter had returned, bringing with them many witnesses to the resurrected Lord, the group had steadily grown, attracting Galileans and Judeans who had come to believe their testimony and that of others who had been at the Lord's appearance to the five hundred.

It could no longer be secret that Joses's residence was the gathering place of the Rabbi's followers. Ironically, though, the very fact that the Teacher's devotees were growing daily in number forestalled any move the authorities might make against the house. Joses and his family were actually safer harboring hundreds than they had been when the upper room housed only the original eleven.

The entire building was now given over to the disciples. The gallery, the mezzanine, even the open space of the court was occupied by cots and bundles. Though the family quarters were still relatively private, the rest of the house was abustle with folk coming, going, eating, sleeping, and talking.

Most of the waking hours were devoted to prayer. Every

morning and evening, one hundred and fifty people congregated on the roof, crowding into the banquet room, where the Lord had observed his last Passover, and spilling over into the adjoining chambers and balustrade. Upon the upper level, at such times, there was standing room only, the mood fervent with anticipation and with enthusiasm for their shared witness.

Again and again they requested the original eleven men to share their story of the last time they had seen Jesus.

The tale had been told to Joses, Mark, and Simon early on. Peter insisted that, as their hosts, they should be privy to the Master's last commission.

"You may choose to disbelieve our testimony," he granted, "but you will hear stranger things from us in the future. It is best to weigh your involvement carefully as you take us into your home."

"Speak," Joses had assented. "We have come too far with you to turn away now."

"Well," the big Galilean began, "it happened the day before our brother, John, came to your doorstep. We had been with the Master one afternoon on Mount Olivet, and when we asked him if he would now restore the kingdom of Israel, he told us, 'It is not for you to know the times or the seasons, which the Father has put in his own power. But you shall receive power, after the Holy Spirit has come upon you; and you shall be my witnesses in Jerusalem, and in all Judea, and in Samaria, and unto the uttermost part of the earth.' "

Peter looked toward heaven as he spoke, and his tone was one of ecstasy. " 'Go and make disciples of all nations,' " he continued, quoting the Master's injunction. " 'Miraculous signs will accompany those who believe: In my name they shall cast out demons. They shall speak in new tongues. They shall pick up serpents. And if they drink any deadly thing, it shall not hurt them. They shall lay hands on the sick and they shall recover!'

"All these things the Lord promised us. And when he had finished, while we looked at him, and even as he blessed us, he was taken from us . . . carried aloft in a cloud . . . and received out of our sight!"

Tears trickled down the big man's cheeks as he told the story, and his hands trembled as he drew them to his chest. "Suddenly," he continued, his voice almost failing with emotion, "there were two men in white apparel standing by us. 'You men of Galilee,' they said, 'why do you stand gazing up into heaven? This same Jesus, who has been taken up from you, shall come again, just as you have seen him go.' "

The men of the House Ben Haman had witnessed too much to question Peter's story.

"We do not know what this 'power' is, of which Jesus spoke," Peter concluded. "Nor do we know how it will be bestowed. But it is for this we will wait in your house. And for this you must be prepared."

Power! Mark liked the word. It registered well with his Roman sensibilities. And it revived memories of the Nazarene's supernatural strength displayed that memorable night in the garden.

Knowing that many of the Master's followers had expected his kingdom to mean the vanquishing of Rome, Mark wondered, now, just how the power would be wielded.

He had come to believe that Jesus was divine, but he did not know just where he might fit in the pantheon of all nations. And, his heart still bound to the empire, he was curious about the disciples' intentions.

Nonetheless, a slumbering chord had been aroused in Mark's spirit the evening he saw the resurrected Lord. A dormant nerve had been pricked, sparking to a small but growing flame. Mark was beginning to yearn for things greater than Rome could offer.

Whatever the disciples' movement might portend for Caesar, Mark was increasingly drawn to them.

It was the dawn of the Feast of Pentecost, fifty days after Passover. Had anyone told Mark, when he first entered Israel, that he would be around for yet another festival, he would have scoffed. But here he was, sitting down to a Jewish breakfast in the Ben Haman house, surrounded by Jewish friends.

After the meal, Mary refused assistance from her guests, allowing the disciples to spend the day in prayer. And so they retired to the upper room once again to seek the Master's guidance and the power promised for the commission they were to fulfill.

Mark had been asked to oversee the servants as they cleared the tables and stored the leftovers. Mary bustled about the kitchen, and Joses and Simon lingered over the parlor fire.

Several times, Mark had sat in on the disciples' prayer sessions, listening to the strange minor chords of the hymns and to the rehearsal of psalms traditional to synagogue meetings. The few Sabbaths he had accompanied his mother to her Jewish house of worship he had not found the sessions exciting and had failed to appreciate whatever messages were delivered. Likewise, nothing much seemed to come of the prayer meetings in the upper room. They varied little from Jewish custom, except that the name of Jesus predominated.

Usually Mark slipped away early from the drawn-out gatherings, preferring a soft pillow to a hard bench. Today, however, he wished he were free at least to attend as an observer. The sounds filtering down from the rooftop sanctuary seemed louder and more emotional than ever before.

Rhoda stood at his elbow, her easily dazed eyes spellbound as she looked toward the highest balustrade.

"What is it, Master?" she lisped, trembling at the chanting sound spilling toward the court.

"Nothing, I am sure." Mark shrugged.

But his hesitant tone troubled her, and when she clutched his sleeve for reassurance, he quickly withdrew his arm.

"Clear the dishes!" he snapped, gesturing impatiently toward the cluttered sideboard.

Then, going to the foot of the court stairs, he cocked his head and listened more intently.

Rhoda turned, downcast, to her work, but watched Mark from the corner of one eye.

When the house began to quiver, the two of them stood
dead still. And when a strange whistling sound drifted
through the gallery, Mary and the servants emerged from the
kitchen.

Joses and Simon, likewise, left the parlor to join the family,
and everyone stared fearfully at the trembling rafters.

Never one to guess when he could know, Mark ascended
the stairs. His stride was cautious, but, as the quaking grew
more intense, he shot up the steps at a run.

By the time he reached the upper room, the wind had
escalated to a rushing howl, filling the whole house, from
roof to court, and the songs and supplications of the disciples
had become a mighty chorus.

No simple prayer meeting, this! When Mark burst into the
chamber, he was met with an incredible swell of sound.

He could not interpret the various voices. Each disciple
seemed to speak a different language, hands lifted heavenward, faces transfixed with glory.

As he stood watching, he rubbed his eyes. Every man and
woman in the room was touched with light as though cloven
tongues of flame rested on each head.

For a long while, the chorus of foreign languages continued, the sound of rushing wind shot through every corner of
the old mansion—heard, but unseen.

Mark fell back against the doorjamb and surveyed the
scene. If this was the beginning of "the power," nothing could
stop the followers of Jesus.

CHAPTER

5

The phenomenon of the tongues, wind, and flames continued for an hour. When at midmorning the disciples dispersed to the temple, the entire populace of the city picked up their fervor.

Mark and his family accompanied the ecstatic worshipers to the Outer Court, where pilgrims from every nation were convening to celebrate Pentecost. Circulating fearlessly among the growing crowd, the followers of Jesus boldly attested to the resurrection of their Lord—each in a new language, each in the tongue of his listeners.

Joses and Mary observed in amazement as they saw Parthians, Medes, Elamites, Mesopotamians, and Asians receiving the witness in their own brogues and dialects. And Simon and Mark were awestruck as even fellow Libyans and Cyrenians were addressed in their African languages. Egyptians, Cretes and Arabs, Romans, and Phrygians marveled at the miracle. Nor did the audience know how to respond, asking one another, "What is the meaning of this?"

Of course, there were skeptics. "These people are full of

new wine!" they mocked, staggering about, mimicking a hoard of drunkards.

Mark's anger flared. Had he had authority, he would have silenced the scorners.

But Peter, hearing their derisive epithets, climbed up on one of the temple's broad stone banisters. As he began to address the congregation, Mark was spellbound.

He could not have imagined anything more provoking than the sight of the risen Master or the phenomenon of the tongues. But now, as Peter expounded the Jewish Scriptures, Mark's conscience was pricked, his heart burning like a hot coal.

"Men of Judea, and all who dwell in Jerusalem!" the Galilean began, his sturdy arms wide open, his rugged face full of conviction. "Listen to my words!"

The crowd ceased its milling about as clusters assembled near the banister.

Peter spoke in the language most common to all, his native Aramaic, and as he preached the throng grew until they filled the porch and the stairs.

"These are not drunken, as you suppose," he cried, indicating his fellow believers with a sweep of the hand, "for it is only nine o'clock in the morning! But this is the prediction given by the prophet Joel!"

Was he about to claim the witness of one of Jehovah's venerable spokesmen in support of his doctrines? The audience became scrupulously attentive, and around the perimeters of the congregation outraged Pharisees gathered.

As the uneducated fisherman quoted the prophet, a hush overcame the listeners.

" 'And it shall come to pass in the last days, saith God, I will pour out of my Spirit upon all flesh!' " Peter began. " 'Your sons and your daughters shall prophesy, your young men shall see visions, and your old men shall dream dreams.

" 'And in those days I will pour out my Spirit upon my servants and my handmaidens. And they shall prophesy.' "

Fascination and anger riddled the multitude. But unlike the day Jesus was tried before Pilate, the majority could clearly see the truth and would not be swayed by the Master's enemies. In fact, the teachers of the law kept silent, for during the weeks since the crucifixion, believers had multiplied fearsomely throughout Palestine. And even the sentiments of those who had not joined the faith were generally in the disciples' favor.

Therefore, the rulers and elders of the people held their tongues, as Peter went on with his "blasphemy."

" 'I will show wonders in heaven above, and signs in the earth beneath!' " he asserted, his voice ringing through the temple's pillared halls like that of an avenging angel. " 'Blood! Fire! And vaporous smoke!' " he shouted, looking toward the gables. " 'The sun shall be turned into darkness and the moon into blood before that great and terrible day of the Lord!' "

Each word was scriptural. The first clearly related to the miracle of the Spirit-inspired languages and the messages brought this day by the humble folk who followed the Nazarene. Could it be that the rest of the prophecy was about to come true as well?

Trembling, folk of diverse nations glanced about them, expecting at any moment to see the walls of the holy mount quake.

But like the mighty evangelist Peter was proving himself to be, the fisherman held out the very hope that Joel had promised. " 'And it shall come to pass,' " he concluded, looking at his audience with penetrating eyes, " 'that whosoever shall call on the name of the Lord shall be saved!' "

These men knew the Scriptures. They knew Peter had added nothing to the prophet's words. And they knew their application to the events of the day was a likely interpretation. Stunned, they stood unmoving.

"Men of Israel!" Peter cried. "Hear me! Jesus of Nazareth, a man proven of God by miracles and wonders and signs, was delivered over to you by God himself. And you seized him with wicked hands, crucified, and killed him! But God raised him up! He freed him from the pains of death! For it was impossible for death to hold him!

"Even King David spoke concerning him when he said, 'I saw the Lord always before my face. . . . Therefore did my heart rejoice, and my tongue was glad . . . because you will not leave my soul in hell, neither suffer your Holy One to see corruption. You have made known to me the ways of life!' "

Again he was using Scripture to verify his position. But he stood in grave danger, calling upon the words of Israel's most popular monarch for his defense.

Scanning the crowd, he realized that his enemies chafed at his presumption.

"Men and brethren," he implored them, "let me freely speak to you of the patriarch David, reminding you that he is both dead and buried, and his sepulcher is with us to this day. But being a prophet, and knowing that God had sworn by an oath that one of his descendants would be crowned Messiah, he spoke of the resurrection of Christ! He foretold that his soul would not be left in hell, and that his body would not see decay."

The audience understood his logic. But they were hardly prepared to have it put plainly to them.

"He was speaking of Jesus, whom God has raised up, and whose resurrection we have witnessed! And what you now see and hear is his gift of the Holy Spirit that he has poured out on us."

Mixed response rippled through the crowd. Some were more angry than ever, but by far the greater number were moved to accept Peter's assertions.

Once more eyeing his opponents, the Galilean warned, by way of David's words, "Indeed brethren, 'The Lord says to my Lord, "Sit on my right hand, until I make your foes your footstool!" ' "

Incensed, the priests and Pharisees muttered among themselves, scowling at Peter. But the preacher concluded, beads of sweat dotting his forehead, "Let all the house of Israel know that God has made this Jesus, whom you crucified, both Lord and Messiah!"

Never had the claims of Jesus been so clearly presented to the public. If the fledgling body of believers had set out to put themselves in jeopardy, they could not have chosen a more effective way of doing so than to defend from the Scriptures the assertion that Jesus was God.

But the majority of listeners were troubled, and many began to ask Peter and the other leaders, "Brothers, what shall we do?"

Mark, his mother, and companions listened carefully as Peter explained how to enter the faith. And the young Cyrenian's soul surged eagerly.

"Repent!" the Galilean cried, prophetlike. "And be baptized every one of you in the name of Jesus the Messiah, for the remission of sins. And you shall receive the gift of the Holy Spirit. For the promise spoken by Joel is for you and your children, and to all who are yet to come, for as many as the Lord our God shall call!"

Mark did not look behind him to see what Joses or Simon or Mary would do. Propelled as by an unseen hand, he went forward, until he stood directly beneath Peter's gaze.

Falling to his knees, he lifted a tear-stained face to the great disciple.

Mark did not know much about sin. He only knew he had an empty heart. He did not know much about prophecy or Messiahs. But he yearned for a more fulfilling life than he had known.

Spreading his hands across the stone steps, he wept like a child. And believing utterly, he breathed in life for the first time.

CHAPTER

6

All night sounds of celebration and rejoicing rang through the city streets, thousands of converts singing and dancing and telling the world of their new faith.

It was an infant faith, not catechized, not dogmatized or even sealed in its own Scripture. Believers, full of childlike spontaneity, were speaking and singing a very simple gospel from newborn hearts.

Largely because it was so uncluttered, their message would catch on quickly, spreading like fire through virgin forest— clean, searing, and white of heat. Unsullied by confusion, preconception, or prejudice, it was, for now, spoken with one spirit, though told by many tongues.

About three thousand people embraced Peter's message, and hundreds of the very folk who days before had shouted for the death of Jesus entered into the faith.

Mark, Joses, Simon, and even the previously reticent Mary Ben Haman were baptized by Peter and other leaders.

When they returned home, Mark found it impossible to rest. Not only did the excitement of the day come home with them, but the decision Mark had made on the temple steps still surged through him.

He did not know just what that commitment portended. He had never been committed to anything or anyone but Rome and his own father.

Jesus, though, was forever. Mark could no longer doubt that the Nazarene was God incarnate. Since his Jewish mother had always said there was only one God, Mark knew there were no other gods beside him.

When others from the temple returned to the house, Mark slipped to his room, preferring to dwell privately on the morning's events.

The chamber was cool and tranquil, its heavy shades closed against the midday sun, the thick walls muffling the din of music and revelry in the streets. But sounds of the temple throng still rang in his ears.

He wondered how the enemies of Jesus were feeling now—the One they had martyred having returned in force to haunt them, his followers multiplied like stalks of grain from a single, fallen seed.

As in solitude he sifted through the impressions of the day, the figure of Peter, strong and dynamic, dominated his thoughts.

How much the fisherman is like Brutus! Mark considered, recalling his friend of Cyrene. Physically imposing and commanding in personality, the two would have either ardently loved or violently hated one another.

And . . . how much like Quintus . . .

This comparison was not an easy one to admit, for he had never admired anyone more than his father.

Somehow, Mark knew that he and Peter could be fast friends, given the chance.

But he had alienated the big Galilean since the day the disciples had set foot in the House Ben Haman. Already Mark sensed that his first duty to this new commitment must be to go to Peter—to make things right between them.

Such a notion was antithetical to Roman pride. But he must

begin to think in terms other than those of Rome.

As he reclined on his bed, his head on his hands, familiar voices reached him from the hall.

Peter and Joses stood on the gallery watching the court fill with returning guests. "They will not sleep tonight," Peter predicted.

"Likely not," Joses said, smiling. "I know that I will find sleep hard to come by."

"This is a glorious day—the birth of Christ's church!" Peter declared. "No one *should* sleep on this day!"

Mark's eyes grew wide with wonder as he tiptoed to the door and leaned against it, listening. "Church . . . ," he marveled. It was a Greek word, implying an "assembly" or "body of citizens," a term Quintus had often used of senators and provincial delegates when they gathered in Cyrene. When Peter used it, it spoke volumes regarding his expectations for the future.

Reluctant to eavesdrop another second, Mark opened the door and joined his uncle.

"Welcome," Joses nodded. "We were just discussing . . ."

"I heard," Mark confessed. "Your comments, Peter, are curious. Did Jesus often speak of such things?"

"He said the gospel must be taken to all nations," Peter explained. "This is only the beginning."

Mark surveyed the group milling around the patio and recalled again the enormous temple crowd. Chanting and laughter filled the halls and streets as people dispersed to their homes. Peter and the leaders who had been with Jesus would doubtless go back to the Outer Court tomorrow, where yet hundreds more would enter the faith.

"To all nations?" he whispered. "How shall they ever be a unit?"

Peter studied his incredulous face. The young man's Roman practicality apparently balked at applying the concept of "body" to such a diverse and unorganized group.

"Marcus Quintus," he said with a smile, gently alluding to Mark's imperial roots, "your uncle says your Israelite name is

John. When I first met the Master, my name was Simon Bar Jona, but he designated me 'Peter,' a 'rock,' saying that he would build his church upon me."

No condescension was evinced in Peter's gentle humor, and in his assertion that Jesus had appointed him such a prominent position, he spoke with humility. Indeed, it was apparent that the fellowship was being founded upon his preaching.

"Perhaps," he continued, "we shall abide by your preference for 'Mark.' For I see in you a shining strength—'shining' for the Master, and therefore imbued with new meaning."

The interpretation embarrassed him, though Peter had meant it as praise. Just moments ago Mark had remembered his abuse of the great disciple.

He lowered his head as Peter turned his attention to his uncle. "And you, Joses," the Galilean went on, "you have been a friend at our weakest moments, compassionate before you knew us, and generous even when we put your house in danger. You shall be called 'Barnabas,' 'son of comfort,' the kindest of men."

Mark's eyes filled with tears as he looked at his uncle's radiant countenance. How often he had privately scorned the very traits in Joses that Peter commended.

Again he felt the inadequacy of his own character. Lacking both Peter's dynamism and his uncle's warm spirit, he saw little hope that he could ever be of use to the church. Joses, called away by his head servant, grasped Peter's hand in gratitude, his own eyes tear filled as he left his companions on the gallery. Mark, alone with the fisherman, stood speechless with remorse.

Peter said nothing for a long while. When Mark finally found his voice, the big man listened quietly.

"I . . . I wish to ask forgiveness," Mark stammered. "I was never kind or generous to you. . . ."

Peter heard the confession dwindle to a choke, and as the contrite young Roman stood paralyzed before him, he stepped near to put a warm hand on his shoulder.

"You are not unlike me," he said. "In fact, we have much in

common. But Jesus has lifted us beyond ourselves and sees only his own image in our faces."

Mark looked into Peter's eyes and saw true empathy, and in that instant something was born between them that only years and many trials would clarify.

PART FOUR

Persecution

*In this world
you will have trouble.
But take heart!
I have overcome the world.*

JOHN 16:33

CHAPTER

1

It seemed years had passed since Mark had left Cyrene. In reality, he had been away only six months. But it might have been a lifetime.

Today he stood on the deck of a two-tiered sailing vessel, heading for his homeland. As he gripped the rail against the ship's gentle sway, his dark hair was blown back from his ruddy face in strands longer than the style to which he had been accustomed in his native land. And a lustrous beard, short-cropped but full, adorned his normally clean-shaven chin.

The red cape that he had carried into Israel, concealed in a satchel, had been left behind at the House Ben Haman. He had not worn it since leaving home, and though he was on his way to Cyrenaica, he would not need it there.

In the few weeks since his conversion under Peter's preaching, he had adopted his mentor's ways from soul to shoe-latchet, and could now have passed for a Galilean.

Considering him the final authority in all matters of faith and conduct, he devoted to Peter the energies that he had, at one time, expended on pleasing Quintus. Peter did not discourage Mark's youthful enthusiasm.

Joses, or Barnabas as the church called him, had gone with Mark from Jerusalem as far as Joppa. There the two had boarded separate vessels—Barnabas heading for his native Cyprus, and Mark for Cyrene.

Since the day of Pentecost, believers in the Holy City had daily assembled at the temple, hearing the preaching of the original twelve—now called apostles or "sent out ones"—learning their doctrine and witnessing countless miracles of healing. Many of the foreigners who had been present in Jerusalem during the feast had remained there, or were relocating from distant provinces and native lands to be near the center of church events.

As the body of believers grew, now numbering about five thousand, accommodations to house the influx were in great demand. The community quickly came to rely on one another as an extended family, and because camaraderie was so high, no one thought of his house or possessions as belonging to himself but rather as being at the disposal of his friends as need arose.

Barnabas determined that, as a Levite, he should not own property and set out to sell his lands, houses, and business in Cyprus. He would give the proceeds to the church. Mark and Mary decided to do the same with their home in Cyrenaica. Though they were under no compulsion to do this, believers in Jerusalem, by the droves, were taking the same action, giving up life savings, inheritances, and properties for the good of the community.

Mary and Mark arrived at their decision from the heart. When they made the determination, it was no light commitment; it was a sacrifice. But the choice had been mutual, followed by a deep sense of joy.

As the prow of the vessel plowed the Mediterranean, casting up salt spray into Mark's face, he remembered his Cyrenian friend Simon's fervent petition: "Find my two sons and tell them to sell our home and businesses in Cyrene and Alexandria. They will think me mad, but they will obey. Then bring them to Jerusalem where they may hear the gospel."

Simon would remain in the Holy City to stand in Barnabas's place as keeper of the House Ben Haman and as helper to Mark's mother.

The young convert knew the task before him would be a difficult one—explaining to Rufus and Alexander why their father gave this command, and explaining to his own friends the change in his life. But he was determined to have the boldness of Peter, to speak confidently as the big fisherman had done on Pentecost.

And since the hour he had turned his face for his native home, thoughts of Philea had dominated all others.

Along the horizon the African sun, rising through a fog-shrouded morning, burned away the haze of dawn and high-lighted the distant white walls of Cyrene. The broad, winding road leading up from the beach drew his thoughts to Villa Ponti, and his breath caught in his throat.

The city streets, yet separated from him by miles of azure waves and thick green jungle, could be viewed only in imagination. But already he walked them, past the courts of Zeus and Apollo, past the precinct where his father had died. For a moment he lingered over that harsh remembrance, and then walked farther—toward the mansion that housed the girl of his dreams.

He glanced down at his simple homespun cloak and untooled leather sandals. His only adornment was a tiny Star of David, suspended by a silver chain about his throat, a farewell gift from his mother. Raising a finger, he stroked the pendant, felt the brush of his beard and long hair against his neck, and wondered what Philea would think of him.

But outward appearance was only a mirror for deeper changes. He would speak to her of his new faith. It would be that, and not the rough tunic or the beard, with which she must contend!

Lifting his face resolutely, he surveyed the beloved coast of his childhood. Visions of hungry souls clamoring for his message thrilled through him, and he imagined himself their deliverer.

CHAPTER

2

The maiden stood in the doorway to her parlor appearing poised and confident. She hoped that in the muted light of the chamber Mark would not see the stubborn flush that had risen to her cheeks when the butler announced his visit.

Though it was still summer, autumn was not far away, and already a nip in the air had invaded the elegant sitting room. Mark had not heard her footstep on the threshold as he stooped over the parlor fire, prodding it with an iron poker. His back was to her, but she imagined his handsome face and dark eyes beckoning as they often seemed to do. And she faltered as she called his name.

Turning about, Mark wiped the soot from his hands and nodded. "It is I," he replied, trying to hide his own uneasiness with a smile.

For a long while they studied one another, he impressed as never before with her delicate beauty, and she stunned at the unexpected alteration in his appearance.

Twilight spilled past her from the garden court, enveloping her in a coral blush, but as she drew closer he saw that her gown was white, not rose. A slender golden chain holding one tiny pearl graced her neck, perfectly complementing her smooth skin. Everything about her was fragile but compelling.

For a moment Mark's eyes lingered on the sweet curve of her lips, but then, remembering himself, he shifted his gaze to the floor.

The girl was circling him, surveying him up and down.

"Had you not told me, I would not be certain it was you," she said, bemused.

In her expression there was no scorn, only ardent curiosity. Mark stood still, his face raised to the ceiling, his jaw tight, as she drew back and studied him again.

"You have questions?" he asked, trying to recapture the sense of resolution he had achieved on the boat.

"I do," she sighed. "Shall we start with this strange transformation, or shall I ask where you have been all these months?"

"Whichever," he gently replied. "The two go together."

"Then let us begin with your promise to me as you departed Cyrene."

With that reminder, Mark's calculated confidence fled. Philea was a lady, but she could confront when occasion demanded. Indeed, he had broken a vow. And he must answer for it.

"I . . . I was caught away," he said, beginning badly. "Israel is a . . . mysterious place."

Philea considered this patiently but was not convinced. "I have heard the Jewish women are beautiful," she offered with hollow generosity. "Perhaps . . ."

"No," Mark interrupted. Then laughing, he said, "You do not understand."

The girl turned from him, finding it more and more difficult to conceal her anger. Her throat constricted, she managed, "You missed a wonderful festival. The 'coming out' was full of color—music, dancing . . ."

Suddenly, she wheeled about. "Oh, Marcus, why weren't you here?"

The question stung, draining him of all purpose. Reaching

for her, Mark tried to hush the soft crying she could not stifle. Though she resisted, he enfolded her in his arms and pressed her cheek to the rough fabric of his cloak.

"Now, now, my lady," he pleaded, "please forgive me. I had planned to be here. I thought of you every day I was away. But . . . I had my own coming out to do."

If the explanation was insufficient, he knew of no other way to put it. Could Philea understand if he spoke of the Messiah, of the Resurrection, or his own rebirth?

"You play games!" she cried, pushing away.

Composing herself, she wiped the tears from her face, determined to maintain her pride.

"Why the strange attire—the beard, the hair?" She changed topics. "And what is this ornament about your neck?" she asked, flicking his Jewish medallion with one finger. "You no longer look Roman."

It was a barb, but Mark managed to take it graciously. "Perhaps this observation, more than anything, gets to the point," he said, willing now to reveal all. "In my heart, I no longer belong to Rome."

Philea heard the syllables but rejected their meaning. The very thought was abhorrent—implying her own loss of Mark.

With wide eyes, the girl insisted, "Speak no more in riddles! In the past you saved my life. Save now my heart!"

Yes, Mark, speak plainly, he rebuked himself.

"Caesar is no longer my god," he declared. "There is another who has won me."

Philea, trembling, turned for the divan near the fire. Her hands perched like small birds upon her narrow lap as she pondered the statement.

Brows arched, she finally shrugged. "There are many gods. Why must you reject one and embrace another?"

"But you are wrong!" Mark asserted, his voice rising more than he intended.

Philea recoiled, stunned as Mark began to pace the room.

"Have you heard of Jesus the Rabbi, the miracle-worker who caused such a stir in Israel?"

The girl searched her memory. News from Roman provinces all about the Mediterranean flitted through Cyrene with the passage of vessels through its port and commerce through its streets. She could recall vague references to such a character.

When she nodded quietly, Mark proclaimed, "He was more than a magician, more than a healer or philosopher! Jesus is the Son of God Most High!"

The maiden reflected. "But did we not hear that this Rabbi was crucified—an enemy of the state? Surely, you cannot think him divine?"

"He rose again!" the young man cried. "I have seen him with my own eyes!"

Philea dropped her gaze, embarrassed for the one she loved.

Carefully choosing her words, so as not to further unravel the tattered edges of his mind, she suggested, "Perhaps Israel has bewitched you. A few weeks at home will do you good. See your friends, your acquaintances . . ."

Mark realized he had not handled this well. Casting about for a way to reconstruct his testimony, he gritted his teeth, causing her further fear.

Philea stood up and cautiously stepped toward the door. Seeing that he had lost her, Mark suppressed panic and held his tongue.

When the butler appeared announcing another guest, Mark straightened his shoulders. "It is best that I go now," he said. "Perhaps another day . . ."

The young woman nodded. As she walked with him from the parlor, the new visitor was approaching down the hall. Mark instantly knew him.

"Brutus!" he cried. "I was coming to see you this evening!"

The soldier at first did not recognize his old friend. When the identity dawned on him, he stammered a greeting, a hundred questions racing through his mind.

"Marcus has come home," Philea interjected. Her strained enthusiasm did not escape Brutus, nor did her covert gesture, implying that Mark needed gentle handling.

"Welcome!" the sergeant repeated, clapping him on the back. "You missed a great coming out! You should have been here!"

"So I hear," Mark assured him, wondering why Brutus was calling on Sergius's daughter.

"This kind man was my escort," Philea explained, patting the big fellow on the arm.

There was no malice toward Mark in her tone. But he could not interpret her feelings for the soldier. It was evident that Brutus was now a regular caller at the Villa Ponti.

Remembering his friend's assertion that he would one day court Philea, Mark bowed his head and excused himself. As he headed for the door, Brutus suggested a rendezvous at the taverns.

Mark did not reply.

CHAPTER

3

The Cyrenian caravan, carts, and wagons loaded with the goods and furnishings of two households, wound its way slowly toward the Herodian Towers. It had been a long trip from Cyrenaica to Joppa. Mark had chosen a freight vessel rather than a speedier passenger ship to carry Simon's belongings and the balance of his own possessions to Israel.

The top-heavy vehicles tottered up the steep incline toward the Holy City, Simon's servants pulling on the oxen's harnesses to keep them from sliding backward.

Rufus and Alexander, who walked beside Mark at the head of the train, had never seen Jerusalem. They had heard their father and Joses speak of its splendor. But they, like Mark upon first seeing it, were unprepared for the gleaming spectacle.

Had the son of Quintus been disposed to focus on his companions, he would have noted the same wide-eyed awe in their faces as he himself had manifest the day he first entered the capital.

But since the moment he had left Philea his thoughts had been a jumble. With the strength of conviction he had gone to her home, and, feeling a fool, he had fled from her.

It would have been easier to take a strong stand if only Brutus had mocked him—if only Philea had scorned him. But the look of pity in their faces was humiliating.

Therefore, the return to Jerusalem, an event which should have heralded the shedding of the past and the embracing of a new direction, was overcast with doubt.

Why had he run from his friends? Was he incapable of boldly maintaining his witness? Surely he had not doubted the reality of Christ. Never could he do that, having once seen the risen Lord in the upper room of his uncle's house!

As the caravan neared the center of town, the temple compound looming before them, Mark remembered Peter's address on the steps of the Outer Court. Flashes of the apostle's bold countenance and courageous stand caused Mark to question of what mettle he was made. But his sad introspection was interrupted by Rufus's voice. The lad's black face was shining, and his eyes glistened with excitement. "Where is the Cyrenian synagogue?" he asked. "Father has spoken of it often, saying that it is near the temple."

"Yes," Mark agreed. "He has attended Sabbath meetings there since coming here. It is on the next street."

"Will we pass by it?" Alexander asked, full of expectancy.

"We shall make it a point to do so," Mark said with a smile.

Along the many blocks ringing the holy compound, meeting halls for different nations had been erected through the years, allowing pilgrims and Jerusalem's foreign residents to worship in their own languages and with their own kind. The Cyrenian synagogue was one of the most prestigious, noted not only for its finery but for the high thinking that went on within its walls.

Here, as in Cyrene, the people of Mark's province loved philosophy. Though it was kept within a Judaic framework, Cyrenians brought to their discussions of the Law and the Torah a taste for debate even more sharply honed than that of the Jewish scribes. As a result, men of many nations were attracted to this meetinghouse where mental reasoning was encouraged and given liberal rein. In fact, members of this fraternity were called "the Libertines" for their freedom of thought.

The noon sun illumined the synagogue precinct with white light as the caravan came near. Mark shielded his eyes against the glare, trying to make out the source of a disturbance in the vicinity. "What is it?" Rufus inquired, hearing the sounds of shouting and ruckus down the way.

The doors to the Cyrenian sanctuary had been thrown open, and from the hall a great body of men was emerging, pushing and shoving against each other as they spilled into the street.

They seemed to pursue someone, fists raised and faces contorted in angry remonstrance. But no one could be seen running from them.

When Mark and his companions drew near, it became evident that whoever their victim was, he was being pushed along with the throng as they yelled venomous threats.

The caravan could do nothing but proceed behind the crowd as the angry mob coursed through the narrow viaducts leading back toward the temple. By now the larger community had entered the street following the disturbance and asking questions.

Once they reached the gate to the holy compound, Mark and Simon's sons abandoned the train to the care of the servants. The throng, now numbering in the hundreds, rushed as a body up the wide steps leading to the court of the Sanhedrin and jostled along the wall separating them from the inner sanctum.

As yet few of the newcomers knew the reason for the gathering. "Lawbreaker . . ." "Moses-hater . . ." and similar epithets were slung into the air on curses and spittle. But Mark did not know whom they accused until he saw a white-haired gentleman being dragged up the stairs to the court-room.

Blinking his eyes, he whispered, "Stephen!" And turning to

his companions he explained, "It is Stephen, an elder of our church! They are taking him for trial!"

Rufus tipped his turban back, and Alexander rose on tiptoe to view the situation. "What has he done?" they asked.

"Surely nothing evil!" Mark asserted. "He is a good man!"

Someone overhearing him snarled from the crowd, "He speaks against this holy place and against the Law!"

Like a mad chorus other voices threw in yet other accusations, all ludicrous.

Mark had heard Stephen speak often. A wise and mighty orator he was and a miracle-worker.

But the young convert knew better than to fight against so many. He knew these people had once put a better man than Stephen to death, and, though the Libertines loved "reason," they would not hear it now.

By sunset the congregation had grown so large, the people spilled into the porches ringing the courtroom building. Along with thousands of curious onlookers who had followed the Libertines to the site, nearly everyone who had joined the church since the day of Pentecost was outside the meeting place of the Sanhedrin, awaiting word of their friend Stephen.

Mark sat with Rufus and Alexander against the stone partition separating the public from the courts of law. All around them were men and women of the church, singing and chanting, praying for the well-being of the brave preacher who now stood trial.

Most could only speculate on what had transpired at the Cyrenian synagogue to instigate the arrest. Leaders of the Libertines were in the courtroom, and their followers had been allowed into the patio beyond the partition, so no one was available to give a clear explanation.

Rufus and Alexander watched Mark and his fellow believers as they waited through the long hours of the trial, holding hands and swaying as one great body to the chords of a psalm.

"O God," they sang, "do not remain quiet; do not be silent, and, O God, do not be still. For behold, your enemies make an uproar; and those who hate you have exalted themselves. They make shrewd plans against your people and conspire together against your treasured ones. . . ."

The young Cyrenians knew this Scripture, but they were amazed to hear it put to such use. Awed by the fellowship and single-mindedness of those about them, they sat silent, sensing that some great or very terrible thing was about to happen. "O my God," the chorus continued, tears streaming down men's faces, "make them like the whirling dust; like chaff before the wind. . . . Pursue them with your tempest, and terrify them with your storm . . . that they may know that you alone . . . are the Most High over all the earth."

The red glow of a large, descending sun was just touching the bronze gates of the Sanhedrin compound when suddenly the large doors were thrust open and one lone man stepped before the waiting crowd.

Several voices accosted him. "Simon, were you in the synagogue? What goes on in there?"

Mark nudged his companions, and the two young black men peered speechlessly across the heads of the throng into the tear-streaked face of their own father!

Rufus jolted to his feet and began flashing his wide-sleeved arms back and forth until he caught Simon's eye, and Alexander stumbled across the veranda, picking his way through the crowd until he clung to his father's embrace.

"Oh, my boys!" the Cyrenian wept. "I had expected to rejoice when you came to Jerusalem. But this is a sad, sad day!"

Peter, who had sat with his followers through the long afternoon vigil, stood and demanded, "Friend, how does Stephen fare?"

Simon's sons, their own faces wet with tears though they did not yet understand what transpired, fearfully absorbed their father's words.

"I was in the house of worship today," he began. "The Libertines had invited Stephen to address us and to explain the doctrines of Jesus, so that our thinkers might ponder them."

Here his shoulders stooped and he shook his head. "But my people did not wish to hear the truth! They wished only to dispute with him!"

"What charges have been brought against him?" Peter shouted.

"False ones!" Simon declared. "Lies! They claim he speaks blasphemies and destruction! That he says Jesus will change the laws of Moses!"

The unchurched in the crowd murmured at this, and believers themselves shook their heads in fear.

But Simon was not finished. Staring back toward the courthouse, he shuddered. "When the Libertines gave their accusation," he cried, "Stephen sat straight as Jerusalem's gates! And his face . . . oh, his face was like that of an angel!"

A thrill passed through the company. Most folk here, whether believers or not, had heard Stephen speak from time to time. And they could imagine such a statement to be true.

When a mighty swell of sound from the direction of the courtroom spilled toward the crowd, Simon's voice broke. "He has finished his defense!" he shouted. "They will have him now!"

Suddenly the gates swung wide open behind the Cyrenian, pushing him aside. Out from the house of the Sanhedrin a body of angry men filled the porch, shoving Stephen before them.

The court elders, as well as leaders of the Libertines, rudely pushed him through the streets until they reached an exit along the city walls.

Mark, together with Simon and his sons, rushed through the great doors of Jerusalem's eastern boundary until they stood with the throng outside.

Everything happened quickly. Unlike a Roman crucifixion, this sentence would be accompanied with speed. Boldly, men of the Sanhedrin and of the Libertine synagogue stripped off their cloaks and threw them at the feet of one of their supporters. Then, picking up stones from the ground, they began to hurl them at the preacher.

Stephen's white hair and beard blew back in the wind as he remained still and tall a long moment. He did not go down with the first blows but kept his face upturned to the setting sun.

"Lord Jesus, receive my spirit!" he cried at last, as the blood streamed from his forehead. Slowly he slumped to his knees, his countenance lost to all save those who ringed him. Still they continued to throw rock upon rock at his battered body.

Kneeling upright, his voice loud as a trumpet, he prayed, "Lord, do not hold this sin against them!"

Mark could not see the broken victim. But his words tightened about his throat like a tourniquet. For a long while he stood, mesmerized by the haunting challenge.

The crowd was dispersing when Simon took him by the arm, pleading with him to come away.

But Mark could not leave.

Dark descended on the pile of rubble and rock that marked the end of Stephen's life. Here and there a tatter of the prophet's clothing could be seen between the stones, and blood trickled in gaudy gashes across the ground.

Mark cursed his fellow Cyrenians, shamed to be called by that name.

As he turned to go, the executioners were gathering up their clothes, lingering in muted conversation with the one who had kept their cloaks.

With a knife-like stare, Mark studied the coat-keeper who had taken great pleasure in the stoning. Handing out the last garment, the fellow wiped his fingers across his tunic, and as he did so, his gaze was caught by the solitary figure beside the rock pile.

Perhaps he sensed the hatred in Mark's spirit. Perhaps he did not. But his smile, as he flashed it, was a shard of ice.

CHAPTER

4

It was midnight when Peter sent men from the House Ben Haman to fetch the body of Stephen. The apostle may have hoped to insure his people's safety by waiting for cover of dark, but he would not presume to hush the great lamentation that accompanied the preacher's interment.

Amid much weeping, the church placed Stephen in a sepulcher outside the city, and for days the first martyr for the cause of Christ was mourned, believers burning black candles in their homes and wearing sackcloth about the streets.

Mark had not slept well for many nights. Somehow, the witness of Stephen's death had affected him as profoundly as the crucifixion of Jesus.

Although stoning was more a Jewish form of execution than Roman, Mark had seen a few such killings in Cyrene. They had not troubled him then any more than the sight of criminals suspended from crosses.

But he was not the same man now as he had been when he lived with Quintus. Nor was he the same man who had observed the Master's crucifixion.

Since Mark's conversion, he saw things differently. Life was precious. And he loved the brethren, among whom Stephen had been a prince.

The memory of the martyr's torture haunted him. But that was not all. He could not erase from his mind the face of the Jew who had held the cloaks.

The stranger's calculated smile seemed to portend dreadful things, just as Judas's dark exit from the Lord's Passover had foreshadowed treachery.

Tonight Mark held a glass of red wine before the parlor fire, tipping it this way and that, blankly staring at the ruby light that bounced off the glass. Perhaps there were others in the house who found sleep hard to come by. But the place was quiet; even the streets were hushed with foreboding.

Did they all fear, as he did? Did they sense oppression in the air?

Drawing his shoulders into a huddle, he tried to shake the pall. When he heard a footstep on the tiles, he turned with a jerk.

"It is only I . . . Peter," the big Galilean greeted. "I see you, too, are restless."

Mark managed a vague smile and faced the fire again. "Do you believe in wandering spirits?" he asked.

Peter did not reply without thought. "The Master spoke of such things . . . yes, I do."

"These nights since Stephen's death," Mark said, "I have believed in them, too. Evil things, which inhabit the dark . . ." Sighing, he drew his back up straight. "Sometimes when I cannot sleep, when the house is very still, I feel them every-where."

"Are you afraid?" Peter inquired.

The young disciple looked at him squarely. "Yes, teacher. I am afraid."

"I have also known fear," Peter confessed.

Mark, recalling the Gethsemane night and the torments that followed, nodded. "Then perhaps you, too, have seen the evil one. I think that I, twice, have seen him," he said with a shudder.

Peter could not guess what he meant, so leaned close. "Do you speak of flesh and blood?" he asked.

The young Roman, unused to speaking in such terms, peered about the room. "Judas was flesh and blood," he whispered, "and yet he was evil."

The apostle stroked his brief beard with thick fingers. "Judas is gone," he reflected. "He has gone to his own place."

Mark's gaze drifted through the flames. "Perhaps Judas has a brother," he suggested. "If there are wandering evils, can they not leap from heart to heart?"

The Galilean sat back, his skin bristling. "I suppose they could," he replied.

"Then," Mark exclaimed, his voice tremulous, "it is this which I have seen—in the eyes of a man!"

The affinity of apostle for student prevented doubt on Peter's part. "Who is the man?" he asked.

"He guarded the cloaks of Stephen's persecutors," Mark replied. "I was there, alone with him, beside the rock pile. You had departed and so had the others."

Peter listened respectfully, considering every word.

"He means ill for the church . . . I know it," the young Roman declared. "I do not know his name, but we will soon hear it every day. All of us!"

CHAPTER
5

When the persecution came, it was a whirlwind—rending families, crushing faith, shedding blood.

The persecutor's name was Saul, and as Mark had predicted, it quickly became the most notorious name spoken among believers.

"Great" the name meant. And so Saul was—great in wreaking havoc, a master of terror.

With the power of the Sanhedrin behind him, he began to break down doors throughout Jerusalem, leading troops from the temple and soldiers from the high priests. Armed with letters of indictment from the religious court, he took men and women captive, committing most to prison, and many . . . to death.

Simon, who had heard Saul speak often in the Cyrenian synagogue, told Mark that the fiend who decimated the believers had once been a student of Gamaliel, the most profound Jewish scholar of the generation. Raised in Tarsus, a city of Cilicia, the son of a very wealthy and devout Jew, Saul had been privileged to sit at the renowned rabbi's feet for years, studying the Law in Jerusalem and cutting his teeth on Judaism.

While Gamaliel himself leaned toward liberalism, his brilliant young student had thrived on the traditions and presuppositions gleaned from the theologian's more orthodox teachings. While Saul's genius was enlarged under the tutelage of Gamaliel, so was his ability to argue defense of the Law and the cause of conservativism.

For years Saul had been a favorite of the Libertines, not because they agreed with him, but because he had a keen wit. Often the young Jew had been invited to debate in their meeting hall, and gradually, though they made strange bedfellows, Saul and the "free thinkers" had become friendly antagonists. No wonder, then, that he had been present the day the Libertines hauled Stephen to trial.

Mark pondered the perversion that had arisen from Saul's intensive study and devotion to tradition. How like the vain reasonings of Cyrene's babblers! While Cyrenaica's mental jousting led always to a dead end, Saul's brand of Judaism, followed for its own sake, had led to hatred and violence.

For months, fear hounded the church. Believers never knew when the next raid might occur, or where. Because so many homes in Jerusalem housed groups of converts, including countless foreigners who had joined them since the Day of Pentecost, Saul's invasions were often random, his troops tramping from door to door, seeking out telltale activities and signs that this place or that sheltered "heretics."

His cleansings were sporadic, coming with no warning, frequently at night, sometimes simultaneously throughout town, and sometimes concentrated within one sector. But behind his seemingly haphazard approach was a solid plan of action. The church could never rest, knowing that at any moment a knock at the door could prelude disaster, that sleep or daily routine might at any hour be interrupted by a violent hand. Nerves were kept constantly on edge, tempers and infant faith strained to the snapping point.

Believers began to meet in secret, speaking in whispers and

singing without instruments. They invented symbols and greetings to which only the initiated were privy, but which would allow them to greet one another on the streets, or to designate themselves silently as Followers of the Way.

"Curl your fingers thus, hold your hands thus, use this password, etch this sign upon your doorstep" . . . so they instructed one another. "Tonight we meet at Amon's house, tomorrow at Judah's. We meet beneath this street, or in that cave. But we meet."

As the church continued to grow, Saul's severe face, his swagger, his wild red beard and flint-black eyes haunted everyone. Jerusalem had become a military state, crippled not by Rome alone but by religious inquisition.

Those who had never joined the church, who had never succumbed to the powerful preaching of the apostles or to the winsome brotherhood of their disciples, those who had resisted the popular gospel, now began to avoid contact with its adherents. Neighbor shunned neighbor, friend betrayed friend, fingers were pointed, leaving the tormented city a society in shreds.

As for the House Ben Haman, it had remained strangely untouched. As day by day word was brought to the apostles of homes broken into, families divided, believers incarcerated, the door of the old hostel never felt a soldier's kick or opened on a foe.

But the very fact that Peter's domain was granted such immunity magnified the certain threat against it.

Very early one morning Mark awakened to the sound of quiet sobbing. Listening through his door, he heard someone pass by his chamber and down the court stairs.

Quickly donning his dayclothes, he left his room and followed the sound to the kitchen. There he found his mother, alone and weeping. She stood over the meat spit in the center of the room, wiping it again and again with an oily rag. When Mark entered she lifted a pale face to him and tried quickly to dab away her tears.

She was thinner of late than Mark liked to see her. Always precise about her grooming, she had, even at this early hour, combed her hair smooth and even against her head and had moistened her lips with berry juice. But she did not look well, her forehead lined with strain and anxiety, her frame a little stooped.

Gently, Mark pried the rag from her cold fingers and wiped them with the edge of his cloak. Then taking her in his arms, he held her close.

"You work harder than your maids," he whispered. "Always you have done so."

"I could not rest," she replied. "Not when so many are in danger."

"Times are not easy," Mark said weakly, still embracing her.

"Oh, but they are!" she cried, drawing back. "They are much too easy for us . . . for this house!"

Pulling away, she grabbed the rag again and began to twist it in her fists.

"Saul plays with us, like a cat with pathetic mice!" she insisted. "I would rather he burst through the door this moment, than dangle blood-bought safety before us another day! Oh," she sighed, throwing her head back, "I weep every night for the children whose mamas have been torn from them . . . for the women whose husbands . . ."

Mark could not bear another word. He cupped her mouth with his hand and kissed her white cheek.

"Enough, Mother," he begged through gritted teeth. "There is nothing we can do. . . ."

"And Saul delights in the fact!" she blurted out, wrenching from his grasp.

Her hot eyes seared him until, seeing him wither, she suddenly rebuked herself.

"Oh, Mark," she pleaded, "I am not myself. I lash out at you in my anger because I am helpless."

The young man nodded, showing empathy for his mother's frustration.

"You have sacrificed much to be here," she finally whispered. "Your birthright in Cyrene, your career with Rome, friends . . . love . . ."

Mark looked at her in surprise, wondering how she knew about Philea.

"I am not blind," she assured him. "You think that because you have not spoken of her, I do not know? It has been your silence that spoke the loudest," she admitted. "I only hope that as others leave Jerusalem, you will still remain . . . with me."

Mark knew that, daily, believers were fleeing the Holy City. Though the church was growing despite persecution, families were, by the hundreds, seeking refuge in distant places, abandoning their homes for asylum. And since Joses had not yet returned from Cyprus where he was selling off his properties, Mary truly would be abandoned should Mark ever leave.

Holding his mother close again, he breathed into her hair. "I have given up nothing, Mother. I have found everything."

Then looking toward the front door of the house, through which the Lord himself had once walked and the fledgling church had later emerged into the world, he felt a thrill pass through him.

"Who knows?" he offered. "Perhaps this place has been spared not by Saul but by God because it is the seedplot of the faith." And holding her at arm's length, he promised, "I intend to remain until I am uprooted."

CHAPTER

6

For months Saul made havoc of the church until nearly every believer had evacuated the Holy City.

To the persecutor's consternation, however, the forced dispersion only spread the doctrines of Jesus beyond the boundaries of Israel. As the converts told their story, Jews who inhabited far-flung parts of the Roman Empire were turning to the faith.

It started with Samaria, the province to the north of Judea, where the deacon Philip preached as powerfully as Stephen had done in Jerusalem. Again, by hundreds, men and women accepted the witness that was confirmed by miracles at Philip's hands.

And this was followed by the conversion of an Ethiopian, south in Gaza—yet another seed by which the gospel would spread beyond Egypt.

Meanwhile, folk who had fled Jerusalem for their original homelands or who left their native Judea to take up new lives in Syria, Asia, and throughout the Mediterranean world declared Christ to hundreds who eagerly embraced the powerful story.

Barnabas, who had been in Cyprus when the persecution began, had felt he should remain there when he saw the influx of leaderless believers who fled to the island. Letters from him reported that there were now congregations throughout the region.

Similar news came from Damascus and Antioch.

Saul seethed with desire to annihilate them. Threatening slaughter, he procured more summons from the high priest giving him authority to ferret out Jews of the new "cult" beyond Palestine. On a rampage, he began to invade village after village, town after town, proceeding north toward the Syrian desert.

Jerusalem was quiet—too quiet. Fear reigned among the few believers who had stayed with the apostles. Sorrow for the days of past glory and for their departed companions was pervasive.

Mark and his Cyrenian friend, Simon, hugged the shadows as they walked through the streets this evening. They were returning from a secret meeting across town and were careful to step softly as they hastened through the twilight.

The young Roman had been given increasing responsibilities as a member of the house where the apostles dwelt. As an intimate disciple of the great fisherman, he was considered a leader of some authority.

Nevertheless, he was essentially a deacon, a servant of tables. He longed to be of "higher" service to the church.

Gritting his teeth, he gazed through the gloaming in frustration. Unable to vindicate his friends, helpless to right the persistent evils brought against his family and fellow-believers, he expressed his anger with a clenched fist.

"Simon," he whispered, "I want to do more than work in the kitchen! Our people live in torment, and all I do is cook and clean. I have given up Rome, and yet, perhaps the Roman way is not entirely bad."

The black man, who of all people knew Mark's proud heritage, listened respectfully.

"We are many in number—thousands upon thousands!"

Mark expostulated. "We are spreading across the empire! If we were to organize . . ."

Simon sensed his fervent anxiety, his grasping for action, and added, "If we were to take up arms?"

"Yes, yes!" Mark enthused. "Take up arms! I know something about the military! I could be of great help."

When Simon shook his head, whispering *Heis ho Theos,* the Roman's youthful zeal sputtered to a sigh.

"So the church should go to war?" the sandal merchant probed. "The church exists to kill and to avenge?"

Mark's fist tingled, the knotted finger joints fiery. Rubbing his knuckles against his thigh, he felt his face redden.

"So," he muttered, "I return to the kitchen! Where is the power in such service? Were we not promised *power* at Pentecost?"

Simon studied the darkening street. He understood Mark's ambition, his inbred desire to be a hero. "I do not know what the Lord has ahead for you," he answered gently. "But for now you have a work. Even mundane tasks take on glory when done from the heart. Yes," he insisted, "the heart has everything to do with it."

CHAPTER

7

Strange rumors were filtering south from Syria, from the distant church of Damascus.

"Insanity," Peter called the reports. And all the apostles agreed. The men and women of the Ben Haman house had lived in choking fear for months. They had seen their friends murdered in the streets and were not about to believe hearsay.

Whatever substance there was to reports of Saul's conversion, it was a plot. The naive church of Damascus, so far removed from the seedplot of Jerusalem, lacked guidance and was easy prey for the Deceiver.

Word did have it that Saul's dreaded venture north to assail the Syrian congregations had ended peaceably. He had taken no prisoners, no lives. But apparently, in his craftiness, he had managed to penetrate the confidence of Damascus believers, posing as a transformed man, humbled by some devastation, and seeking the truth of Jesus.

Even Barnabas, who had met Saul on a visit from Cyprus to Damascus, contended that the stories were true, writing to the mother church that if they would but talk with Saul, they would know.

"Ludicrous!" Thomas asserted. "Blasphemy against the Lord!"

The rumors continued for three years, and though, during that time, the persecution ceased, brethren of Israel scorned reports of the enemy's growing Syrian "ministry."

The day Saul returned to Jerusalem, asking to see the apostles, fear sprang up afresh with memories of his holocaust.

"He is the very Devil's son!" John's brother, James, asserted. "Son of the Father of Lies! Does he expect to perpetrate such foolishness in the very city of God?"

The upper room was stifling hot. A merciless sun beat through the summer sky past reed blinds drawn over the open skylights. Tempers were short and easily provoked.

"Perhaps someone should at least visit him," John ventured.

James turned toward him with a jerk; incredulous faces scowled in every corner.

"Are you mad?" Thomas glowered. "Are you mad?"

John shook his head and stared at the floor. "Judge as you like," he simply said. "But would Barnabas lie to us? He has worked with the man!"

Mark leaned into a breezeless shadow and bit his tongue. He could feel his temperature rising, and it was not due to the heatwave.

More than once since abiding in the House Ben Haman, he had been embarrassed and even angered by his uncle's careless generosity. In the past, he had regretted such feelings, wishing to be more like the kindly Levite. But this time, he knew Barnabas had gone too far. Recollections of Saul's horror, staged in the very streets outside this building—visions of bodies dragged half-alive to prison and of corpses smearing blood from the heels—could never be blotted away. Nor could Mark forget the sounds of crying children and pleading women.

Tensely he shut and opened his fists, his stomach knotting. Whatever Barnabas thought he had observed in Damascus, he was deluded!

Another blast of steamy air shot through the overhead blind.

Peter sat quiet for a long time, his hands on his knees. "Barnabas is not with us, so we cannot question him," the big fisherman concluded. "We must follow our own judgment."

John settled back with a helpless shrug, as his companions sneered at him.

And Mark sided with them.

A week later, Barnabas opened the door to the House Ben Haman and peered into the patio. James, the Lord's brother, Mark, and some of the church leaders lounged near the fountain, hoping for respite from yet another oppressively hot evening. Peter was not among them.

Glancing over his shoulder, Barnabas whispered to a hooded figure, bidding him to take his arm.

Having rehearsed again and again what he would say to the apostles when he introduced his guest, he cleared his throat and walked as confidently as possible into the courtyard of his own home.

Mark, the first to notice his arrival, bolted upright. "Uncle!" he cried. "What are you doing in Jerusalem?"

The men surrounding the fountain looked curiously at Barnabas's companion, and James, expecting an introduction, went forward in eager greeting.

"Welcome, friend!" he exclaimed. "We had not expected . . ."

"Call Peter," the Levite simply said.

Caught short, James studied the newcomers uneasily, then, bowing, sent a servant upstairs to fetch the apostle.

In a moment, the Galilean stood on the mezzanine.

Barnabas brought his guest forward, and confronting the leader, announced, "Peter, this is Saul of Tarsus, a believer in Jesus Christ."

The men began to whisper to each other, glaring with contempt at the shadowy alien. They would have seized him, but something—either his strangely quiet demeanor or his brazen foolhardiness—prevented them.

The big fisherman leaned against the gallery rail, saying

nothing, the tension in the room broken only by Barnabas's firm assertion.

"Saul *has* received Jesus," he declared. "You are just too stiff-necked to believe it!"

With this he related the persecutor's own peculiar account of his conversion, while the man of Tarsus gazed at the floor. Out of respect for Barnabas, the apostles listened to the incredible tale of Saul being knocked to the earth on the road to Damascus, of seeing a blinding light from heaven and hearing a voice.

" 'Saul, Saul, why do you persecute me?' " Barnabas continued, full of urgency, as though he himself had been there. " 'I am Jesus, whom you are persecuting. It is hard for you to kick against the goads!' "

The Cilician nodded his head, and Mark thought he saw him shudder.

For a long moment there was silence. "Why does he cover his head?" someone snarled. "Does he still live in shame?"

Barnabas, sighing, whispered to his companion, to pull the mantle back from his face.

It seemed to take Saul a moment to focus on the men. As he looked in their direction, Mark scrutinized him.

Yes—it was Saul! He could never forget his angular nose and rusty beard. But, memorable as the fellow was, something about him was now different.

From face to face, Saul's gaze traveled, dimly tracing each disciple's features, as with a broken stylus.

When his searching eyes found Mark's, the young man puzzled, for they were no longer fearsome but soft beneath a bleary haze. And though he looked for their icy splinter, he found none.

"For three days after he saw Jesus," Barnabas explained, "our friend was blind. Even now his vision is not what it once was."

With this the Levite took his companion's cold hand in his own.

"My sight returns day by day," Saul said, speaking his first words to the Jerusalem leaders. "But I need my brothers to guide me."

Approaching the gallery, he stood at the bottom of the staircase, and looked up at Peter.

"Sir," he said with respect, "I have heard that your people often receive new names when they enter the faith. Is this so?"

Mark could see that his mentor was confounded, his expression half a sneer and half pity as he looked into his enemy's filmy eyes.

"This is so," was all he replied.

"Then," Saul insisted, kneeling on the step and throwing his head back, "I wish no longer to be called Saul but Paul."

The listeners quickly interpreted that the professed convert no longer wished to be called "great," but "little."

Everyone knew that however Peter responded to this request would seal Saul's status with the church. From then on he must be either accepted or rejected by the brethren.

When the apostle finally made a move, coming cautiously down the stairs, no one breathed. And when at last he pressed confirming hands upon Saul's head, only the penitent's soft weeping broke the silence.

PART FIVE

Growth

Then Peter began to speak:
"I now realize how true it is that
God does not show favoritism
but accepts men from
every nation who fear him
and do what is right."

ACTS 10:34-35

CHAPTER

1

There had never been a schism in the church. The times of fear and persecution had served only to bind believers tightly together, resulting in the spread of the gospel beyond the bounds of Palestine.

But when Saul's persecution ended and the church relaxed, division followed.

Though Peter had welcomed him, others would not believe Saul had been converted. So strong was their antipathy that they set about to kill him.

It was not surprising that if any of the disciples were to reject Paul, it would be the Grecians, Greek-speaking Jews born outside Palestine and not reared in the strictest traditions of Judaism. It had been against the liberal philosophies of such Hellenists that Paul had set his teeth since his early days under Gamaliel. The fact that so many of them had joined the ranks of the infant church had only convinced him of their heretical tendencies, and when he had gone about to destroy the believers, he had been particularly vengeful against these folk.

Though Paul remained with Peter and the others for fifteen days, he made quick enemies for himself. It could be expected that the Pharisees and priests would turn against him, as he spoke now in the temple in defense of the church, using the same oratorical skills with which he had once lambasted the doctrines of Jesus. But when the Grecians likewise disputed with him, Peter and the apostles were chagrined.

Paul was a highly educated man, but he was ill-prepared to argue the teachings of a faith so new to him. He especially was at a disadvantage in discussing such matters with those who had been converted long before he had.

Mark was present the day Paul's antagonists rose up against him. "You are not one of us!" the Grecians cried. "You only know the Law! What do you know of Christ?"

Standing at Peter's side, Mark saw the fisherman fidget nervously as Paul defended his belief in Jesus on the grounds that the Nazarene had fulfilled the requirements of Law and prophecy for the anticipated Messiah.

"Does this forgive your cruelties?" the Grecians cried. "Behold, he believes the prophets!" they mocked. "So all is forgiven!"

Mark glanced anxiously at the priests and scribes who lined the porch. It was obvious that they scorned Paul's attempts to reconcile his previous stance with the new doctrine. But they kept silent, content to let the followers of Jesus dispute among themselves.

"This is not good," Peter whispered, leaning toward his student. "Paul is sincere. But he stumbles over too much logic."

As much to save the church as to save Paul the apostles agreed to send him away.

"Return for a season to Tarsus," Peter counseled the new convert. "We will supply your passage if you will only go home to study. There you will be safe, and your brilliant mind, guided by the Spirit, will be led into all truth."

Humbly the former persecutor took Peter's advice and, his satchels full of scrolls, set off on a ship bound for Cilicia. He would study—indeed, he would. And when he was confident, he would return.

Mark had reserved judgment on Paul. He had tried in vain to accept him, but his feelings leaned toward distrust of the man. He had been relieved to see him go.

That had been six years ago.

Meanwhile, the church had flourished. Apostles and elders spread the gospel in cities about the empire, where dispersed Jews of the persecution cried out for leadership and teaching. Even Simon had returned to Cyrene with his sons, hoping to establish a fellowship there.

Peter had rarely set foot beyond Jerusalem during this time, but as folk in distant cities clamored to meet the "rock of the church," the apostle determined to visit congregations scattered throughout Palestine.

So it was that the son of Quintus came to abide by the Mediterranean this evening, just outside Joppa.

Curled in his cloak, he tried to find a comfortable position in which to lie on the pebbly beach. A cool breeze heading in the direction of the setting sun wafted through the flames of a small campfire, and dancing shadows emphasized the moody features of Mark's comrades.

In the distance a narrow path led to the tiny cottage in which Peter lodged. There had been room in the little house for only one guest, and while the apostle could have stayed outside with his friends, he had chosen to accept the hospitality of the poor brother who lived here.

His choice to do so had created no small stir among those traveling with him. Mark, unversed in matters of Jewish kosher law, had not at first understood the squabble, except that it had something to do with the host's occupation.

Leaning on one elbow, he glanced toward the cottage and tried to ignore the conversation around the fire. Whatever the problem posed by Peter's lodging inside, Mark was tired of hearing about it.

A long rope, suspended above the yard of the house, sported

several cowhides, freshly stripped. Like flat ghosts they fluttered in the breeze, sending malodorous confirmation that the resident of the cottage was a tanner. And with each reminder the squeamish Jews shuddered.

"It was hard enough to accept Saul," someone complained. "But now our leader cohabits with the unclean!"

"He used to be so scrupulous," another recalled. "I have seen him clean a catch after a day's fishing. He never hesitates to throw back a catfish or an eel, though they will bring a good coin from a Gentile buyer."

"Humph!" yet another exclaimed. "I fear what this will lead to. Sooner or later he will open his arms to embrace Gentile converts!"

Raucous laughter followed this comment, and Mark sat straight up on his sandy bed.

Never had it occurred to him that Gentiles should not be admitted to the church. Certainly until now the gospel had been preached only in Jewish assemblies throughout Palestine and in other provinces. Until now there had never been an unproselytized Gentile pressing to join. But Mark had not been aware of any edict against the possibility.

Though identifying more and more with his Jewish heritage, Mark understood the Gentile world better. And he was still half Roman.

The comforting unity of the church seemed daily to be challenged on a new front. First, the dispute over Paul, then the contention between the Grecians and the Hebrews. Would racial prejudice now confine the gospel to an elite corp?

Disgusted, Mark rose and shook the grit from his garments, giving no explanation as he walked away from the fire.

Trekking solitary down the beach, he filled his lungs with sea air and cast his gaze across the moonlit waters toward his distant homeland.

Though he had committed himself to these peculiar folk, he sometimes missed his people sorely. And he wondered if Jesus would likewise have rejected them.

CHAPTER

2

There were men at the tanner's gate seeking Peter.

They were not Jews. They were Romans, servants of some wealthy house, it appeared. While they were not dressed in the robes of nobility, two of them were well attired, the third outfitted in military garb, and they represented their master, a man of Caesarea.

Mark pushed open the humble gate and led the callers to the door. Having slept for the third night on the beach, he brushed the sand from his robes and smoothed his hair. It had been a long time since he had been with Gentiles, and even longer since he had spoken Latin.

These men, like himself, were fluent in Aramaic, but they seemed pleased to be greeted by one of their own.

"I am a guest here with Peter," Mark explained, using the language of his father. "How does your master know the Galilean?"

"Oh, he does not know him," the soldier corrected. "He only sent us to find him."

Mark would have inquired further, but, silenced by the

men's authoritative posture, he realized that their mission must be very sensitive.

Because it was a warm day, the cottage's front door was open. Flies buzzed in and out, energized by the ripe aromas of drying blood and leather in the tanner's shop.

The incongruity of these fine-garmented folk paying a call on such a lowly place did not escape Mark. Embarrassed for himself and Peter and gripped with fear, he led the visitors inside.

Simon the tanner sat hunched at his sunlit workbench mending a hole in a piece of hide where the butcher's cleaver had left its mark. Because he could not see well, he did his best work here where the afternoon light poured through a small window.

And because he was also hard of hearing, he did not realize he had callers until Mark loudly addressed him.

"Simon," he called, bending close to his ear, "men are here, looking for Peter."

The tanner's elderly wife, plump and harried, bustled from the pantry where she had been preparing the midday meal. She was not used to a houseful of company. It was well past noon, and dinner was still not ready.

Sighing heavily as she entered the room, she rubbed her hands together as if to say, "Oh, no! Not more mouths to feed!" And when she saw a Roman soldier in her parlor, she grew even more concerned.

"These are men of Caesarea," Mark said, sympathetic with her uneasiness. "They seek Peter."

Housing followers of Jesus had been a risky undertaking for these Jewish believers, bringing the censure of their synagogue and many neighbors. A visit from an imperial soldier made them even more uncomfortable.

"Is he still on the roof?" Mark inquired.

"He came down earlier to see if it was mealtime," Simon's wife replied, blushing. "I had to tell him it was not. And so he retired again to his chamber."

Mark glanced at the rickety stairs, no more than a ladder,

ascending to the low housetop. Peter had kept to himself much of the time since arriving here. Praying, his followers assumed.

"I thought you or one of your friends must be with him," the woman continued, eyeing Mark nervously. "I have heard Peter's voice off and on, as though he spoke with someone."

The young disciple shook his head. "No one has been with him. Are you certain . . ."

"My *husband's* hearing is impaired," she snapped. "Not mine!"

The tanner clearly heard this and was about to object when a pair of sandaled feet appeared at the head of the ladder.

"I am the one you seek," Peter greeted the callers. "Why have you come?"

When he was in full view, the soldier dropped his austere demeanor and bowed humbly before him.

Now Mark, the tanner, and his wife were even more bewildered. And when the fellow proceeded to explain the visit, they listened in awe.

"We are sent from Cornelius, a centurion of Caesarea," he began. "He is a just man, one who fears God, a man of good reputation among all the Jews." This was said with sincerity and with an edge of anxiety, as if the soldier needed to convince Peter that he spoke the truth.

The apostle nodded as though he knew of Cornelius, and so the visitor went on in terms Mark had never heard spoken by an imperialist.

"My master was told by God," he explained, "through a holy angel . . . to send for you to come to his house that he might hear you speak."

Mark glanced at his mentor, wondering how he would respond. Something in Peter's expression since stepping into the room puzzled the young disciple, as though the Galilean had indeed spoken only moments before with someone on the roof—someone . . .

"I would be honored to meet your master," Peter replied, stepping forward and grasping the soldier's hand in a warm grip. "My men and I will accompany you to Caesarea tomorrow."

Leading them out the door and toward the gate, Peter hailed his other companions, introducing them to the Romans.

As Mark followed him, he could not help but overhear the reaction of the host and hostess.

"Why would the apostle visit a Gentile?" the tanner questioned, his voice, due to his deafness, louder than he intended.

"Why would he visit a tanner?" his wife jibed, poking him good-naturedly in the ribs.

CHAPTER

3

Caesarea reminded Mark of Cyrene. Though it sat beside the sea and not inland like his hometown, it bore the imperial touch in architecture and ambiance.

"Belonging to Caesar," the name meant. Built by Herod the Great for Augustus, it was designed to be a gesture of goodwill and deference by the Jewish king to the higher world power and was a showcase of Roman culture.

Clean and white like Joppa, it sat as a crown jewel among Herod's many achievements. It was said that in building Caesarea, Herod had overcome nature, for he had created a safe harbor on a storm-battered and unstable shore, invading the sea itself and artificially constructing his own bay.

It was a wealthy city, its enormous amphitheater and temple graced with countless slender columns and statues to the emperor.

Nowhere was its privileged economic status more clearly seen than in the homes of its noblemen. It was to such a home that Mark and Peter came to visit Cornelius.

Accompanying the apostle were several Jewish converts from Joppa as well as the small group who had traveled from

Jerusalem to greet congregations in distant cities.

When they arrived at the city gate, they were met by gilded carriages ready to take them to the centurion's residence.

As the son of a Cyrenacian legate, Mark had once been accustomed to riding in glamorous vehicles. But having adopted the church's communal spirit, he had long ago relegated such luxury to the past. Stepping into the carpeted carriage and sinking into an upholstered seat, he found memories of his father's life-style hard to resist.

Peter was very quiet as they rode through the city's finest sector. Mark sensed that he, too, was full of memories— memories of a lesser life-style, the lot of the Galilean fisherman. The big man's large, work-knotted hands lay still in his lap as the carriage passed monuments and statues to Greek and Roman heroes, emperors and gods of the greatest power on earth.

When the carriage at last pulled in front of a pillared entry, Peter cleared his throat a time or two. And when he and Mark were guided through the portal, the disciple saw him rub his palms on his cloak.

Pressing against Mark's back were his fellow travelers. They halted inside the entry, fearing to touch anything Gentile, and, once again unprepared for what they saw.

Rushing out to meet them was a handsome man, dressed in a pleated tunic and high-strapped shoes, his hair close-cropped and curled Romanlike about his forehead.

Mark recognized his cape as signifying the Palestinian legion and knew that the bronze eagle on his breast symbolized years of power and prestige in the ranks of Caesar's army.

The centurion stopped in front of Peter, trembling as he studied the apostle's rugged features. When he suddenly fell to his knees, pressing his face to the floor, a hush and then a worried murmur passed among the Jews.

The Galilean, more distressed than ever, gazed down at the worshiper who clung to his feet and knew not what move to make. At last, brow furrowed, he bent over and pulled the centurion upright.

"Stand up," he pleaded. "I am only a man like you."

The centurion, though tall as Peter, looked into the apostle's eyes like a small child. His voice had commanded thousands, but today, he was soft-spoken and humble as he addressed the man of God.

"Come, then," Cornelius implored. "Meet my friends and teach us."

As the company entered the patio, they were overwhelmed, not only by the grandeur of the place, but by the number of people gathered there.

All along the several galleries and mezzanines, people waited. There must have been hundreds—kin, friends, and associates of the statesman.

Women in fluid gowns, shoulders bare and hair coiffed high, leaned over the railing, watching for the entrance of the fisherman. Children playing on the patio and splashing in the many fountains grew quiet at the arrival of the guests. And men in fine apparel, legati and senators, military leaders and wealthy merchants, whispered among themselves, studying the apostle from head to toe.

"Friends!" Cornelius called, hushing the crowd. "I summoned you here today to meet Simon Peter. I have told you little about him because I know little myself, except that an angel of the Lord impressed upon me that he should speak to us."

Again murmuring filled the house, the centurion's audience wondering at the strange pronouncement. Had they not known Cornelius for years and thought of him with great respect and admiration, they would have questioned his mental health. As it was, they had gathered here out of love for the man and out of deference to his convictions.

Still it was strange, not at all Romanlike, to speak of visions and angels. The Caesareans were as curious as they were respectful.

Quiet descended on the court. Peter, not knowing just what was expected, shuffled his feet and looked about him awkwardly.

When at last he spoke, Mark studied the floor self-consciously, wondering why Peter did not approach these people in a more gracious way.

"You know that it is unlawful for a man who is a Jew to keep company or to even visit folk of another nation. . . ." His voice, due to anxiety, was quite trumpetlike, and the listeners understandably interpreted his opening as a rebuke.

Turning to one another, they began again to whisper, flashing angry glances at the speaker and his companions. The fisherman, fumbling for diplomacy, cleared his throat again and quickly added, "But God has shown me that I should not call any man common or unclean."

Though intended as a kindness, this statement was no better than the first, and it stung the Gentiles.

Mark wondered when and how God had revealed such unusual insight to this devout and kosher Jew. But as it was, he could only relate to the discomfort of the Romans.

Peter, surveying the jostling crowd on the patio and hearing the hissing scorn of women on the galleries, tried to recover the goodwill that had been procured by Cornelius's testimony.

"Because God has shown me this, I came without argument as soon as I was sent for," he explained, trying to speak above the noise. "So, tell me, why have you asked me to come?"

No one but Cornelius knew the answer to that. Heads shook and unkind things were shouted from the mezzanine before the centurion intervened.

Hoping to save the moment, he stepped in front of the apostle and raised his hands, calling for quiet.

"Four days ago," he cried, "I was fasting!"

Everyone hushed at the sound of their friend's voice.

"I was praying here in my house in the afternoon," he reiterated as the din subsided, "and, behold, a man stood before me in bright clothing!"

The strength in his tone was riveting, and the crowd hung on each syllable.

"This being said to me, 'Cornelius, your prayer has been heard, and your gifts to the poor have been noticed by God.' "

Cornelius was a powerful man, but well known for charity and humility. His audience knew he would not have pointed to his own generosity without good reason.

" 'Send to Joppa,' " he continued to quote the visiting angel, " 'and call for Simon, also known as Peter. He is staying in the house of a tanner, who lives by the sea. When he comes, he will speak to you and tell you what you ought to do.' "

Silence reigned as Cornelius turned to the apostle, bowing. "Immediately I sent for you. And you have done well to come."

As his gaze locked on the Galilean's, the big fisherman sensed the gravity of the meeting.

"Now, we are all here," Cornelius concluded, "present before God . . . to hear whatever God would have you say."

Though some, no doubt, were present who did not have any yearning for such guidance, no one challenged the centurion's assessment.

Peter had spoken to thousands of Jews in Jerusalem and had addressed proselytes and fellow believers in other cities. But this was something new. These folk were alien, not only religiously, but racially, politically, and culturally. He had confronted his enemies at home with the Scriptures. With what should he convince these pagans who knew nothing of the God of Israel?

Still, something *had* transpired at the tanner's house, something which he had revealed to no one. And he knew he must share Jesus with these people.

Raising sweaty hands, he shook his head and shrugged. "Truly," he began, his voice unsteady, "I clearly see that God is no respector of persons. In every nation, whoever fears him and does what is right is accepted by him!"

This time the gathering heeded his words graciously. They

may have realized that such a sentiment spoken by a Jew was rare. But they did not know how revolutionary it seemed to those who had accompanied Peter from Jerusalem.

The friends gathered behind the apostle knew, however. It was their turn to squirm angrily.

"You have all heard what transpired in Israel," he continued, trying to find a common ground for his message. "Peace was preached to the Israelites by Jesus Christ, who is Lord of all! Surely you have heard what happened throughout Judea, beginning in Galilee—how God anointed Jesus of Nazareth with the Holy Spirit and with power. He went about doing good and healing all who were oppressed by the Devil. For God was with him!"

Angels and devils were somewhat foreign to these folk, but they knew about the miracle worker and the treatment he received from his own countrymen.

"We are all witnesses, both you and we, of all the things that he did throughout the land of the Jews and in Jerusalem. Jesus . . . whom they murdered . . . and crucified."

It did not escape the listeners that crucifixion was a Roman execution. Was Peter saying they must share the blame?

But the preacher was not finished.

"God raised up Jesus the third day and caused him to be plainly seen. This you have all heard!"

The audience remembered the reports and nodded.

"Not everyone saw the risen Master," Peter went on, "but certain witnesses whom God had chosen did. We did!" he cried, gesturing to Mark and the others who had come from the Holy City.

Mark's skin tingled. As if it were only yesterday he could see Jesus standing in the upper room.

"We even ate and drank with him after he rose from the dead," Peter declared. Then suddenly, as though struck by a great revelation, he asserted, "And he commanded us to preach to all people everywhere, and to testify that he is ordained by God to judge the living and the dead! All the prophets testify that whoever believes in him receives forgiveness of sins!"

Truly, Jesus had commanded that the gospel be preached everywhere! How could the brothers have forgotten this? How could even Peter be overwhelmed by the thought?

But now as Peter's voice still echoed in the rafters, a shaking filled the house as an eerie wind moved down the walls and through the galleries. Folk about the court, both those who had come with Peter and the Caesareans, began to quiver.

It was happening again! Just as it had happened on the Day of Pentecost.

Mark poised himself for the refrain, and soon enough it came.

He and all those about him, Jew and Gentile, clean and unclean, began to speak in other tongues—together, in ecstasy, in fellowship.

For many moments the phenomenon continued. Then Peter turned to his companions, his face tear-streaked, and placing his hands on their shoulders, cried above the din, "Can any of you forbid that these should be baptized in water? Have they not received the Holy Spirit just as we did?"

The brothers laughed. And they cried. There would be a celebration at the edge of the briny Mediterranean that very afternoon, and the church would be opened to the world.

CHAPTER

4

The church did not stretch beyond its Jewish origins without growing pains.

When Peter arrived home from Caesarea, he was greeted with angry inquisition from the Jerusalem believers. "You visited with Gentiles? You ate with them?" they cried. "How could you pollute the gospel so?"

During their stay with the tanner of Joppa, and after Peter had preached to the people of Caesarea, Mark had noticed that the apostle was unusually deep in thought. He did not converse easily with his friends and was not available to the disciples for fellowship and instruction. Mark sensed something strange had occurred on the tanner's roof just before Cornelius's servants arrived, but he had never felt free to ask about it.

When the Jerusalem converts quizzed the apostle concerning his mingling with Gentiles, he spoke of his housetop experience for the first time.

"I was in Joppa," he began, "praying in the afternoon. And in a trance, I saw a vision."

His masculine face turned upward at the memory, and something like fear shone in his eyes.

"A container, like a great sheet, descended . . . let down from heaven by the four corners. It came directly to me," he asserted, "and upon it were animals of various kinds, and reptiles, and birds."

The believers, seated about Peter in a circle, wondered what such a tale could preclude. And Mark glanced up at the rafters of the Ben Haman house, trying to imagine such a sight.

"Then I heard a voice say to me, 'Rise up, Peter! Kill and eat!' "

The apostle's fists clenched, and he declared, "But the creatures were not all kosher. And I said, 'Never, Lord! For nothing common or unclean has ever entered my mouth!' "

At this the listeners did not know whether to nod approval or to marvel at his daring.

"But the voice answered me again from heaven," he went on, " 'What God has made clean, you must not call unclean!' "

Now the audience was speechless. They had not always agreed with Peter's decisions. He had offered Saul the hand of fellowship, and now he was admitting Gentiles to the faith. But they had not forgotten that the Lord himself had given this apostle "keys to the kingdom," to establish the church on earth. And they listened with due respect.

"This happened three times," he said, "before the sheet was taken up again. And immediately there were three men calling on the house where I was staying, sent from Caesarea."

The rest of the story was familiar to Mark. And when Peter relayed it, telling of the Spirit's visitation upon the centurion's home, the scorners were silent.

Mark sat on the edge of a low stool, waiting for their assessment of the account. When they finally spoke, it was not to rebuke, nor to approve, but to praise the Lord.

"Then it must be!" Thomas, famed for his skepticism, declared. "God has granted salvation not only to the Jews, but to the Gentiles as well!"

So the church was broadened. The Great Commission, which had been somewhat forgotten, began to be fulfilled, and the faith grew beyond the boundaries of race and tradition. Not all the Hebrew constituency liked the notion. But over time they would be forced to make concessions.

The stretching began, appropriately, among the churches that the dispersed believers had established outside Israel following Stephen's martyrdom.

Mark had long ago promised his mother that he would never leave the House Ben Haman until he himself was uprooted. He began to itch now for a change. As he heard of the growth of evangelism in Gentile lands, he began to wish himself free to revel in the experience.

For years now he had submerged the Gentile part of himself beneath the Jewish. He had willingly taken on the appearance and culture of a Hebrew. He had done so out of admiration for Peter and his other companions. And he had been content to sever himself from his Roman past. Indeed, he had come to be ashamed of it.

But it had never completely died. As much as he once needed to remember his Jewish heritage, he now needed to identify with the Gentiles.

He kept this longing to himself, thinking it somehow unclean as Peter had once spoken of unclean foods and beasts. He had thrilled to the apostle's liberating message, but grasping it required reviving a part of himself that he had, for the sake of holiness, come to scorn.

When his uncle, Barnabas, was sent to Antioch, Syria, to look into reports of conversion among Gentiles in that city, envy magnified longing. And the envy was compounded by news that Barnabas had asked Paul to return from Tarsus, inviting him to minister in Antioch alongside him.

Often these days Mark's thoughts turned to his homeland. Though he was estranged from it, North Africa was the cradle of his youth, and people still lived there whom he loved.

Visions of the dense palm forest that fringed the coast beckoned as he watched the tumbling waters of his uncle's fountain this evening.

Peter, John, and most of the other residents of the house were out on church business. James, the brother of John, was upstairs preparing a Sunday sermon. Mark appreciated the quiet house. Only the sounds of his mother puttering about the kitchen disturbed the silence.

"I hope they return within the hour," she was saying as she entered the patio, wiping flour on her apron. "The roast will soon be done, and the wheat cakes are already out of the oven."

Mark, preoccupied, did not look away from the fountain and did not acknowledge her comment.

Drawing near, Mary placed a light hand on his shoulder. "Your mind is far away," she said gently. "Of what do you think?"

"Home."

The woman sighed. "I, too, think of Cyrene, often."

"You do?" Mark responded, very surprised.

"Of course. And I wonder why we never hear from Simon. Three years have gone by. I hope he is well."

Recalling the sandal merchant's dark face and bright smile, Mary shook her head. "Can you imagine? A church in Cyrene? Do you suppose he has won many converts?"

Mark stood up from the stone bench as if to say he cared not to know. Always it shamed him to think of his friend's witness as he remembered his own faltering attempt to speak of Jesus at Villa Ponti.

"Perhaps we could take a trip to visit him," Mary suggested.

Mark wheeled about. "Stop, Mother!" he cried. "You torment me!"

Mary, astonished at his reaction, sat down and watched him pace the pavement. "I . . . I only thought . . ."

"I know what you thought. But, it would not be pleasant for me to return there," he asserted.

Mary, wounded, looked at the floor. Mark studied her miserably. Any apology he might have made, however, was precluded by the sound of feet in the entryway.

Peter was running through the portal, dozens of other disciples close behind.

The big fisherman's face was drained and his voice husky.

"Mary," he called, "where is James?"

"Upstairs . . . studying," she replied.

"See that the doors are fastened! See that no one goes out again tonight!" the apostle ordered.

"Dinner is ready," she offered weakly, thinking of nothing better to say as her guests hastened to their chambers.

"James!" Peter called down the gallery. "Herod is after you! The church is under siege!"

Mark stood riveted to the patio floor, his mind ahead of his feet in receiving the news. As he headed for his own room, his mother clutched at his sleeve.

"I am frightened!" she confessed.

"I am with you," Mark assured her.

CHAPTER

5

There was no saving James Bar Zebedee. Late that night Herod's men broke into the House Ben Haman and, overwhelming the residents, hauled the apostle away.

Now he was dead—killed by an executioner's sword.

Herod Agrippa, who loved the praises of his people, especially wanted to please the Sanhedrin. Since the church, these days, boldly associated with Gentiles, he knew the timing was more opportune than ever to take a stand against it. Doing so, he won the applause of the Pharisees, the most powerful body of Jewish legislators in Israel.

The Jerusalem congregation knew Herod would not stop with one death. James's brother, John, and Peter would be prime targets. And though the church tried to keep their whereabouts a secret, Herod set out to track them down like a hunter's hound.

The extra house across the alley had not been opened for years. Peter could hide there, and if the lights were kept low, the place might not be suspected. It was a slim chance, but the big fisherman insisted on being near his congregation.

Mark, Mary, and a bevy of servants were visiting him a few

nights after he moved in. Rhoda and two butlers bustled about, lifting dusty coverings from the furniture and sweeping the floors in the dim candlelight.

So far the tiny hideout had not been detected, and they were thinking it might never be. John, holed up at his family home across town, had not been accosted. Perhaps Peter could emerge from the apartment in a few days, they told each other.

But that was before they heard the tramping of soldier feet in the alleyway. That was before the door was hammered with heavy fists and kicked open with iron-tipped boots.

Under Saul's persecution, the House Ben Haman had never been invaded. Until James's abduction, Mark had speculated that it was secure. And perhaps while the church was in its infancy, it had been supernaturally spared. But not under Herod.

Finding the old residence vacant, the king's troops proceed-ed down the alley, and, observing that the little cottage was of similar architecture, they deduced that it was part of the property.

When they blasted in, Mark clutched Mary to his side. But as they laid hold of his master, the one who had nurtured his fledgling faith from the first day and under whose preaching he had received Christ, he jumped to intervene.

Throwing himself between the arresting officer and his teacher, he tried vainly to protect Peter.

But the Galilean did not struggle against his captors. "Enough, Mark," he commanded. "Our Lord went quietly. Let them have their way."

That had been two days ago. Since then, the little apart-ment had been the scene of a continuous prayer meeting.

John, being notified of Peter's arrest, had called for the vigil to be shared by groups throughout the city. And he conducted the session at the apartment.

Mark was glad for the apostle's guidance. He himself did not have the faith to lead the little company.

The son of Quintus had lived through Saul's persecution.

He had witnessed the martyrdom of Stephen and the crucifix-ion of Christ. But that had been in company with stronger men. Now his favorite uncle was hundreds of miles from home. His supportive friend, Simon, was across the sea. And Peter, his beloved teacher, the man he admired most on earth, had been torn from him.

Full of fear and self-doubt, he was ill prepared to endure this test.

Tonight, as John urged his followers to lift their hands, to praise God for this trial, and to petition for Peter's safety, Mark suddenly rebelled.

He loved Peter as he had loved his own father. Memories of Quintus's death flooded over him and he shivered.

Sinking into a shadow of the darkened room, Mark kept his arms folded on his breast and wondered how he had gotten here.

CHAPTER

6

News of Peter's arrest by Herod was disheartening for the praying church. It was rumored that the king had placed four quaternions of soldiers in guard over the apostle, that he was chained day and night with double chains between two overseers. Not only this, but the door to his dungeon cell, in the lowest level of the underground prison, was under special guard.

"What does Herod fear?" the believers wondered. "He must remember the resurrection!"

Of course, Mark agreed. It would never be forgotten by the Jerusalem community, by the province, or by Rome itself, that the setting of guards over the tomb of Christ had been in vain. Herod would see to it this time that all restraints possible were used with Peter.

Still the church appealed to heaven for the apostle's deliverance.

Now and then, as the hours passed, even Mark found strength to whisper longing for his friend.

It was past midnight of the fourth day. John had divided the group into shifts, and when it was time for Mark's company to rest, the young deacon managed to doze. But horrific dreams of his teacher locked behind bars in darkness and in pain always woke him.

Just now he had seen with his dreaming eyes a vision of Peter's dead form being buried beside James's, beside Stephen's. And as he stared into the grave, watching the shovels of dirt tumbling on the apostle's ravaged body, the corpse became that of Quintus.

Lurching awake, he leaned against the back wall of the little apartment, and hoping no one noticed, trembled quietly, tears spilling down his cheeks.

Unfortunately, someone *had* noticed. He could have borne scrutiny by anyone but Rhoda.

Walking across the room, she drew near and looked intrusively into his troubled eyes.

Her imbecilic face tried to convey compassion. But the poor girl knew not how to help him.

"I am all right, Rhoda," Mark said, shaking his head. "Go now . . ."

"But sir," she whispered, "do you not hear? There is a knocking at the door!"

Sitting upright, the stupor of his dream evaporating, he noticed that, indeed, everyone in the apartment was looking toward the entryway. And as he listened, the knock came again.

"See who it is!" he commanded. "But be careful!"

The girl crossed the room and stood leaning against the door. At last, whoever it was called out softly, and, as though hit with lightening, Rhoda raced back into the parlor.

"It is Peter!" she cried, her shrill voice piercing the anxious congregation.

"Who?" Mark asked incredulously, leaping to his feet.

"Peter!" she insisted, jumping about and clapping. "I heard his voice in the alleyway!"

"You are mad!" her master retorted.

Crestfallen, the servant gazed at him sadly. "No, sir, I am not mad," she lisped.

"Maybe it is Peter's angel!" Thomas jibed, typically skeptical.

Mary Ben Haman, catching John's eye, gestured to him.

Quickly the blond Galilean, who like the others sat paralyzed with fear and disbelief, rose and went to the entry.

As the knocking continued, he opened the door a crack. Within seconds the big fisherman stood before his friends.

"It is I—Peter," he assured them. "No angel, no phantom!"

Suddenly the petitions that for days had been sent heavenward turned into genuine praise. And as the ex-prisoner told of his miraculous release, Mark slowly emerged from his dark corner.

Barely did the tale impress him—of an angel's visitation to Herod's dungeon, of riven chains, of Peter's unimpeded journey through jailhouse wards, or of the stockade's iron gate swinging mysteriously open for his freedom.

To Mark, the greatest miracle was that his teacher stood before him.

Embracing him fondly, Mark wept. And Peter stroked his dark head with a compassionate hand.

CHAPTER

7

If Mark had hoped to be granted Peter's companionship once again, his hopes were quickly cut short. The disciples insisted that the big fisherman find a safe place to stay until the ravaging winds of Herod's spite blew over. So he went away, telling no one of his whereabouts.

Had not Barnabas returned about that time from Antioch, bringing Paul for a visit, Mark might have tracked Peter down with as much determination as had Herod. "He will want me with him," he insisted. "He needs someone to tend to details."

"But it would not be wise," Barnabas argued. "If you go seeking him, Herod's men may follow."

"Then, I should continue here . . . to assist my mother?"

Barnabas could not miss his nephew's tone of disappointment. Paul had just entered the courtyard, and as he sat down, Barnabas directed Paul's attention to the crestfallen young man across from them.

"Mark has been a blessing to the House Ben Haman since coming here twelve years ago. Did you know that he was present in the garden when our Lord was arrested? And that he witnessed the crucifixion?"

Paul's eyes, which had once pierced the young convert like knife blades, were wide and warm now. The blurred vision had gradually receded, the glow of faith replacing it. "Indeed?" he marveled. "Were you there at Pentecost as well?"

Though Pentecost was an annual feast of the Jews, reference to it among believers recalled the hour the church was born.

"I was," Mark replied. "In fact, like Barnabas, I was born again when Peter preached that morning."

Paul nodded congenially, and Mark wondered if he remembered his presence at the death of Stephen.

It almost seemed that the "Saul" part of Paul's life had never existed. So freely did the former persecutor of the church circulate among the brethren, and so dynamically did he declare the gospel, that he was hardly recognizable as the one who had imprisoned and murdered hundreds of believers.

His years in Cilicia, after he was sent away by the apostles, must have been spent in intensive study of the Scriptures. His sermons were highly reasoned and scrupulously supported by the writings of the prophets.

Still, Mark had never felt completely comfortable with the man.

Perhaps because he had been the first to encounter the evil scheming in the persecutor's eyes, Mark had never been able to forget his abuses. Perhaps because it seemed he had too easily transferred his zeal for the church from hatred to love, Mark still suspected him.

He had not at first cared for Peter either. Having been a witness to the apostle's impetuosity in Gethsemane, and then knowing that he had been in hiding during the crucifixion, Mark had found it impossible to respect the man. But in time, hearing his powerful speech in the temple, and then being his personal disciple, he had come to adore him.

He doubted, however, that he could ever feel the same commitment to Paul. Something in his personality grated

Mark. And it seemed, sometimes, that he spoke with too much authority.

But Barnabas was talking again.

"Not only has Mark been with the church since its inception, but he has been an able deacon."

Paul listened respectfully, his stocky torso bent forward in rapt attention.

"I was thinking," Barnabas went on, "that we could use someone like Mark in our ministry."

"You wish to bring him to Antioch?" Paul asked.

"Just so."

When the Cilician smiled broadly, Mark knew they had previously discussed the possibility. He stared at the two elders in astonishment. Promises of freedom and adventure beckoned to him.

His feelings toward Paul would just have to be overcome. Perhaps, in time, he could rise above them. Meanwhile, he would grasp opportunity with eager hands.

PART SIX

Mission

He said to them,
"Go into all the world and preach
the good news to all creation."

MARK 16:15

CHAPTER

1

Antioch-on-the-Orontes spread like a green and white shawl over the feet of the Amanus Range. Sixteen miles inland, it sat resplendent beneath a seaward sun and blushed coral the evening Mark first saw it.

His mother had resisted his leaving Jerusalem, as he had known she would. But when she finally submitted to his insistence that he was, at last, being uprooted, she had pressed his hand to her cheek. "Perhaps Antioch will be good to you," she sighed. "It was, after all, founded by Jews."

This was not altogether true. The first settlers had been Macedonian sailors. It had been colonized by Athenians and by Jews, sent there by Seleucus Nicator, three hundred years before. It still boasted a large Jewish population, with a total of three settlements inside and outside the walls, and the race had always been highly favored. Beneath Antioch's superficial glory, however, the social life was sensual and debased.

Known as "The Queen of the East," with a census of half a million, it was the third largest city in the Roman Empire, surpassed only by Alexandria and Rome. But it was not a place one would have expected the early church to bloom.

As Mark rode beside Paul and his uncle along the Roman highway that made Antioch a main terminal for the world, he noticed the infamous Groves of Daphne, hotbed of idolatry and every kind of perversion.

Fed by a thousand springs and waterfalls, this plateau suburb, crowned by a temple to Apollo, was a miniature of Cyrene. Its baths, public buildings, and Olympic stadium, as well as countless orchards and flower gardens, had made it a haven of licentiousness and a favorite vacation spot for people from as far away as Egypt.

The five-mile drop from Daphne presented a spectacular view of the Syrian capital. Mark could see that the gridlike arrangement of Antioch's streets was designed to funnel the daily sea breeze into the heart of the city—a breeze that wafted the fragrance of Daphne's rose arbors over the metropolis when it blew from the southwest.

Reining his horse the few remaining yards to the southern gate, Mark hugged his coat close. The wind this evening was a little too cool. It was fall, and he shivered as the gargantuan wall loomed before him. Atop the fortified gate at the far end of town was an enormous stone representation of the legendary she-wolf nursing the foundlings, Romulus and Remus, forefathers of Rome. The point at which he would enter was likewise crowned with gigantic likenesses of Zeus and Athena, the sea god leaning cavalierly against his pronged spear, and the goddess adoring him at his feet.

As a child he had always thrilled to tales of Rome's founding. And he had been captivated by the immense statuary to Greek and Roman heroes when he lived in Cyrene. Even now their imposing grandeur moved him.

Through the enormous doors the three travelers passed. Not one of them could name their mutual love, Israel, as his homeland. While Mark was a North African, Barnabas was Cypriot and Paul a Cilician. Yet each claimed a higher heritage.

Once inside the gates, they were greeted by a broad avenue stretching straight ahead for four and a half miles. Paved with sparkling Egyptian granite and lined on each side by thirty-foot wide colonnades, it made anyone traversing it feel important.

Mark blinked his eyes beneath the glow of a thousand streetlamps. Antioch was the only city in the world with fully lit avenues every night. Though the sun had now dipped below the rim of the Great Sea, this city shone like midday.

Even side streets intersecting the main avenue were colonnaded, so that a pedestrian might literally walk the town untouched by sun or rain.

This silent fanfare of architecture and fountain, statuary and light, evoked images of monarchs on parade. Mark could almost hear the shouts of onlookers and the din of marching bands. Conquerors in triumphal procession flashed across his imagination. And he drew his shoulders back, sitting tall in his saddle.

Indeed, a sense of anticipation and adventure had settled over him, as though several parts of himself might be brought together here. As though Antioch might answer questions for him.

Still, he must not forget that this was a pagan place. As he followed Barnabas and Paul through the center of town, his horse flared its nostrils at the perfumed aromas spilling from the brothels. Magnificent private mansions fronted the street, tribute to the materialism and conspicuous consumption of resources dominating everyday life here.

Hundreds of converts had fled here after Stephen's death. If not for that exodus, it could have been several generations before the church took root in this place.

Mark glanced at Paul, who rode a dark, husky mount, and he considered how ironic were the ways of God. He shook his head at the incongruity—that the former enemy of the church should minister to those he once pursued, and in the very place of their refuge!

In fact, Paul's work had created such a stir in this city that the brethren here had come to be called Christians, a name that was catching on throughout the world. At first a term of derision, it was quickly becoming respectable for Antiochans to identify with the movement. Many of the first local adherents had been from prestigious and influential Jewish families.

Barnabas had explained that, although the early leaders of this church had been from Jerusalem, the host of the house where they would be lodging was a prominent Gentile convert, in fact a Syrian legate, named Perus.

Mark, anticipating that he would like the man, smoothed his hair, his beard, and his travel-rumpled coat.

As they came upon Perus's house, in the very heart of mansion row, he was reminded of the day he had accompanied Peter to Cornelius's residence.

Dismounting before an elaborate archway that spanned two street columns, they stepped into an ornate, mosaic-tiled portico and waited for the butler.

When the door was opened, however, it was not a servant who met them, but the host himself.

Suddenly Mark had even more reason to remember Cornelius. Not only in appearance did Perus resemble the centurion, but, as that ill-informed Roman had done to Peter, this one appeared ready to cast himself at Paul's feet.

Intensely reverent, he led the evangelist into the courtyard.

Barnabas followed close behind and, catching the host's ear, announced, "This is my nephew, John Mark. He will be assisting us in the work."

"Wonderful!" Perus smiled.

Mark extended a hand to greet the Syrian, but the man's glance had been cursory. Already his attention was again on Paul.

"A light to the Gentiles!" the legate exclaimed. "We have missed you, Brother Paul!"

Then, as though it were an afterthought, he added, "And you, Barnabas! We have missed you, too."

Mark rankled, keenly disappointed in his first meeting with a Roman Christian. Had not Barnabas first nursed the Antioch church? Was Perus saying Paul had now replaced him?

And hadn't Peter first opened the door through which all nations could enter the church? Since when had Paul been designated prophet to the Gentile realm?

Barnabas was not one to take offense, and it was not Mark's place to say anything. Since Paul only nodded graciously, the matter went unchallenged.

CHAPTER

2

As in Jerusalem, the church of Antioch was composed of smaller congregations that met in individual homes for fellowship and for meals. The communal spirit was not so predominant here as in the Holy City, however, because that social form had been born largely out of persecution.

In the first months of Antioch's Christian movement, when the church was composed mainly of folk fleeing Israel, there had been much sharing of goods and shelter. But as the church grew to encompass Gentiles, the new converts had kept their properties, with open doors to fellow Christians.

When the city's numerous congregations wanted to meet together, however, there were no homes that could accommodate the crowd. Unlike the temple at Jerusalem, Antioch's temple was not the place for a Christian gathering. Because it was utterly pagan, its worship devoted to Zeus, both Gentile and Jewish converts scrupulously avoided it. Nor would local authorities approve renting the stadium or other public auditoriums to those who scorned the state religion.

There were many squares and marketplaces where philosophers taught and entertainers drew spectators. Since new religions and new ideas were not unusual in Antioch, the Christians were allowed to meet unhampered in such places.

They were not always appreciated, however. They attracted scoffers and ridicule. But there were few fanatically Orthodox Jews in the city, certainly not enough to threaten danger, as in Jerusalem. In fact, in a society debauched with excess and starving for ethics, the monotheistic and highly moral code of Jews and Christians was rather appealing.

The church, of course, was considered by outsiders to be nothing more than a subculture of Judaism, but because it had won the allegiance of many wealthy and important Hellenistic Hebrews, it could not be discounted.

Mark was spending his first Sunday in Antioch. As in Jerusalem, this day of the week had come to be the Lord's Day, reminiscent of Jesus' resurrection. Throughout the Christian world, Sunday had gradually replaced the Jewish Sabbath as a time for gathering together, for hearing the Scriptures expounded, and for breaking bread.

An afternoon breeze blew off the Orontes River, cooling the autumn marketplace. Bundles of golden wheat, piles of pears and pomegranates spoke of harvest time, and Mark remembered his first Feast of Tabernacles, or Feast of Ingathering, in Israel.

He was seated on a grain sack in the middle of Antioch's main plaza. Around him were the uplifted and celebrant faces of Antioch Christians. Bread and wine were passed from hand to hand as Barnabas stood at the head of the congregation, reminding them of the Lord's last Passover and of the words he gave his disciples that night.

" 'Take, eat,' " he quoted, " 'this is my body, which is broken for you. Drink . . . this is my blood, which is shed for many, for the remission of sins.' "

Around the edges of the square were the booths and carts of a thousand merchants. Business went on as usual, despite the impeding crowd of worshipers, except that many of the booths stood unattended, their owners among the faithful converts.

Mark had never forgotten the Day of Pentecost, when the Pharisees and priests had looked in contempt at the birth of the church. Yet, though a huge bronze statue to Tiberius Caesar dominated this place, there was little hostility toward believers.

Jerusalem, which had stoned Stephen and driven Peter from its gates, was crowned by the temple to God Almighty, the house of Jesus' Father. And yet, in this city, where a temple to Zeus of the Greeks dominated, and another to Jupiter of the Romans overshadowed all religious exercise, the worshipers of the Nazarene were allowed perfect freedom.

Before his eager audience, Barnabas rehearsed the story of the Last Supper, just as he had heard it given by Peter and the other apostles at countless Lord's Day meetings. Though he had not been present in the upper room to hear the words of Jesus, they were as familiar to him as if he had been there. And they were becoming familiar to thousands throughout the Roman world, as they were taught by elders and preachers.

It was said, "All roads lead to Rome." But, likewise, all roads of the empire led through Antioch. And this afternoon, the city's main thoroughfare brought travelers of every nation directly under the sound of Barnabas's voice. Syrians, Greeks, Persians, Scythians—all journeyed through this part of town on business and as tourists. There could not have been a better site for the spread of the gospel.

But there could have been a better spokesman, Mark thought, chafing as Paul walked to the makeshift podium after Barnabas had served the bread and wine.

In Jerusalem the ex-persecutor was still not well-received. He was allowed to speak and had been endorsed as an apostle, but many Christians were still suspicious, and the Sanhedrin, of course, considered him a traitor.

Antioch had warmly embraced him. After eight years of contemplation and virtual exile in Cilicia, he had been summoned by Barnabas to take up a new life as leader of the first Jewish/Gentile congregation. Those in Jerusalem who still whispered unkind things about him considered, with a sneer, that this was appropriate for him. To minister to pagans and Hellenist Jews, when he had once been a pietist Pharisee, was just deserts for the likes of Paul.

Perhaps Mark, like those in Jerusalem who criticized Paul, had hoped he was unhappy with his assignment. But it was evident that he was not only content, he reveled in the Antiochans' reception.

Applause rose from the crowd as the man of Tarsus took the podium. A full year he had ministered here, and love exuded toward him from the congregation.

Mark could not understand it, for some of these very people had been chased to Syria by Saul's persecution—some had even lost loved ones and friends to his soldiers' swords.

They had forgiven. But Mark did not know how. In fact, bitterness festered in him daily as he jealously guarded Peter's position as head of the church, fearing Paul's growing popularity.

Looking around him, he could easily see that this was a wealthy church. Antioch itself had few poor residents. Handsome clothing and gold jewelry punctuated the fact that most in the crowd lived in luxury.

No wonder Saul loves it here, Mark thought, inwardly smirking, still thinking of him by his given name.

He began to listen to Paul's message, however, and as it reached his hard heart, he had difficulty knowing what to do with it.

Paul was speaking of his dreams for the Antioch church. He was saying that this congregation, like the one in Jerusalem, must become a seed plot for expansion of the gospel.

"Brother Barnabas and I have prayed for many weeks," he cried, his voice tight with urgency. "We believe God has let us be your ministers for this little while so that you might help us minister to the world."

Something in his tone told the audience this was no ordinary exhortation. Something of great importance was afoot.

"You have been blessed with abundance, both spiritually

and materially. It is time to share your abundance with the regions which still sit in darkness. It is time to send the light into lands where the name of Jesus has not been heard!"

The crowd murmured, wondering at the direction of Paul's message. "Brother," Perus asked, rising to his feet, "tell us plainly, of what do you speak?"

"We feel the call to take the word into other lands," he replied, "just as Jonah of old was compelled to go to Nineveh."

Christians were not prepared for this. For months they had basked in rich teaching and fatherly nurture. They could not easily give the apostles up.

"Where would you go?" Perus asked, verbalizing the question in everyone's mind.

"First to the isles of the sea, and then through Asia Minor," Paul announced.

"But such places are steeped in idolatry!" Niger, one of the elders, objected. "You could encounter grave dangers."

"Yes, Brother Paul," Lucius, another elder, agreed. "Why not send someone else? Why must you—our fathers . . . ?"

Mark quietly observed as love-torn converts pleaded with their mentors not to depart. He remembered well how he had felt when Peter had gone away.

"Friends," Paul countered, "are there not those among us who not so long ago sat in the shadow of paganism? Were not some of us worshipers of idols, and were not the rest bound by Jewish law to the blinding of their souls?"

The crowd grew quiet. They remembered their neediness when folk bearing the gospel had come their way. Would they leave other human beings to wander in spiritual deserts?

"Of course," Barnabas said, rising now to stand beside Paul, "without your blessing, we will do nothing. Without your prayers and financial support, such an undertaking would be impossible."

Suddenly Mark realized that the outcome of today's meeting could have a profound impact on himself.

Paul was not seeking to dally in the luxury of Antioch.

Rather, the former persecutor was seeking approval from the Antioch church to go into spiritually uncharted territory, risking all for the spread of the faith. Mark could, perhaps, have admired him for this. But when he had been invited to serve alongside his uncle and the Cilician in the ministry, he had never dreamed it would lead to fields more foreign than Syria.

As the congregation considered Paul's request with tears in their eyes, Mark waged his own battle. While the Antiochans were not ready to give up their two pastors, Mark was facing a greater sacrifice. He would have to give up everything—his future, his safety, perhaps even his life—for the gospel.

CHAPTER

3

For the unchurched of Antioch, Sunday was not a holy day. All afternoon, cargo boats moved in and out of the city's port, situated on an island midriver. And barges plied the waterway until dusk.

It was on one of the piers at the southeast edge of the island that Barnabas found Mark, lingering in the sunset. The young man had not shown up for the afternoon repast at Perus's house, and had been nowhere among the congregation following the morning service.

Barnabas wasted no time ferreting out the problem his nephew faced. He, in fact, had expected such a reaction to Paul's presentation.

"You are angry with me," he guessed, greeting Mark. Walking toward him on the pier, he waited for the rebuke. Mark turned about, scowling.

"Should I not be?" was the cryptic reply.

"I suppose you have good reason," Barnabas conceded.

"Ha!" his nephew replied, nodding. "You have virtually abducted me, leading me to Antioch under false pretext! I thought I was to serve with you, in *this city!* Why did you not tell me you wished to make a missionary of me?"

"We believed you would be willing to serve, in whatever capacity."

"That is not fair!" Mark asserted. "Once before, years ago, you got me to stay on in Jerusalem when I would have returned home, by tempting me with stories of the Nazarene! Now you would have me sail to who-knows-where . . . to give up . . ."

"To give up what?" Barnabas challenged. "Did you not tell us you yearned for new horizons? Did I not detect that your mother's house was a confinement?"

"You avoid the issue!" Mark insisted.

Tense silence followed as Barnabas studied the rippling wakes where bundle-laden boats pushed off from the dock.

"There is a big world out there," the Cypriot said, a lump in his throat. "I had hoped . . ."

As he sensed his uncle's shame, Mark's anger began to soften. Still, he did have a legitimate complaint and wondered which way to turn.

"Of course, you know I shall be eternally grateful to you for persuading me to stay in the Holy City, to learn of Jesus and all. . . ." Mark was a proud man, and concessions did not come easily. "You know I have gained everything and lost nothing of worth."

Barnabas looked at his nephew, tears glimmering in his eyes. With a sigh, he nodded.

"I must confess something, Uncle," he went on. "When I saw the wealth and ease in which the Antiochans live, I assumed Paul's motives here were material. After hearing his appeal, I know that they are anything but."

"He is a good man, Mark," Barnabas proclaimed. And then, hesitantly he added, "Sometimes the faults we attach to others—love of safety, love of luxury—are projections of our own weaknesses."

Remembering the finery of his mother's Jerusalem home and the opulence in which he had been raised, Mark blushed. Never had he been accountable for his life-style. It had simply been handed to him. He had never considered it a temptation. But now, as he realized how hard it was to let go, a dart of revelation speared his heart.

He looked down at his homespun robe, donned years ago out of preference, not duty. As he fingered the Star of David on his neck, he realized that his life had been full of choice. He had been pampered from birth, and even self-denial had been a luxury.

"This is all very sudden . . . ," he whispered.

"The ways of Jesus sometimes are," Barnabas acknowledged. " 'Sharper than a two-edged sword. . .' "

Mark raised his chin, laughing a little. "Now, Uncle, please don't preach."

Barnabas smiled broadly.

"Very well," Mark shrugged. "Where do we begin?"

"The elders meet this evening. They will pray about our going, but I believe they cannot say no. And our plans are to sail in the spring for Cyprus."

Relief spilled over Mark's hesitant spirit. "Your own homeland!" he sighed. "That should not be so bad." Heading for the comforts of Perus's house, he called over his shoulder, "Cyprus! Why didn't you tell me?"

Barnabas watched his departure numbly. His nephew had much growing to do, and he hoped he did it quickly.

CHAPTER

4

The bow of the tramp merchant ship bounced over a sea of chopped silver when Cyprus came into view. It had been a foggy spring afternoon when the three missionaries set out for the big island, and though the spindly piece of land that was their destination could often be seen from the shores of Asia Minor, it had been cloaked in vapor until now.

A large, square sail billowed in a fine breeze, the topsail above it waving eagerly toward port. The trip from Seleucia to Salamis had taken twenty-four hours, but it had been a leisurely one, the lulling wind and swaying of the vessel rocking Mark to sleep in his small deck tent.

When he emerged from his shady sanctuary, he was just in time to see the sunrise against the leaping gray-pink limestone of the island's northern range. That pinnacled coast formed a distant frame for Salamis, its seaward side profuse with trees and flowering vegetation. But the cliffs nearest the port itself were virtually barren, white plateaus stepping down to the beach in a confusion of steep-flanked mountains.

Salamis and the south coast, however, could claim Mount

Olympus for its own, a smaller but revered version of Greece's famed "home of the gods."

As Mark looked over the edge of the beamy merchant vessel, he spied the upcoming port, and though he was a Christian, could not help but recall with a thrill the tales his father had told of the Greek hero Ulysses. Homer's *Odyssey* had been his favorite literature once he learned to read, but he had always loved it best when recited by Quintus. "Ulysses and all his mighty men, returning from the Battle of Troy, settled on Cyprus," the story went. "And they founded there Salamis, Curium, Nea Paphos, and the halls of Aphrodite."

If Quintus had a favorite deity, it must have been Aphrodite, or Venus, as the Romans insisted on calling her. Cyprus was her island, the site of her emergence from the sea, borne upon the waves in a shell, born of seafoam. When Rome had taken the gem-like isle from the Greeks, it had been a glory for the empire. If Quintus had had his choice of places to govern, it would have been Cyprus.

It troubled Mark, however, that the tales of Greece and Rome and their many gods still had power to move him. *Why,* he wondered, *did old attachments die so hard?*

It seemed everything was a muddle these days. Something deep within longed to do more than merely observe the working of the church. He wanted to be useful, either to shed the things of the past or to find a way to make them serve him.

Barnabas emerged from his shelter when the bowman called out for anchor. He stood now at Mark's side, full of emotion at the sight of Cyprus.

For the Levite, the island was home. He had friends and loved ones here. But it was easy to see, by the wistful gleam in the man's eyes, that he was apprehensive over this homecoming. He knew the Cypriot mind as no other apostle might know it. And he knew there was a battle ahead.

Never had a missionary set foot in a foreign place solely for the purpose of heralding the Christian message to the public. Where it had spread in the early years, it had been by happenstance, as with the dispersion of believers following Stephen's death. Joppa and Caesarea had been milestones, and Antioch a nobly successful experiment. But in these cases, the gospel had been welcomed by the populace, landing in fields fertile for the taking.

Now Christians were presuming to move into the world, to herald a message where it had not been sought, and to preach repentance to people who hardly knew the meaning of the word.

Paganism was rampant on Cyprus. The cults of Aphrodite and Apollo dominated. Jews here were not as prosperous as in Antioch, and they did not hold as much power.

Of course, a sizable group of believers already existed on the island. In fact, some of those who had evangelized Antioch had been Cypriots. But it was an untaught church, sorely requiring the guidance and instruction the missionaries could give.

Christians of Cyprus had not separated themselves from the local synagogues. Viewing their faith as an intimate outgrowth of their inherited Judaism, they still worshiped with Orthodox Jews—when they were allowed to do so.

They were not always allowed. It was inevitable that Followers of the Way would alienate themselves from traditional Jewish congregations. With no one to lead them, they were often confused, and sometimes it seemed the gospel would be lost to dominant synagogue doctrines.

Paul and Barnabas, therefore, considered it their primary duty to visit Jewish houses of worship—to look in on the small groups of Christians who struggled to uphold their faith without a teacher.

In the process, Gentiles would doubtless be won for Christ, for throughout the Jewish world there had always been Gentile "God-fearers" and also proselytes, converts to Judaism. And since proselytes mixed with the greater Gentile community, to reach the synagogue was to reach the island.

Having the experience of Antioch under their belts, the apostles would use this as their strategy when they took on the task of evangelizing Cyprus. It was not only deference to their Jewish brothers that led them to speak first in the synagogues. It was good planning.

But good planning would not forestall conflict. This Barnabas knew.

And doubtless Paul knew it too. For when he joined Mark and Barnabas on deck, he was very quiet.

If Mark had expected an easy time on Cyprus, his expectations were quickly dashed.

It was a tangled scene on which Barnabas, Paul, and Mark entered. And it was a battlefield of some dimension.

For four months the two missionaries and their assistant trekked the length of the island, following the interior highway which led from Salamis, the largest port, to Paphos, the capital. Mark's duties were simple: see that the food supplies were in order, that clothing and shoes were in repair, that Barnabas had a fresh quill for his journal each evening, and that Paul had salve for his eyes, which still troubled him from time to time.

Each time they entered a new town Mark had to find lodging for them. More often than not, they were greeted by an unfriendly rabbi, who suspected they had come to proselytize his flock, and who preferred they speak and sleep outside the synagogue walls, if not outside the town itself.

Though Mark longed for a more prominent position in the church, he was content, of late, to keep a low profile. Everywhere he went he was confronted with the complexity of being a Christian.

Tonight Barnabas and Paul had settled for a sleeping post in the market square of a tiny Cypriot village. The afternoon had been spent in the steamy hot sanctuary of a little Jewish meeting house. Only bits and pieces of the day's events coalesced in Mark's mind. What lingered as potent memories, beyond the blur of words and faces, were the looks of hatred in threatened Jewish eyes, indecision in the mien of young Christians, and the tentative smiles of sympathetic Gentiles.

Overspreading all this would be the haunting insistence of the Roman world outside—the gleam of sun off pagan shrines, the lilt of Aphrodite's smile on grotto statuettes, the strength of Apollo's arm revealed in village sculpture.

Night had moved in on the audience hall, and cold had descended from the northern and southern mountains before the synagogue meeting broke up. No one had invited the trio home, so they had staked claim to a corner of the public square.

Not all towns were like this. Sometimes the apostles were welcomed by liberal rabbis and embraced by believers hungry for instruction.

But today's experience was more typical.

Mark rested his head upon a wadded flour sack and gazed into the slate black sky. He knew that the same sliver of moon that drifted over Cyprus touched Cyrene, hovered over Villa Ponti, and lit a nook of Philea's room. He wondered if she had ever married—if she ever thought of him—or did Brutus sleep beside her?

It seemed, as he considered the twists and turns of life, that there were only a few questions that required answering. Sometimes, in recent days, when he had seen pure joy light the countenance of some new believer, he was convinced that the answer to all questions was Jesus.

Nevertheless, in reverie he enfolded Philea in his arms and drifted off to sleep. He would think of her again tomorrow when he trekked the world in search of himself. And he would dream of her each night when he wondered what his mission was.

He guessed he had a mission. He guessed he had a calling. But it was yet elusive, like the girl he had kissed just once before he had been set adrift.

CHAPTER

5

Remnants of the spring festival of Aphrodite still remained in Paphos weeks after the rites of the three-day orgy had been fulfilled. But even as the goddess had led her processional through the groves, gardens, and sanctuaries of the southern coast, leaving marks of excess and debauchery in every nook and grotto, so did the apostles leave their influence on the island.

For four months they had been loved, hated, received, rejected; they had liberated, confounded, uplifted, perplexed town after town from end to end of Cyprus. And at last they had arrived in the capital where the queen of Roman harlotry held her court.

Some of Mark's ambivalence regarding his Gentile heritage and his privilege as a son of Israel lay in the fact that he had never taken the religion and the deities of Greece and Rome to heart. For him the empire was a political and cultural phenomenon, not a spiritual entity.

If this tour through Cyprus would do anything for him, it would act as a scalpel, peeling away layer upon layer of blindness, as the skin of an onion is peeled, until the inner eye is left open, seen and seeing.

Hundreds of little temples to Aphrodite graced the hillocks outside Paphos, tattered ribbons flapping against their make-shift sides where children had hung them. Made of cowhide and sticks, the tabernacles were studded with colored rocks and trinkets, the best poor peasants could afford. And the closer the apostles drew to the city, the more elaborate were the shrines, evidence of the wealth of the townspeople.

There was no synagogue in Paphos. The city was so pagan that Judaism had never flourished here. There was a small Jewish congregation that met in a home. But there were no Christians. It was an antagonistic brotherhood that lived here, and a powerful heathen society, ruled by the proconsul, Sergi-us Paulus.

Mark doubted that he was becoming more spiritually sensi-tive. Perhaps it was simple paranoia that made his skin bristle as the three men approached the walled city.

Paphos was quiet enough. A gentle sea breeze licked her flat-roofed buildings. Magnificent temple complexes and gov-ernment quarters touched a coral sky like sentinels of peace.

But Mark did not feel peaceful.

All the Greek gods were worshiped here, the Venus of love, beauty, and fertility reigning supreme. Thousands of devotees had come here to abide beneath her banner, calling her by many names: Astarte, Ishtar, Cybele, but most of all Aphro-dite. And Paphos had become a sanctuary for Oriental, Greek, and Roman worship of the goddess.

Countless pilgrims passed through Paphos each year to celebrate the rites of their deity. Always the practice revolved around religious prostitution, the sale of virgins for the en-hancement of the soul.

From miles out at sea, the grand structure that was Aphro-dite's temple could be seen on the cliffs at Old Paphos, the original city, so that the pervasive sense of her presence was unmistakable whether one arrived here by land or water.

But Mark sensed no maternal protection here. Something

warned him that danger lurked ahead as the visitors passed beneath the sunset shadow of the Paphos gate.

He could remember feeling this way only two other times in his life: when he had seen Judas slink through the alley, and when he had first looked into Saul's eyes the night Stephen was killed. Judas was dead, and Saul was an apostle. So it must be Paphos that troubled him.

They were not far inside the gate when the fear took on flesh.

"Saul of Tarsus," a voice hailed them, each *s* coming in a hiss. "Sergius would see you."

The apostles and their companion wheeled about, goose bumps raised on each man's skin.

"Who goes there?" Paul demanded.

"You who have killed Christians and now are one yourself," the voice continued, "Sergius Paulus would speak with you."

As the newcomers surveyed the darkness beneath the shadowed wall, a figure even more shadowy stepped into the light of the street torch.

Paul, stricken by the accusatory greeting, stared at the stranger in silence, and as he drew near, Barnabas leaned close to his friend.

"It is one of the Cinyradae," the Levite whispered, his breath shallow, "a priest of Aphrodite."

Barnabas had seen the like often at rites of the goddess in Salamis. The priestly family, old as the island's most ancient Greek cult, was more than a religious caste. It was next to Rome itself in Cyprus's governmental authority, and in the minds of the people even more powerful. Because Rome knew it could never eradicate the priesthood, it had allowed it to retain its station, just as the Hebrew priests had retained authority in Israel.

"How do you know me?" Paul challenged, surveying the long-robed stranger.

The priest drew his dark hood back, revealing a sinister countenance, small, pea-black eyes and hooked nose. "I know many things about you," he replied, his voice a rattle.

Then edging even closer, he repeated, "I am the deputy's minister. We have heard of your doings throughout our island. The proconsul would have you present your case to him."

"We have no case," Paul retorted. "We speak only the message of salvation."

The wiry fellow pulled his embroidered caftan tight to his thin frame, and its numerous sequined emblems shimmered in the pale yellow light.

Symbols of moon and stars, sun and earth, fire and water, death and fertility glinted on the black shroud, just like flashes from his narrow eyes.

Almost a caricature he was, with his crooked staff and pointed finger. "So you will come?" he insisted.

Paul looked at Barnabas. Seeing the invitation as an opportunity, the Cypriot nodded.

"If I go, my friends go with me," Paul declared. "I will not speak without witnesses."

He was claiming the right of a Roman citizen to a just hearing. Sergius Paulus was no small authority here. He was the voice of Rome in the island, and Paul did not deceive himself that this would be a light meeting.

Part of Mark wished not to be involved, but the larger part of him would not miss this encounter for the world.

"Very well," the priest agreed. "Come this way."

He turned to lead them toward the palace. However Paul would not follow just yet.

"You seem to know much about me," he reminded the guide. "But we know very little about you. We go with no man unless we know his name."

The wizened old fellow turned his head over one bent shoulder and croaked, "Elymas . . . I am called Elymas . . . Bar Jesus." The last words were given great weight, as though the fellow wished to impress them especially upon the visitors.

"A Jew?" Mark whispered, turning furtively toward Barnabas.

"So it would seem . . . a Galilean at that."

The two apostles and Mark followed the stooped guide with more questions burning in their minds than they had anticipated.

"Elymas . . . 'wise man.' Bar Jesus . . . 'son of Jesus,' " Mark interpreted.

A Jew who had traded the oracles of Moses for the sorcery of Aphrodite! Could even Judas have been more evil?

CHAPTER

6

A fire burned brightly at one end of the council chamber where Sergius Paulus, mightiest man on the island, waited.

This was the only light, the only warmth in the otherwise dank and dim hall.

When the apostles and Mark entered behind Elymas, guards lifted spears above their heads as though the visitors could actually harm the deputy. As they passed beneath the weapons, they saw that very few other people were in the room.

The proconsul sat near the fire, elevated upon a marble throne. But he did not sit erect, or kingly. He slumped, his elbows spread lethargically on the chair's broad arms, his head leaning wearily on one fist.

Sergius did not look up when Elymas entered. When the "wise man" announced the visitors, however, the deputy suddenly lurched to attention.

It had not escaped Mark that this man bore the same given name as Proconsul Ponti had borne. He was younger than the magistrate of Cyrene had been and was a larger, more athletic-looking fellow. But there were certain traits that went with being Roman, that went with being an imperial governor, that could be expected in any proconsul.

The short-cropped, tight-curled hair, the fine linen tunic, and the breast chain bearing the provincial medallion—all these were reminiscent of Sergius Ponti. And the look of boredom, of material ease—these were common.

However, when this Sergius motioned to Paul and Barnabas to come near, and then introduced some of the people in the room, Mark felt as if time had sped backward.

One of the members of the audience was a young woman, fair of countenance, light of hair. And she was presented as the magistrate's daughter. Sergia Paula was her name, and she stood next to her brother, Lucius Sergius Paulus the Younger.

The girl was not as beautiful as Philea. No one could be, Mark considered. But the devotion she exhibited toward her father in coming here at this late hour—how like Philea that was!

Mark tried to shake the feeling that all this was more than coincidence. Focusing on the elders whom he served, he endeavored to give his mind to more important things.

Paul and Barnabas stood straight and tall before the deputy, and as Elymas stepped back into the shadows, Sergius leaned forward.

"I understand that one of you is a Cypriot," the Roman said.

"I am," Barnabas replied, bowing from the waist.

"Of Salamis?"

"Yes."

"And you have lived in Israel from time to time."

Barnabas knew the empire had ways of learning about its subjects, but he had not expected such full disclosure.

"I am an Israelite by birth, Your Lordship," he answered.

"And you must be Saul of Tarsus," Sergius noted, facing Paul with marked interest. "A Cypriot and a Cilician here to promote a new god!"

Mark thought the man sounded angry, but perhaps he only presumed he would. The more Sergius spoke, the more apparent it became that his interest in the case was not so much to protect his country from rabble-rousers as it was to appease his own curiosity.

Paul shook his head, beginning without further introduction to present his doctrine.

"It is no new god we proclaim, Sergius, but the *only* God, and his Son, Jesus the Christ."

The concept of a Christ or Messiah was not solely a Hebrew idea. Most nations longed for a redeemer, one who would bring peace and prosperity to all. Some, like the Egyptians, saw him as a spiritual figure who would promote brotherhood and equity. The Greeks considered that he would be the ultimate philosopher, a herald of final truth. And the Romans typically saw him as a political champion, a redeemer-king, who would rule with untarnished authority.

Sergius, therefore, was not foreign to the concept and probably had heard of many such messiahs in his time. Perhaps it was Paul's confident tone which piqued his attention. Looking into the apostle's eyes, he demanded, "This Jesus, is he not dead? My friend Pontius Pilate suffered many things because of this upstart!"

"Yes—he was killed. By Rome and by Israel. But he lives! You have surely heard of his resurrection."

Sergius smirked and sat back in his chair, flicking a finger in the air. "Come now, Saul. Is this the childish prattle that has stirred up my people? You know, as well as anyone, that this story was the invention of the Christians to keep their dreams alive!"

"It was first spoken by Roman guards, sire," Paul reminded him, "when they failed in their mission to guard the tomb. My own brethren among the Pharisees paid the guards to say otherwise."

At this, Elymas, who had kept silent, stepped again into the firelight. "Such fables can neither be proven nor disproven, Your Lordship," he asserted. "Is it not enough that these men have subverted the worship of our beloved Aphrodite?"

"It is indeed of concern to me, Elymas, that there is contention brewing in our streets over these men's teachings," Sergius agreed. "But I am not here to judge them so much as to hear what they have to say."

The three comrades received this information with no little relief. If Sergius were not putting them on trial, they could speak boldly.

But Elymas seemed bent on overshadowing them. Grasping again for an opportunity, he reiterated, "These fellows speak of matters that cannot be proven. And yet, Governor, you have seen miracles wrought through the goddess by my own fingers!"

Throwing his hands in the air, he turned his palms this way and that as though he would even now conjure up some illusion to make his point.

Mark watched him uneasily and studied the young woman across the room. Transfixed with fear, she trembled as the magician began to mutter some incantation beneath his breath.

But Sergius, surprisingly unmoved by the show, snapped his own fingers at the priest. "Enough, Brother Elymas," he commanded. "We have been privy to your marvelous works plenty of times. Let these men have their say!"

The old wizard resentfully bowed his head and slunk again to the edge of the chamber, where he listened in seething silence.

This time Barnabas took the floor, coming to the heart of things quickly. "I perceive, sire," he began, "that you are a prudent man, one who respects truth, wherever it may be found. But what salvation is to be had in Aphrodite or Apollo? Has the debauchery of her shrines, or the excess of his high places filled your spirit with serenity? Do you draw closer to goodness for having been with your gods?"

Sergius made no reply, but a twitch at the edge of his mouth was answer enough.

"For a moment's pleasure you would sell your soul and the souls of a thousand beside. You trade the truth of God Almighty for paltry tokens of a sorcerer's power," he asserted, gesturing toward the huddled Elymas.

The wizard's breathing could be heard in the corner as clearly as though he stood at Barnabas's shoulder, and everyone in the room looked uncomfortably at the priest.

Everyone but Sergius. It seemed he had had his fill of the old conjurer and was not afraid of him.

"Christian, our friend finds your words distasteful," the governor laughed. "Do you not worry that he might turn you into a toad?"

Barnabas knew the statement was made in jest, but he took advantage of it.

"I am the possession of Christ himself!" he declared. "Bought by his blood, redeemed by his resurrection! No one can wrest me from his hand, for in truth, I and my companions are sons of Jesus, unlike some who bear the name only in the flesh!"

He alluded, of course, to Elymas's surname, something which the priest would not lightly overlook.

Suddenly the old Jew leapt again from the corner, his fingers spread menacingly. "In the name of the goddess!" he shrieked, stabbing the air with his crook. But just as he was about to mouth some demonic curse, Paul wheeled about and stared him square in the eye.

"O wicked one!" he countered. "Full of every lie and all mischief! You child of the Devil! You enemy of righteousness! Will you not stop hindering the ways of the Lord?"

Elymas fell back, crouching like an attack dog. Moving his feet back and forth, he seemed ready to pounce upon the apostle, when Paul cried out, "Behold! The hand of the Lord is upon you! You shall be blind, not seeing even the sun for a season!"

Unlike the wizard, the missionary did not need to make threatening gestures. Instead he simply looked heavenward, and instantly the old magician groaned with pain, his crabbed hands clutching at his face.

For Elymas, the light of the fire went out. The room became utterly dark to his bemisted eyes. Groping about the chamber, he begged for someone to take him by the arm, but no one would touch him. Come morning he would seek the sun, but he would not find it.

CHAPTER

7

Mark sat beneath the shelter of his small traveling tent, studying the luminous waves of the Mediterranean. Phosphorus played a game of blue and green light against the surf as it nudged the edge of Asia Minor's coast.

The three missionaries were bedded down this evening on a beach in Pamphylia, 180 miles north of Cyprus.

The lights of the Port of Perga could be detected through the thin fog, just a few feet up the shore. But Mark felt as though he were a thousand years from civilization.

Some folk hesitated to even consider Pamphylia part of the civilized world. This province was wild country, famed for pirates in its ports and brigands in the interior. It had resisted subjugation by a long line of would-be conquerors—Persia, Alexander the Great, and the Seleucids, to name a few.

It was Roman territory now, and the metropolis of Perga even sported a 12,000-capacity stadium. But like Pisidia, its sister province to the north, it had never been truly tamed.

Mark kept close within his canvas hut. The beach was notorious for robbers and foul play. He preferred to stay invisible until morning.

An incessant breeze blew in from the sea. He thought he would have heard his companions' sonorous breathing, nonetheless, if they were asleep in the lean-tos nearby. Apparently they were restless, like himself, apprehensive over unfamiliar sounds and shadows.

Despite the circumstances and Paul's choice of countries to visit, this should have been an exciting time for Mark. A great miracle had taken place in Cyprus. The blinding of Elymas caused quite a stir, and it had been followed by the conversion of Sergius and his entire family.

The church was growing. It was no longer a Jewish subcult, but it had become a way of life for many Gentiles. And now for the first time a powerful Roman governor had embraced the faith. With his conversion, the entire isle of Cyprus would be unalterably affected. And from there the influence of Christianity would continue to spread.

Country by country, the Roman world was being invaded—not by any army, for no army would dare; not by political strategy, for no man was greater than Caesar; not by philosophy, for the philosophers had had their day.

Nor was it religion that was felling town after town. For Christianity was not religion. It was a personal, abiding transformation.

Herein lay its power.

Mark himself had sometimes known this power, this transformation. He should be happy, but he was not.

With the witness of the miracle in Paphos, depression had settled over him like a casket cloth. Worse by far than fear of bandits or assassins was the Accuser's voice. Mark's enemy was morbid introspection.

The daughter of the governor of Cyprus may as well have been Philea, so profoundly had her conversion affected Mark. But what should have been a joyful moment had only reminded him of his failure in Cyrene.

Threatening mountains at his back, a cold sea before him, and aliens on every side could not discourage him more than the sight of Barnabas's boldness before the proconsul or Paul's victory over evil.

Even if a path of roses lay ahead—eager hearts and open minds ready to receive the missionaries—Mark would still feel inadequate to the task of evangelism.

As he fed on such thoughts, the haunting image of one man's face confronted him—not Peter's strong countenance or Paul's commanding gaze—but a phantom of Quintus, brooding, disapproving.

Mark had not lived up to his father's expectations. He had not taken a seat in the senate, nor campaigned with Caesar's army. He had hoped he might at least succeed within the church and rise on wings of oratory or miraculous works.

Instead of trophy or applause, however, he was left with nothing but defeat.

Dwelling on this, he found that the phantom of Quintus was exchanged for the mocking visage of Brutus; and then Brutus became Peter, wondering at his weakness; and Peter became Paul, shaking his head, not at all surprised.

The breeze grew to a gale outside Mark's meager tent. All night long he had brooded, and when the sun rose, he was yet more despondent.

It was Barnabas who came to rouse him, thinking him asleep. Standing outside his tent, he called his name softly, and when Mark did not answer, he pulled back the flap.

"We have hired a fine crew of guides," his uncle eagerly informed him. "We head for the Taurus mountains today."

Mark, bleary-eyed, ran cold fingers through his matted beard. "Not I," he whispered.

Barnabas leaned his head in the door.

"I said, 'Not I,' " Mark repeated.

The look of shock and dismay on the elder's face revealed that he had not previously detected Mark's misery.

"What do you mean?" he protested.

"I am turning back—going home," Mark announced.

"But, why, son?"

"I am no man's son," Mark muttered. "I am useless."

Crawling past his uncle he took a deep breath of the ocean air and began to dismantle his tent.

"I don't understand," Barnabas stammered. "What will I tell Paul?"

That other apostle had not yet risen. He still lay beneath his lean-to, only the edge of his cloak visible below the curtain's hem.

Mark sighed, his eyes filling with tears. Stifling them, he turned a determined face to the wind.

"Tell him what you like," he replied, and tossing his knapsack on his back, he headed for the Port of Perga, the seaward ships, and the shelter of Jerusalem.

PART SEVEN

Reconciliation

For he himself is our peace,
who has made the two one
and has destroyed the barrier,
the dividing wall of hostility.

EPHESIANS 2:14

CHAPTER

1

Many days passed after Mark reached Israel and the house of his mother before he talked to anyone about his situation.

Peter had returned to Jerusalem since Mark had been away. Herod's threat against the apostle's life was withdrawn when the monarch suddenly and mysteriously became ill and died.

The great fisher of men, resuming his duties as head of the Jerusalem church, came back to confront a growing number of problems related to the developing doctrines of the faith.

Since the church's birth on Pentecost, it had transcended its Jewish roots, had pulled away from the authority of the Sanhedrin, and was proving itself a force to be reckoned with by Israel, Rome, and society at large. But the more Gentiles it took beneath its banner, the more contention developed over certain matters of ritual, holidays, feast days, and the keeping of the Laws of Moses, which every devout Jew observed.

Quite naturally, the customs of Judaism had attached themselves to the church. In fact, they had never been completely abandoned by those raised in their traditions.

But most Gentile believers failed to see how they applied to the new faith, and having no devotion to the ordinances of

Israel, recoiled when they were enforced.

Thus two camps grew up within the body of believers: the Judaizers, who might accept Gentiles but who insisted they practice the customs and laws of the Jews, and the Freemen, who resisted such imposition.

At times the contention became so strong that there was talk of a split—a Jewish church and a Gentile church. And with the passing months, both camps began to choose leaders.

Because Paul worked more with Gentiles in Syria and on his continuing journeys, he took sharp exception to imposing legalism on his followers. He who of all apostles had carefully observed the Law throughout his life had made as complete a break with his old ways as he could. Eating and drinking with people of every nation, he quickly came to the conclusion that apart from the fundamental code of the Ten Commandments little else in the Old Covenant applied to the life of a Christian. The change in his thinking was as pronounced as his overnight conversion from a murdering persecutor to a believer.

And it provided as much fodder for division among the Christians as had that momentous transformation.

As for Peter, it had been radical enough to accept Cornelius and his kin into the church community. He had been able to extrapolate from the vision of the sheet and the unclean beasts that God was admitting Gentiles to the fold. Beyond this, he preferred not to speculate.

But the matter was demanding attention, and when he returned to Jerusalem, he could not avoid it.

For days he had witnessed the battling of the divergent parties, he had read and reread messages from Paul and Barnabas regarding their work in other countries, and he had heard the reasoning of James, the Lord's brother, and others in the mother church. There was a time when his opinion on matters of the Law would have been quick and cutting. But since his experience in Joppa and his encounter with Cornelius, he was less hasty in making pronouncements.

He had had little time for his disciple, Mark, since he had

come back. This evening he asked the younger man to accompany him on a walk through the Garden of Gethsemane, outside Jerusalem's wall.

A warm breeze filtered through the olive branches, bearing the scent of lilies across the little oasis. It was spring, and thoughts easily turned to the climactic night when Jesus, in this very spot, surrendered his will to the Father.

"A great deal has happened since our Lord prayed here," Peter noted. "None of us dreamed what that might lead to."

Mark carefully considered the teacher's words.

"*I* certainly did not," he agreed. "I was here that evening, you know . . . right over there in those bushes by the stream."

"You saw the arrest?" Peter asked incredulously.

"All of it—the Lord's ordeal from beginning to end."

"Why did you never tell me?"

Mark smiled wistfully. "At first I prided myself on the secret. Later, I guess I wanted to spare you—embarrassment, whatever. . . ."

The apostle's eyes crinkled at the corners. "Ah—so that is how you knew my name when you castigated me in the upper room," he said, recalling Mark's verbal attack following the crucifixion. "You heard Jesus call me Peter, when he made me put up my sword."

Mark nodded, remembering the Galilean's impetuous action that long-ago evening.

"It is a wonder you ever claimed me as your teacher," the elder sighed. "I have not always been respectable."

"You will find no criticism here," Mark assured him. "I am not as cocky as I once was."

Peter sensed the disciple's discouragement. He had heard it in his voice and seen it in his bearing ever since he had returned. Seeking a way to draw him out, he took a seat in the grove and directed him to sit nearby.

"What do you respect, Mark?" he inquired. "What traits in a man are admirable?"

The young Roman moved his finger absently through the dirt and pulled his ankles close to his body.

"Confidence . . . consistency," he reflected. "Honor . . ."

He had just denounced himself, for he was certain he lacked all those qualities.

"I have not asked you why you left Paul in Pamphylia. Do you wish to speak of it?" Peter offered.

A blush burned Mark's cheeks. He was not at all certain he wished to speak of it. But he knew he could not put it off forever.

Recalling his uncle's sad face the morning he had left the shore of Perga, he rested his chin on his knees and sighed.

"There was not one single reason," he began. "There were a multitude. But I suppose, more than anything . . . I was afraid."

Peter knew such a confession came hard.

"Pamphylia is a dangerous land," he acknowledged.

The disciple shook his head. "I wish it were that simple. It was not fear of robbers or wild beasts that drove me away. It was fear of . . . failure."

There—it had been said. The load of anguish slipped down his back and hung close to dropping. But Mark could not let the burden go.

Peter could only speculate as to the nature of Mark's "failure." He had not been with him in Cyrene when both Brutus and Philea had pitied him.

Sitting quietly, he probed Mark's soul with silence. And as one festering memory followed another, he listened like the friend he was.

"I had always hoped I might amount to something," Mark admitted. "But I shall never be a Peter or a Paul. I am not a preacher. No one looks to me for instruction. I am not a teacher."

The apostle did not interrupt. And Mark continued.

"The night Jesus was taken in this very place, I was helpless to help him. I knew Judas was up to no good, but did I warn the Master? No. . . . Did I confront the soldiers? No . . . I ran. Naked as the day I was born!"

Peter did not understand this last allusion but did not question it, aching for the agony in Mark's voice.

"I am good for hauling water and for loading crates. But let me witness the Lord's appearing on my own uncle's rooftop, and it will be days before I speak of it!"

The young man stood now, pacing the ground near the rock where Jesus had wept. "Oh," he sighed, "for the courage of Barnabas! You should have heard him address the governor of Cyprus! Bold and confident! You should have seen Paul denounce the wizard priest in the palace itself! You have heard of this?"

Peter nodded. Tales of miracles at the hands of the missionaries reached Jerusalem almost every day.

"But I cannot speak for the Lord even before my own friends," Mark declared. "When I visited Cyrene, I stumbled over my testimony. And again, like a naked fool, I ran!"

Looking down at the earth, he kicked a root in the ground and clenched his fists.

"I am my mother's son. I am good for keeping house. But I have failed my father."

The venom in his tongue shocked even himself. Peter's countenance registered surprise, but the apostle did not voice disapproval.

"Tell me of your father," the Galilean prodded. "He was a mighty man?"

"Very," Mark asserted, evincing the pride that had never diminished.

And then, as unbidden tears welled in his eyes, he whispered, "He raised me to be a Roman—a senator at least, if not a hero."

Had there not been so much torment in the young man's voice, Peter might have smiled. But as Mark went on, he sensed how grave was the wound the disciple carried, how unresolved the guilt.

"But how did I repay my father?" Mark cried. "I left him to die alone! He died without me, Peter, slain by insurgents when I should have saved him. Burned by fire when I could have . . ."

Peter recalled the story of Quintus's death—how the Libyans had taken over the praetorium and how the governor had been their victim. But, strangely, his face twitched, as if with some hated memory of his own. He stood and, reaching out to grasp Mark's arm, demanded, "You could have *what*? What could you have done?"

Mark glared at the apostle's insistent face. How dare Peter confuse him? Fists angular, he stood rigid and helpless at the confrontation.

At last, dropping his gaze, he trembled. Slowly his head began to move back and forth.

"I don't know . . . ," he whispered.

The Galilean held out strong arms, inviting Mark to enter his embrace.

Like a child, the young Roman did so until he ceased to tremble and his body convulsed with sobs.

Had he been less self-focused, he might have felt Peter's own body quaking.

"We all have failed," the apostle groaned. "Miserably, utterly . . ."

"No!" Mark resisted. "Not like I have. Not so often."

"Worse," Peter declared. "Much worse and more profoundly!"

The disciple could not imagine what he meant. He would have considered the assertion mere kindness had Peter's voice not carried its own boundless load of regret.

Pulling back, Mark studied his teacher's face, wondering how the great leader could relate to such failure and longing to question him.

But Peter would not allow questions. Not just now.

"Perhaps," the apostle suggested, trying to clear his own mind, "perhaps you have spent your life serving the wrong man. Let Quintus go, my son. Let failure go. And enter the rest of Jesus."

CHAPTER

2

Rest—the concept struck Mark as profoundly as had the idea of power on the Day of Pentecost.

But though he longed to believe it was available—rest of heart and soul—he saw little evidence of rest among the Christians.

Contention between the Judaizers and the Freemen intensified with each passing day, until at last it reached a climax of division, threatening the very foundations of the church.

Only a meeting of the key leaders of the Christian world could settle the matter, if indeed it could be settled.

Mary Ben Haman bustled about her commodious house with the energy of a woman twenty years younger. Not since the first weeks of the infant church had her home been filled with so many notables. Every great name among believers, the pillars of a dozen congregations, were gathered here, and the high energy that filled each corner of the old mansion was infectious.

Three years had passed since Mark had left Paul and Barnabas in Pamphylia. In all that time he had not seen his uncle.

He had received letters from him, sent from numerous cities, but none of the communications sent from Paul to the Jerusalem church mentioned Mark by name nor asked about him.

It was therefore of little comfort when he learned that the church at Antioch was sending the two missionaries to the council. Though the young deacon looked forward to seeing Barnabas, he doubted that a reunion with Paul would be pleasant.

Each apostle and many elders had left their work in diverse corners of Palestine and other parts of the Mediterranean world to be here. This first great council would set the pattern for many to follow in coming years when conventions of the church would be called from time to time to settle various disputes.

Mark could have reveled in the history-making that would transpire beneath his own roof. He was invested in the topic emotionally, culturally, and spiritually, for many matters regarding his two heritages were about to be debated. But he preferred to keep in the background while these mighty men gathered in his mother's house.

When Paul and Barnabas arrived, he could have enjoyed the tension of the great drama about to be played out between charismatic figures. He could have enjoyed the raw grating of nerves and tempers.

But he stayed behind the scenes.

All eyes were riveted on Paul when we walked through the front door. Then attention fell on Peter and his plan for the meeting.

Mark would observe from a corner of the room. Over the days that followed he would take his customary station as waiter and server. And he would avoid Paul's gaze.

It never failed to amaze Mark that matters of kosher law should so exercise his Jewish brethren.

It had been a climactic moment for the church when Peter's victory in Cornelius's house had been condoned by Jerusalem believers. But that had not resolved issues of circumcision, of unclean food, or the keeping of holidays. In the intervening years since the Caesarean centurion had come to Christ, the feud between factions over whether Gentiles must bow to the Mosaic commandments had only escalated. Extremists on the side of the Law went so far as to say that if a man was not circumcised, he could not be saved. And if anyone failed to keep the ordinances, he would lose his salvation.

Paul and Barnabas had already dealt with such dissension when they taught in Antioch. Upon returning from their missionary journey, they had been confronted with Judaizers who had come from Jerusalem to stir up the Antioch Christians. Converted Pharisees contended with Paul over issues on which they had once agreed. Paul had been a member of their sect, a teacher of the Law, an assistant to the Sanhedrin. It was inconceivable that he should so utterly have abandoned the regimen of his fellows.

But he had. And he had imposed few restrictions on his Gentile followers.

For three days the Pharisees, the Judaizers, the Freemen, and all gradations between debated in Mary's house.

The courtyard was packed wall to wall with council members. The gallery strained beneath the weight of the audience, folk of the Jerusalem church and pilgrims from throughout the empire.

For three days heads shook, fists clenched, teeth ground.

Peter and James, the Lord's brother, sat at a head table at the far end of the court, while jostling bodies dangled feet above them and hot hands clung to the mezzanine rail. All about the patio, postures denoted tense feelings, while the apostles attempted to keep order.

Paul's main defense, when he did battle with the Judaizers, was the record of miracles performed under the ministry in foreign lands. Often Barnabas spoke as well, giving account after account of healings, deliverances, and conversions among Gentiles in Pisidia, Iconium, Lystra, and Perga.

Still, the Pharisees would quote the Law, Judaizers would quote from Israel's history, and their disciples would raise cracking voices in defense of the prophets, until the very rafters of the old house rattled.

The scene was like a hundred Paul had witnessed when he had sat in on Sanhedrin meetings, or had been invited to debate in the Cyrenian synagogue. The difference was that this time he was the "Devil's advocate." This time he took the side of freedom and did not speak for Moses.

After three days, it seemed inevitable that the church would split.

The Judaizers, gifted in their use of Scripture, continually overrode Paul's more experiential testimony. And though many former Pharisees sought to refute them, they came up with no legal evidence to contradict them.

Mark's emotions were a tangle through it all. Though he had his problems with Paul, he appreciated his stand. When the apostle defended the Gentiles, he could not help but applaud him, and when his enemies had the upper hand, he was downcast.

More than anything, though, he wished the ordeal would conclude. The Law had never done anything for Mark. He had come to Jesus without the code of Moses and would just as soon the Jews kept it to themselves.

Wearily he listened to yet another debate as he walked around the head table, gathering up luncheon dishes and re-filling wine cups. James, who had stood on middle ground, sat to Peter's right, looking through sheaves of scrolls, vainly searching the Scriptures for a definitive solution. And as Mark passed Peter's seat, he noted the big Galilean's stooped posture and sweat-beaded brow.

The great fisherman wished to hear no more. He rested a throbbing head on taut fists, and at last stood up, just as Mark made a move to take his plate.

The young deacon stepped back, sensing that something important was about to happen.

The apostle raised his hands over the squabbling crowd, and they grew quiet. Even James looked up from his hopeless quest.

"Men and brethren," Peter cried, his voice tight as a bow string, "you know that years ago God ordained that the Gentiles should, by my preaching, hear the gospel and believe. And God, who knows all hearts, confirmed their conversion by the gift of the Holy Spirit, even as he did to us!"

Suddenly the room was very still. Here was evidence that could not be denied. God's Spirit would abide only in hallowed souls, and not even the most Orthodox Jew among them could refute what had happened at Cornelius's house.

"There is no difference between us and them!" Peter declared, pronouncing the words with great respect. "God has purified their hearts by faith!"

The thrill that comes as history is made fell on the multitude. Though their minds might resist Peter's challenge, their hearts could not resist the truth.

"Now, therefore," the apostle demanded, "why do you tempt God by putting a yoke upon the neck of the disciples which neither our forefathers nor we ourselves have been able to bear?"

The hush became a shudder, for there was no greater sin than to defy the Almighty.

And so the Galilean fisherman, as though he were a practiced attorney, gave the conclusion.

"We believe that through the grace of the Lord Jesus Christ, both Jews and Gentiles shall be saved!"

Not a word was given in rebuttal. Three days of debates and hatred had in a few syllables been resolved. No one stood to speak until Paul, who had never publicly joined himself to Peter, took a place beside him. And once again recounting with Barnabas evidence from other countries, he supported Peter's contention.

"Our brother has said what no one else had words to say," the man of Tarsus confessed. "The Holy Spirit tried to tell us when he fell on the Gentiles that all our striving is after wind!"

Mark could never have imagined Paul and Peter side by side at the head of a congregation. Though their competition had never been spoken, it had been real. Yet today they were together, champions of one cause.

Behind them he watched, holding a stack of dirty dishes and wishing he might be great as they were.

Even James, who had hoped to find the definitive Scripture, leaped to his feet, blessed with the final word.

"Peter has said rightly," he announced, holding an open scroll before him like a banner. "God *has* visited the Gentiles, separating them to himself! Listen! The prophets agree!"

Slowly he began to quote golden phrases, which he had only now stumbled upon, given him for the conclusion of the council.

" 'After this I will return . . . that the remnant of men may seek after the Lord, along with all the Gentiles who bear my name, says the Lord, who does all these things. Known unto God are all his works from the beginning of the world!' "

They were the words of Amos, the prophet, and they seared the ears of the congregation like cauterizing irons.

Setting the scroll aside, the elder surveyed his audience with tear-filled eyes and lifted one trembling hand, after the manner of a court judge.

"Therefore, my sentence is that we quit troubling our Gentile brothers. Let us send letters to the churches advising them to abstain from idolatry, from fornication, and the shedding of blood, as is the voice of conscience throughout the world. And beyond this, let them judge for themselves."

CHAPTER

3

With the conclusion of the council, a turning point had been reached by the church. But this did not mean there would never again be contention about these matters.

In the climactic moment of unity experienced by Peter and Paul, a certain healing between the two men took place. But there would never be complete agreement between these two strong leaders.

Though the church progressed in spurts of doctrinal understanding, it was made up of human beings. And the heart grows more slowly than the mind. So it was that when Peter accompanied Paul, Barnabas, and Mark back to Antioch, all was not well. They carried a message of unity and freedom but were not themselves totally of one accord.

Peter had given the proclamation that should have forever unified Gentiles and Jews, but he still had a long way to go in overcoming prejudice himself. And though Paul was learning some humility, he was not happy with the letters sent out by the council. He had been content to accept James's assertion, but more restrictions had been inserted into the epistles than he liked.

Nevertheless, fellowship had been warm between the big fisherman and the man of Tarsus since they had entered Syria. For nearly a week they had taught together, speaking in the Antioch assembly and encouraging the Gentile believers.

But trouble was brewing.

Unconvinced Judaizers—men who had not been present at the council—came down to Antioch from Jerusalem, and only yesterday they had entered the church's meeting place to hear what the apostles were saying.

They were certain that freedom could only lead to evil excess and were determined to return home with sensational reports of debauchery and licentiousness.

It was mealtime. Mark worked beside his uncle in the kitchen, cutting onions and cabbage. A fine stew boiled over the cooking pit, and women scurried to and fro preparing to serve the food.

Barnabas did not mind such duties, though Mark had never become accustomed to them. The uncle spoke with enthusiasm as he labored over a pile of leeks.

"Paul and I are planning another journey," he told his nephew. "We intend to visit the congregations we established on the first trip."

Mark wished he could be happy for them, but his face betrayed sour feelings.

"Would you like to go with us?" Barnabas asked.

Suddenly coming alive, Mark stared into the Levite's smiling eyes. Just as quickly, however, his eagerness cooled. "Paul would never consent," he muttered.

"Don't be so certain," Barnabas said. "I have spoken with him."

"And?"

"He is not opposed."

Mark studied the speaker carefully. "He has approved, then?"

Barnabas looked at the bushel of vegetables at his feet.

"He is not opposed," he repeated.

"Ha! Enough said," Mark snarled. "He will never consent!"

Activity was picking up in the kitchen. People were taking seats in the dining hall of Perus's house, and Mark grabbed a ladle to begin dipping stew into a hundred bowls. Loading the food onto a tray, he exited the kitchen and began to help the women serve.

Peter was conversing amiably with a group of Gentile converts at one table, and as people filed into the room, they sat wherever they wished, mingling easily.

Mark's face still burned with anger as he walked from group to group, placing bowls on the linen spreads. Barely did he notice when Judaizers entered the room and stood staring with disapproval over the throng.

It was not until he came to Peter's table that Mark's attention was drawn to them. Peter had stopped speaking for the moment as he uncomfortably observed them.

One long table remained vacant near the entry, and it was to this that the Judaizers turned, clutching their robes close, and sitting apart from the others.

The room was deadly quiet.

Barnabas came from the kitchen and stood at Mark's side. "This is not good," he whispered. "Where is Paul?"

The man of Tarsus had not yet arrived. So it was left to Peter to handle the matter.

Mark, knowing his mentor as he did, shuffled nervously. It had been one thing for him to receive Cornelius and to mingle with the tanner of Joppa. But this was a different situation for it involved the whole church.

Peter was rising to his feet now, and with a weak smile he started across the room toward the visitors.

"Brothers," Peter said, bowing from the waist when he reached their station, "we are glad you have joined us."

The Judaizers were not favorably impressed, their silence more telling than a rebuke.

Waving a shaky hand at Barnabas, Peter called for him to join them.

The Levite, not expecting this, found himself torn. Perhaps it would not hurt simply to greet the men from the Holy

City. He would not sit with them long. He would rise quickly, then busy himself in the kitchen once again.

As Barnabas carefully walked through the hushed crowd, Mark noted the relief on Peter's face, the comfort gained from such a move on the part of another apostle.

Anger fueled anger in Mark's already burning heart. His face hot, he turned toward the pantry.

But the sound of Paul's voice jolted him back. The missionary had arrived and stood in the doorway of the court, livid with indignation.

"Peter!" he was crying, pointing an accusing finger. "If you, being a Jew, live like a Gentile and no longer like a Jew, why do you compel the Gentiles to live like Jews?"

Peter's face was ashen. "I . . . I do no such thing!" he objected.

"Ah, but your actions speak for you!" Paul argued. "We know that a man is not justified by works of the Law, but by faith in Jesus!"

Heading for the visitors' table, Paul continued to confront the big fisherman. "If we go under the Law again, we become sinners!" he shouted. "If we build up again the things that have been destroyed, we are guilty of the Law's demands!"

Paul's dark eyes flashed lightning, his red beard shook. "I am dead to the Law, Peter, that I might live for God! I have been crucified with Christ. Nevertheless, I live. Yet not I, but Christ lives in me. And the life I now live in the flesh, I live by faith in the Son of God, who loved me and gave himself for me!"

The mighty Galilean shrank before the man of Tarsus, his lip quivering, until Paul drew back and shaking his head, sighed, "Oh, Peter, do not frustrate the grace of God! If righteousness comes by the Law, then Christ is dead in vain!"

Sleep would not come easily that night. Everyone in the house of Perus had turned in, but few would find rest, their minds and souls charged with the events of the day.

It must have been past midnight when voices in the court

roused Mark from troubled dreams and brought him to the gallery rail outside his room.

In the dim light of a low-burning lantern, two men engaged in animated conversation near the fountain. It was Paul and Barnabas discussing the dinnertime confrontation.

"I am not a little put out with you, as well!" Paul declared. "How could you have betrayed our Gentile brethren as you did?"

The apostle paced back and forth, pounding his fists against his thighs as Barnabas looked on, defenseless.

"I only meant to greet them," he insisted. "I would not have stayed with them all evening!"

"Perhaps . . . perhaps. I don't know," Paul doubted.

Silence fell between them until Barnabas tried to change the subject.

"About the coming journey . . . ," he said, "we are still going?"

Paul turned to him, shrugging. "Of course! Would you pull away from that as well?"

It took a great deal to prick Barnabas's temper. But now he sat rigid and asserted, "That is not fair, Paul! Can you not forgive?"

The hotheaded Cilician slumped where he stood, his shoulders drooping. "I am sorry," he whispered. "Sometimes I get carried away. . . ."

"Stubborn . . . obsessed," Barnabas rebuked him.

"I suppose so," Paul conceded. But then, not to be dampered for long, he enjoined, "Someone needs to be . . . about some things!"

"All right," Barnabas sighed, knowing it was no use to argue. "About the trip . . ."

Paul was pacing again. "It should be easy to put together the second time. We know how many supplies we need. There is money in the treasury."

"Very well. But we will need a helper," the Levite reminded him. "We spoke earlier of John Mark. . . ."

Paul's volatile temper flared again.

"Helper, indeed! Where was he today when his teacher turned from the truth?"

Barnabas could not believe his ears. And Mark, who had taken in every word, stiffened angrily on the mezzanine.

"Again, you are not fair!" Barnabas defended. "You do not know Mark's mind on these matters. Why, he is himself a Gentile as well as a Jew!"

The Cilician only sneered. "I know his mind well enough! Is he not Peter's disciple? Did he not prove himself untrustworthy in Pamphylia?"

Barnabas leapt to his feet. "You have gone too far!" the Levite cried, his voice ringing through the house. "You speak of my nephew—the son of my sister!"

Doors began to open on the gallery, and bleary-eyed folk emerged from the guest rooms. Mark's cheeks flushed. He knew the argument had been overheard and his reputation was on everyone's mind.

Light from half-a-dozen chambers spilled past him, revealing his presence to the men below. He would have gone down, but his uncle shook his head. "Stay where you are, Mark," he commanded.

"He may stay where he is until we return from our trip," Paul said.

The Cypriot would bear no more. Gathering up his cloak from the bench, he resolutely lifted his chin.

"You will not only need to find a helper," he declared, "but a fellow missionary. I will not accompany you!"

Paul, incredulous, watched his old companion ascend the stairs. "Come, Barnabas. You do not mean it!"

"But I do!" the Levite assured him. And taking his nephew by the arm, he asserted, "If I make another journey, it will be with John Mark!"

Mark, his head spinning and his arm clenched in Barnabas's grasp, followed his uncle down the gallery.

"Nephew, you will go with me to Cyprus, won't you?" the missionary inquired, loudly enough that Paul could hear.

"I guess so . . . ," Mark stammered. "Of course."

CHAPTER

4

Dense fog cloaked the Port of Salamis. Mark stood at the edge of the bay, listening to the lapping tide but barely able to see where it pushed frothy fingers up the sand.

This stint on Cyprus had taxed him to the breaking point. Sometimes he wondered if his choice to become a Christian had been a grave mistake.

Not only had he brought with him all his feelings of failure and self-loathing, his memories of past ineptitudes and Paul's burning accusation, but Salamis contained a microcosm of every battlefield on which the church waged war.

Idolaters fought the faith, Jews fought Gentiles, and Christians fought Christians.

Since the preaching of Paul and Barnabas in this city, a sizable congregation of believers had taken root. But the silversmiths of Aphrodite's cult leveled venomous threats against the young church, as it cut into their popular trade in goddess figurines. Some people had actually been attacked in the streets, when they openly witnessed of their faith in Christ. In broad daylight and under plain view of the authorities they risked their lives. But nothing was done to protect them.

Persecution against Christians was nearly as ferocious from the synagogue, and stubborn enmity between Judaizers and Freemen opened a deepening rift between the brethren themselves.

Barnabas had chosen no easy field when he returned here. But these were his people as much as were the folk of Israel, and he loved them.

Mark as always played a secondary role. His clear-thinking uncle was a forceful evangelist, proving himself to be, in Paul's absence, nearly as great an orator as the man of Tarsus.

In his advancing age, the venerable apostle was a distinguished character, silver-haired, his beard a dignified, patriarchal length. In his early journey the pagans who heard him preach mistook him for Jupiter, father-god of the Romans. Though he had denounced the notion, the nickname was sometimes still applied to him and had become a term of endearment among his followers.

This evening Mark had left the apostle at their small apartment in Salamis. Several blocks away was the synagogue, and even farther toward the city center was the little meeting hall of the church. When he had last seen Barnabas, he had been sitting in the light of the apartment fireplace, a long scroll spread across his lap, and his fingers moving eagerly over it as he read.

The nephew wondered now what the elder had been reading, for it seemed to bring tranquillity to his face.

How Mark wished he might know peace! For a long time, he had yearned for power—for the fulfillment of all his youthful training. But now, peace was more important.

The church did not always represent peace—feuding as it did among its factions. And the Roman world did not exhibit it—filled as it was with greed and the lust for conquest.

As he stood upon the twilight shore, the constant call of the tide a rhythmic balm, it seemed the waves washed this truth into his heart.

"Rest . . . ," they whispered, "Rest . . . ," recalling Peter's advice regarding his ambition. "Perhaps you have spent your life serving the wrong man. . . . Let failure go and enter the rest of Jesus."

He had not come to the shore this evening in quest of a spiritual experience. His yearning was years old, and he had become accustomed to it. Somehow, though, as he reflected upon these words, his soul drew a healing breath. Pulsing through him, the tide of God's love began a new work of grace.

How long he stood thus, drinking in the solace of the Lord, his face upturned, he knew not. When he opened his eyes, they were wet with tears.

As real and as unexpected as the Pentecost experience was the spiritual infusion born of Mark's hour on the beach.

It was of a different sort, however—deeper, quieter, more abiding.

Carefully he carried it home, like a surprise package, eager to share it with Barnabas, but fearful lest the stillness of his soul be shaken by movement among humankind.

He never expected the shaking to take the form it did. As he drew near the fishermen's wharves, an eerie glow permeated the fog. The entire sky above the bowery was fire red. And as he drew closer still, he realized the glow came from the vicinity of his apartment.

"Barnabas!" His pulse drummed.

His feet seemed lead, his heart a dead weight, as he raced toward home. As though he had been catapulted back through time, he remembered the orange sky of Cyrene and the death of his father.

When he reached the building, it was blocked by horrified Christians, women weeping and men battling the flames.

"The Jews," some said.

"The idolmakers," said others.

Mark cared not who the arsonists were. Pushing through the crowd, he raced for the door. His friends warned him not to enter, but he ignored their concern for his safety.

This time he would not fail. Flames would not keep him from a dying man's side.

Amid the leaping holocaust he found his uncle, stomach down, his face black with soot.

Mark's own breathing was shallow, but bending over he pulled Barnabas across the floor and through the curtain of smoke. Once in the street, he cradled his uncle's head in his lap and wept.

In Mark's arms, Barnabas died.

Through the night, and while the sun rose over the charred ruins, Mark held his uncle, until someone, taking pity, gently lifted the body from his grasp.

At midday, as the noon sun penetrated the ashes, Mark scanned the debris.

He asked to be alone as he surveyed the site of the martyrdom. His little flock, honoring his request, let him venture there unattended. But some watched from a distance as he picked through the rubble and kicked at the fallen rafters.

At last, concerned for their pastor's obsessive behavior, one of them went forward and called to him.

"You will stay and be our teacher, won't you?"

This was the last thing Mark wanted to hear. The thought of staying on in Cyprus was abhorrent to him.

Shaking his head, he longed to cry out, "You do not understand. I have no power, no ability."

But just as he was about to reply, his gaze fell on the object of his search.

Stooping, he lifted a fragile corner of parchment from the ashes. It was a fragment of the scroll from which Barnabas had been reading the night before.

The Greek letters were smoked out, but one complete thought was readable: "In quietness and in confidence shall be your strength."

It was the prophet Isaiah speaking across the centuries from the ruins of this place.

As Mark read and reread the words, the same spirit that had infused him with peace on the shore only last evening came to wash away the turmoil of his soul.

"Quietness . . . ," he reflected. "Confidence . . . strength . . ."

It was the *rest* Peter had promised, the rest that equaled power.

Turning to the young convert who had drawn near his side, Mark found himself smiling.

"I will be staying on," he replied, "as long as I am needed."

CHAPTER

5

Mark remained in Cyprus for eight years. During that time the church on the island grew until it was one of the largest in the empire and occupied meeting halls in each Cypriot town.

Mark had become known as "the Evangelist," taking up where his uncle had left off, both as a preacher and a pastor.

Middle-aged now, Mark's face, bearing lines of character, was more handsome than in youth, and his dark hair and beard were streaked with silver.

The day he left the island was both a happy and sad one for the Christians of Cyprus. They knew he went to a needier country, and that his going indicated they were ready to stand on their own. But they also knew they would sorely miss him.

Peter required help in Rome. Several years before, the big fisherman had gone to the imperial capital to start a church. His career in the seven-hilled city had been so successful that the number of Christians was beyond count.

It was an enormously challenging center, head-on in conflict with world government. And Peter had become the most famous and revolutionary force since Jesus himself.

He had called for Mark, reasoning that he could be an invaluable aide with his Roman background. The deacon would work as a translator, not only between his native Latin and Peter's Aramaic, but between cultures. Knowing the Roman mind, Mark often advised the apostle on the content of his sermons and how best to appeal to practical and material-minded imperialists.

This afternoon Mark had stood beside the Galilean as he spoke to a crowd in the market square. Phrase for phrase, he had taken what Peter had said in Aramaic and had restated it in Latin. For years Peter had tried to preach in his own broken version of the imperial tongue, but having a spokesman like Mark was much more effective.

When they got home from the meeting, the apostle suggested that Mark take on an additional project.

"A book!" the big fisherman suggested with enthusiasm. "A book detailing the story of the gospel."

"I am no writer!" Mark protested. "I have never been a reader and was a poor scholar. It is one thing to be your translator, but quite another to be your scribe!"

The two men sat on the veranda of the spacious house the church had provided the apostle. Below, the Tiber River wound like a coral ribbon through the sunset metropolis.

"It will not be difficult," Peter insisted. "You have already heard me tell most of the story. I will recount what happened; you can write it down."

Mark knew that unless he utterly refused, Peter would have his way.

"In Latin or Aramaic?" he asked.

"How about Greek?" Peter ambitiously suggested. "That would reach everyone!"

"Greek?" the disciple said, laughing. "It may as well be Hebrew, so awkward am I with the language!"

Of course, Mark was exaggerating. He had learned both Greek and Latin in Cyrene.

It was true he was no scholar, but it was also true that he was familiar with the account Peter wanted him to write. He knew the story of Jesus almost as well as if he had walked with the Master.

So it came to be that over many months that followed, Mark spent his evenings on the veranda, listening to Peter's account of the greatest story ever told. As he took it down, sharpening his quill, using roll upon roll of papyrus, he did not know that his would be the first "Gospel," the account from which all others would spring and the most popular narrative of the church.

But he knew how difficult a task it was. It was hard work to capture Peter's sense, to condense and rephrase it in the alien Greek tongue.

It would bear Mark's indelible imprint, however, vivid and simple, action-oriented and full of power—a power that could captivate the world.

"You have used *immediately* a bit too often, don't you think?" Peter critiqued as he read over a portion of Mark's manuscript.

Each evening the apostle perused the segment written that day. He did not usually suggest many changes, but as the work was nearing completion, he was more temperamental about it.

"Romans like stories to move quickly," Mark explained. "Sometimes our poets drag on, but their most popular scenes are those of action, as in Homer's *Iliad*. You wish to reach the Roman mind, don't you?"

Peter shrugged. "I like action too. Can you doubt that? But this one word comes up too often."

"Trust me," Mark insisted.

On this point Peter conceded. But taking a seat, he grew very somber.

"We near the crucifixion, Mark," he said. "I was not there." The apostle's husky voice betrayed the shame he still felt for that spineless neglect. "*You* were there," he went on. "You will have to tell that part."

Mark hesitated, ready to object. "I will do my best," he said at last.

Peter sighed and gazed across the rooftops of the city, off into the distance, as though he sought Jerusalem.

"Very well, then. Let us go on. There is a part of my history and the history of Jesus I have never shared before." Looking deep into Mark's eyes, he reiterated, "I have never told it to a living soul. But you are my friend. I know I can trust you to relay it fully and honestly."

Mark nodded, sensing the gravity of the moment.

"Very well," the big man said again.

Folding his hands on his broad lap, he began, his expression intent, his voice low.

"The night of Jesus' trial, I was in the courtyard of the High Priest's palace. Our brother John had been allowed to go inside, as he was the son of a Sanhedrin member."

His tone was shaky as he divulged the most painful memory of his life.

"I was standing by the fire when a maid came forward and, recognizing me as a follower of Jesus, identified me."

His voice broke, but he went on. "I was afraid to be counted with the accused, so I said, 'I don't know what you're talking about!' And I ran out of the place." With a sigh, he proceeded. "Just then, the morning cock crowed, and some other woman spied me, saying, 'This fellow is one of them!' "

Mark listened carefully, jotting down each word. He knew Peter would not want to repeat the story.

"But again I denied it," he admitted. "And later I did so when more people said I must be one of his followers. My Galilean accent gave me away." The apostle's shoulders slumped, and he pounded a fist against his knee.

"I cursed, and I swore! 'I don't know the man!' I lied. But the cock crowed again, and I remembered something Jesus had said at the supper. 'Before the cock crows twice, you shall deny me three times.' "

Tears welled in the fisherman's eyes. "I wept, Mark. I wept

a long time. And I stayed away from the cross. I could not show my face to the one I loved."

Mark ached inside as his teacher stood and walked to the edge of the porch, leaning, dejected, against a pillar.

The Roman remembered with regret how he had accosted Peter the next day in the upper room, thinking him careless of the Lord's suffering.

"I am sorry . . . ," he whispered.

Peter turned to his student.

"Do you see now what I meant," the apostle concluded, "when I told you long ago that we *all* have failed?"

"After I abandoned Paul in Pamphylia?" he recalled.

"Yes. I would have explained myself then, but . . . I could not."

"I understand," Mark said, a sad look in his eyes.

"But for all there is forgiveness," the apostle added, stepping toward his disciple and placing a hand on his shoulder. "This is what you must convey. This is what our preaching and our gospel must be."

Lifting the scroll from Mark's lap, Peter stroked it again and again.

"We have come to the crucifixion," he repeated, his eyes misting. "And then we will tell that he rose again. Herein is our victory and our redemption!"

As Mark took the parchment carefully from Peter's hand, he asked, "Am I adequate to the task?"

"You are adequate." Peter smiled.

CHAPTER

6

As Christianity spread beyond Israel and became more than a minor "cult" among the many religions of the Roman Empire, it met with opposition from Caesar even more threatening than from the Sanhedrin.

Little by little, and sometimes by great leaps, it was encroaching on the power Rome held over its subjects.

At first, the church had been dismissed as a mere spin-off of Judaism, a few idealists or rabble-rousers whose theology was a quaint oddity. When it began to affect the economy of entire cities where guilds of idolmakers and markets of pagan temples were a major source of revenue, Caesar took notice.

Nero, emperor of the world, had claimed deity for himself. State religions, while recognizing other gods, held that worship of Caesar must be pre-eminent.

Christianity and Judaism, alone of all faiths, refused to acknowledge the existence of any God but Jehovah.

Those who did not understand perceived the worship of Jesus as simple polytheism. The notion that he was one with the Father was unintelligible to most. Therefore, when the church refused to bow to Caesar or to any deity, saying that there was only one God, people outside its ranks branded this hypocrisy.

Nevertheless, Christianity was becoming stronger, challenging not only ancient paganism but the worship of Nero.

It was time for the emperor to act. His advisors need not persuade him of this. His megalomania, his self-worship, could not allow such subversion. The insanity that would one day drive him to burn Rome, his "Holy City," to the ground would not permit him to tolerate the defamation of his name by former followers.

His retribution began with an investigation into the activities of Peter and Paul. A bloodbath that would last for months followed, sending hundreds into exile, to unspeakable tortures and certain death.

Already Paul had withstood trials in Palestine before the imperial magistrates Felix and Festus. Now he was being sent to the world's capital to be tried again, this time by Caesar himself.

Rumors of his journey to Rome were broadcast ahead of his arrival, and Mark and Peter awaited his coming with mixed feelings.

As much as they wished him well and prayed for his victory in the courts, the breach between Paul and themselves at Antioch had never been healed. While Peter admitted that he had been wrong to side with the Judaizers, his antagonist had never mellowed toward him. And Mark still remembered the sting of the man's scathing accusations against himself.

The day Paul arrived, Mark was alone in Peter's house.

He had just completed the first draft of his Gospel and sat with it spread on a table out of the cool draft that blew across the veranda.

Peter had been in town all day, meeting with his followers. Mark had asked to stay behind to finish the task begun so hesitantly months before.

As he read the closing phrases once again, a lump came to his throat. They were the words of Jesus himself: "And these signs shall follow those who believe: In my name they shall cast out devils; they shall speak with new tongues, they shall handle serpents and shall not be hurt; they shall lay hands on the sick, and they shall recover."

Powerful, he thought. Words that described the church . . . and would thrill the world.

And true words. Mark had seen such miracles, had even participated in some of them.

With a measure of personal satisfaction, and with trembling hands, he rolled up the scroll. It had been completed fittingly. The project taken on under protest had been accomplished well.

His gaze drifted across the room. Upon the foot of a low sofa was his father's red cape, sent from Jerusalem by his mother along with Mark's other possessions after he had moved permanently to Rome. Day in and day out, as he had worked on his book, he had kept the garment where he might see it, as an inspiration to remember his audience.

He was confident his work would appeal to Gentiles. *Even Quintus would have read it with relish,* he thought, sighing wistfully.

Perhaps he would do well to sign the manuscript. Though it was largely Peter's account, it bore his personality in every line.

But what name should he use? Marcus? Marcus Quintus? Jonah Marcus Quintus?

"John" bespoke his Hebrew heritage and "Mark," the Gentile. That would do, he reasoned, and quickly he drew back the end of the scroll where the last words could be seen. There was room for a signature!

As he took quill in hand and pulled his little ink bottle close, the door to the house opened.

It was Peter, his face full of sadness and fear.

"Paul is in town," he announced. "He is being held prisoner near Nero's palace."

Mark, looking up from the scroll, shook his head. "This is not good. What are his chances?"

"If Nero has his way, he has no chance."

"Have you been to see him?"

Peter drew off his cloak and sat down, heaving a sigh. "I must do that. I *want* to do that! But it will not be easy on my pride."

Mark needed no explanation. The knowledge that the great missionary was in the city put a damper on the self-esteem in which he had just been reveling.

Putting his pen back in its wrapper, he set it on the table and pushed the scroll aside, unsigned.

The big fisherman and his disciple sat silently together, thinking about Paul—with hesitant love.

CHAPTER

7

Mark drew the hood of his cloak over his head as he hurried through the rainy street. The cobblestones were slippery, and the steep descent of the narrow, winding road made his journey uncomfortable.

Not that it would have been an easy trip otherwise. He had put off visiting Paul for nearly a year.

His bolder friend, Peter, had managed to overcome personal pride and had taken the step within a day or two of the prisoner's arrival. But then Peter was the head of the local church. It would have been unforgivable not to show support of the captive apostle.

Besides, Mark reasoned, the big fisherman had less reason to avoid Paul. While the man of Tarsus had challenged his behavior in Antioch, he had not assailed his character. And while Peter had made a move of indiscretion in eating with the Judaizers, he had not deserted Paul on the mission field.

Yesterday, however, a letter addressed to John Mark and bearing the seal of Caesar's penal system had arrived at Peter's house. "Paul requests your company," was all it said. "Please come at once."

"I think you should go," Peter advised, when Mark expressed his unwillingness.

"But such an invitation!" Mark objected. "Does he think that after years of ignoring me, of leaving my reputation in shreds, he can simply have me with a few words? Why, this is not even written by his own hand!" he snarled, waving the paper in the air. "Someone else wrote it for him!"

Peter nodded sympathetically. "Nevertheless, Mark, what harm can be done if you go? After all, he may be ill, or worse. . . ."

During the year since Paul's arrival, the entire church had awaited his trial. Rome's fickle judicial system had sped him here, but no date had been set for the hearing.

Meanwhile, Paul was a prisoner at large, meaning that he was provided lodging and could come and go at will, under surveillance of a round-the-clock guard.

He had become remarkably influential here as folk sought him out and sat at his feet to learn. Some of the people of Caesar's household as well as his own overseers had been converted. And he was fast becoming as strong a leader in Rome as Peter.

Nonetheless, any day might herald the hour of judgment. Once the court moved, it would move quickly.

"You think Caesar may have called for him?" Mark questioned.

Peter only shrugged, and Mark was left to wonder whether he could live with himself if he ignored the summons.

Most days the narrow street outside Paul's door would have been congested with pilgrims hoping to catch a glimpse of him or to hear him teach. Today, the weather being inclement, few would make the trip to the foot of Caesar's hill, the neighborhood bordering the site of the elevated palace.

The fact that Paul's house was near the home of Nero did not mean it was a gracious residence. Slums and squalor existed in many parts of the city regardless of proximity to the upper class.

Seeking the address that coincided with the one on the

letter, Mark at last located a mud-fronted flat with a low door. Chickens, avoiding the drip of the rain gutter, pecked in rivulets of sewage that ran past the place. Mark could not believe the great apostle had come to this, the one who had once been welcome before the Sanhedrin and whose name was known among princes. He knew the man had endured grave trials in his many missionary journeys, but this was an insult no one should bear.

The sentry posted at the door confirmed that, indeed, this was the prisoner's abode. Showing him the letter, Mark was allowed to enter and bowed his tall frame to fit the entry.

Inside the house there was a guard and another young man whom Mark did not know.

"You must be John Mark," the fellow said, rising from a small table. "The master is expecting you."

The guest could not tell if there was enthusiasm or only relief in the man's face.

"I am Epaphras," he introduced himself. "I drafted the note you received."

Mark, seeing several parchments full of characters on the little table, deduced that this was Paul's scribe. "You do all his writing for him?"

"Oh yes." Epaphras nodded. "We are working on letters to several churches. He keeps up a good correspondence."

The evangelist would have asked why he had been summoned, but the host was already leading him toward the only other room in the house.

A tattered curtain covered the doorway, and as Epaphras drew it back, Mark saw that a warm fire lit the dim interior.

"Your visitor is here," the scribe announced.

Near the fire a shadowy figure sat, his head bent against the cold, his fingers hastily scanning the text of yet another scroll.

"John Mark?" His voice was surprisingly cordial.

"It is I," the evangelist answered.

"John Mark . . . ," Paul repeated, "how good to see you."

The guest moved slowly forward as the apostle rose to embrace him.

Fumbling for a response, Mark said awkwardly, "It has been a long time."

"Too long!" Paul agreed.

"We have closely followed the news of your appeal to Caesar," Mark offered, pulling away from his open arms. "Have you heard anything?"

"Not yet," the apostle replied. "I pray that my time may be extended, though I would like a conclusion to the matter."

So, the urgency in Paul's summons had not been related to the coming trial. If the man of Tarsus simply wanted to clear all his accounts before nearing the end, he could have waited longer.

The apostle drew close, and as he looked into the visitor's face, Mark realized that his eyesight had worsened with the years.

"You have changed little," Paul noted. "Come near the fire so I can see you more clearly."

Mark pulled a stool beside the flames, and Paul sat down, studying him. "Epaphras has been a real boon," he said. "I cannot see well enough to write anymore. I only sign my name at the end of documents, with very large letters!" he explained, tracing the figures through the air. Paul was smiling, coming as close to humor as Mark had ever heard him.

The guest fidgeted, his cheeks reddening as he recalled how angry he had been at the impersonal note he received. "I see," he said, with a nod.

Now Paul laughed. "Is that a play on words?" he teased. " 'I see. . . .' "

Mark did not remember ever hearing Paul laugh, and he did not know how to respond.

Suddenly, however, the typical somberness returned, and Paul picked up the scroll he had been reading.

"This is very good," he said simply, pointing to the manuscript.

Mark, assuming it was one of Paul's epistles, glanced at the work, and his breath came sharply. It was a copy of his own Gospel!

He should not have been surprised that it had come Paul's way. Several copies were circulating throughout the church, having been carefully reproduced by many hands.

"You like it?" he asked.

"I would not change a word!"

Now Mark was even more astounded by the peculiar change in Paul's attitude. And the apostle, perhaps sensing this, leaned forward.

"I have heard of your work on Cyprus," he said. "I know your service to Barnabas and now to Peter has been impeccable . . . devoted. You are a mighty evangelist, I am told."

Mark, unmoving, absorbed the praise incredulously. He still did not trust Paul and wondered what might motivate such an admission.

"Son," Paul went on, "I am rarely a completely selfless man. I may preach crucifixion of the flesh and total submission to Jesus, but it is hard for me to do what I preach."

Mark listened thoughtfully, waiting for the interpretation.

"I would like to think my inviting you here was an act of pure obedience, a desire for healing between us. I do desire that, but I also desire peace of mind for myself," Paul confessed. "This I shall never have without your forgiveness."

The evangelist sat back. "You are asking my—"

"Forgiveness, Mark," Paul repeated. "I have been a fool."

Mark knew that whatever else might motivate the man of Tarsus, such words indicated true repentance. Paul, a paragon of intellectual attainment, could never be a "fool" otherwise.

"I . . . I don't know what to say," he stammered.

"Do not forgive me easily." Paul smiled. "I could not trust such forgiveness. For my sin against you is too great."

The apostle was standing now, pacing the floor as he had done in Perus's court the night he accosted Barnabas. His demeanor was softer though, and if he beat his fist against his thigh, it was in self-castigation.

"I am heralded as a powerful man," he said, "a focused man, a deliberate man—one of strength and conviction. But such traits are not always godly. In my single-mindedness, I often lack the more important graces—patience, tolerance . . . humility."

"It takes all kinds . . . ," Mark offered, a flush rising to his cheeks.

"No! No!" Paul corrected. And then more tenderly, "No . . . it takes the mind of Christ to be a good man. And this I do not always possess."

Mark could feel the pain in Paul's voice. There was a time when he would have reveled in such a sound. Now it only confounded him.

"A rider of causes, I am," Paul continued, his brow knit, "a driven man—both before and since I met the Lord. Jesus once said that he who hates his brother is the same as a murderer. . . . I was once a murderer. . . . Perhaps I still am."

Mark's heart ached. The torment in Paul's eyes was the same as that in Peter's the day he spoke of his betrayal of the Lord. And the fevered brow, the lined face, witnessed that Paul was not always able to keep the past buried. Sometimes it resurrected itself. The ghosts of those he had slain still cried out in the night, and he who preached justification by faith alone needed more than most to feel it.

Perhaps this, then, was the power behind his preaching—the need to assert that all of his sins were forgiven and to sense the cleansing that lifted him on eagle's wings. Who but a man like Paul, once driven by the Law to the point of killing, could find such release in redemption? And who would have taken up the pursuit of liberty as vehemently as he?

" 'Old things have passed away, and all things have become new,' " Mark reminded him. "Do you not preach so yourself?"

It seemed the apostle did not hear. "The chiefest of sinners," he replied, applying the term to himself that he often used in his sermons. "A loving man, a man like Barnabas, would have asked you why you left Pamphylia!" Paul suddenly cried. And turning to Mark he pleaded, "Why, my son, why did you go?"

Mark, his throat tight, could only sit silent. When the words came, they surprised him, for he had never so clearly framed the thoughts before.

"I suppose we are all driven," he admitted. "All my life I have lived beneath the shadow of mighty men—but they all, in one way or another, represented my father."

As Paul listened closely, Mark felt tension grip his neck.

"As much as any Jew was ever bound by the law of Moses, I was bound by the expectations of my father," he confessed. "After my conversion, I decided that if I could not be a great imperialist, I would be a great reformer, and I took it upon myself to convert my friends in Cyrene—with devastating results. I was not a great preacher, not a fit witness for the Lord. And being with you on Cyprus only drove home that fact."

The apostle looked at the floor, hearing the analysis sadly.

"It was cowardice that sent me flying home to Mama," Mark continued. "But a sense of worthlessness, most of all."

With a sigh he grew quiet, contemplating the embers in the smoldering pit. As they sent curls of hot ash up the chimney, his spirit lightened.

"So," he concluded, "it is I who must ask forgiveness of you."

"It is granted," Paul replied without hesitation. Then, placing a hand on Mark's knee, he spoke barely above a whisper, "And now will you forgive *me*? And will you consent to be my helper as well as Peter's? You would be useful to me in the ministry."

Mark's gaze met the former persecutor's just as it had the night of Stephen's martyrdom. The apostle's eyes, once sharp as shards of ice, were now mellow and compassionate.

"I may work beside you?" the younger marveled.

"My bodyguard . . . my emissary." Paul smiled. "And may I, like Peter, be your teacher?"

"You *may*," Mark said, laughing. "I need all the teachers I can get. And you shall also be my father, for one can never have too many good ones."

PART EIGHT

Rest

*Take my yoke upon you and learn
from me, for I am gentle and
humble in heart, and you will find
rest for your souls.*

MATTHEW 11:29

CHAPTER

1

The prow of the Roman cargo freighter slowly pushed toward Africa's north shore. The large square sail and topsail hung listlessly in the quiet sky, leaving the propelling of the 1200-ton vessel to banks of one hundred oars.

For the first time since his aborted attempt to be a witness in Cyrene, Mark was returning to his native land.

He had been away for thirty-four years, and he knew the time had come to reconcile himself with the past.

Like the shadow of a sundial, which must make a full circle to complete its purpose, Mark knew this was his destiny.

Two weeks ago he had boarded the enormous ship, buying the cheapest passage available and checking all his worldly goods with the cargomaster. As it had hauled up anchor leaving the Port of Rome, it had torn his heart from the mooring of great men. Not that they could have helped him now were he to stay. Peter and Paul were dead, martyred at the hands of Nero. They abided at Rome only in the spirits of the people.

For four years Mark had served Paul and had continued to serve Peter. The trial before Caesar, so long dreaded by the church, had ended in victory for the man of Tarsus. Nero's courts had waited a full twenty-four months before summoning the apostle, and when they did, they found no fault in him. No longer a prisoner, Paul had ventured forth on yet another missionary journey, calling Mark along the way. Paul sent him to Colossae and to Ephesus in Asia Minor, where Mark ministered at his side or with other mighty preachers—the convert Timothy and fellow laborers Tychicus and Aquila.

When he was not on some errand for Paul, Mark stayed with Peter and kept Rome as his home base. But with three years of journeys he had become a world traveler.

Though, since his conversion, he had been a right-hand man to several apostles, had served on half-a-dozen fields, and had written the first Gospel, he had never been as prominent as others. Except for his period of ministry on Cyprus following the death of Barnabas, he had always labored in the shadow of bigger names.

But he had come to be content with his lot.

The memory of his uncle's death was almost as fresh as the martyrdom of Peter and Paul. The three bereavements brought feelings of fear and loss that he must continually surrender to the Lord.

Though Paul had been released from the court of Caesar the first time, neither he nor the big fisherman had long survived Nero's maniacal behavior.

For nine months Peter had been held in the cruelest of Roman prisons, the Mamertine, bound to a post in the center of a subterranean cavern, unable to bend over, sit, or lie down. When he was taken out to be executed in the Roman circus, his death was cheered by ten thousand irate citizens and a demonically driven emperor. Since crucifixion was Peter's designated punishment, he requested that he be hung on the cross head down so as not to emulate his Lord.

Mark, able only to sit by helpless all those months while his teacher suffered, not allowed to visit his pitlike prison or speak to him before his death, had tried to forget the horror when he worked with Timothy in Ephesus.

But soon enough Paul sent for him again to minister to him "in his bonds." And Mark had stood by in great distress when Nero called for the end of this second apostle's life.

"Death by beheading," read the certificate that the executioners brought, notifying Paul of his imminent demise.

The church knew that Mark would probably be next on the most-wanted list and pleaded with him to return to Israel.

There was little in the Holy Land, however, for him to do. His mother had died peacefully months before, never having remarried and having served all these years at the House Ben Haman. Since John, the Beloved, maintained the church at Jerusalem, Mark could be more useful elsewhere.

The work established by Simon, the black evangelist, in Cyrene had not blossomed. In fact, no one had heard from Simon for a long time.

The church leaders decided someone must go and look into matters there. And Mark was the obvious choice.

So, with a heavy heart and a sense of anticipation, he left the seven-hilled city.

Two more weeks on the sea would bring him to the palm-lined shore where he, in dreams, had often sought sanctuary.

When Mark arrived, he had no difficulty in finding the house of Quintus, though the area bore little resemblance to the luxurious neighborhood in which he had been reared.

The native son made his way down the littered street that had once been pristine as a new coin, and he marveled at the number of children who played in its shadowy doorways. Their tattered clothes were out of place here, their dirty faces an oddity.

Was this not the neighborhood of the legati? Did not the wealthy inhabit these houses?

But there were no fine chariots beneath the porticoes, no linen curtains draped from the columns.

Mark smiled at the little ones who followed him down the avenue. There were many more black children among them than he had ever played with. Black folk lived across town when he was a boy. Only the sons of monied black merchants like Simon ever set foot in this part of the city.

"Where are you going?" they asked as he passed by.

His ears, unaccustomed to the hybrid Greek they spoke, detected a Libyan flavor to their speech.

"To the house of Quintus," he replied.

The children looked at one another blankly, and shrugging their shoulders, said, "We do not know this Quintus."

Quite a gathering milled about him now as he proceeded down the street.

"Of course . . . he has been dead for some time," Mark explained. "His house belongs to another now."

Mark could not remember the name of the man to whom he had sold the old residence years ago when he and his mother had parted with their properties.

I'm sure he was a Roman, he thought to himself. Catching the children's curious expressions, he repeated, "It belongs to a Roman, a member of the Senate. But then . . . that was also some time ago. It may have passed to his sons by now. Still . . . it would be a Roman house."

The intrigued escorts giggled among themselves, breaking into their native tongue.

"What is it?" Mark asked, stopping in his tracks.

"There are no Romans here!" one small boy declared, his eyes wide.

"Right!" the others chimed in. "No Romans anymore!"

Then whooping and jumping about, they mimicked war, making slashing gestures against one anothers' throats.

Mark, glancing down the avenue, walked faster now. Surely that was it, the great bronze door of the old estate. Green with corrosion, the heavy gate was barely recognizable, neglected of polish for a very long time.

When he drew near, he saw that it teetered on a loose hinge and that, clearly, no one lived here.

Pushing his way inside, his heart drumming, he stopped dead, his face etched with horror.

Leaves and rubbish blew across the courtyard once kept

spotless by his mother. Squirrels scurried up the stairs, and a rat burrowed in a corner.

Clutching his cloak to his chest, he headed for the back door, across the pavement where Mary Ben Haman had once piled crates to take on her trip to Palestine, and he entered the porch where he and Philea had once shared their love.

The columns leaned awkwardly, the crevices where the stones were joined worn by rainwater from an unkept roof.

Beyond he could see the stables of his father's horses, the place where the Roman had spent many a leisure hour.

This part of the estate was even more dilapidated. No horse stamped a greeting. No valet called a friendly word. The stalls were broken down where careless children had played. Ancient feed had rotted to dust in the bins.

Heavy-hearted, Mark turned about, facing the dozen questioning faces of his little companions.

"What happened here?" he whispered.

Just then a shabbily dressed woman entered the vacant court and fearfully called for her children. Three or four jumped at the sound of their names and went running to her.

"A strange man," they chattered. "He looks neither Roman nor Greek. . . ."

The mother, peering out at the stables, drew the children behind her skirts and called, "Who are you and what do you want?"

Mark came forward, and when she saw his strange Hebrew robes, his Star of David, silver-streaked beard, and Galilean sandals, she was even more suspicious.

"I am sorry to frighten you," he said, speaking Greek the best he could. "I once lived in this place."

The woman, her black face doubtful, shook her head.

"Leave my children alone," she warned, turning toward the door and the street.

"Madam," Mark hailed her. "Please . . . a few questions."

Stopping hesitantly, the woman listened as one unfamiliar name after another, one strange inquiry after another, was put to her.

"I have never heard of this Quintus," she said, "or the Pontis, or Brutus, or Mary Ben Haman. Simon, you say? A black man? I do not know him. Who did you say you are?"

Mark sighed. "Can you tell me what has happened to this neighborhood?" He did not mean to offend her, but surely she knew it had not always looked like this.

The woman, staring at the broken mosaic of the court floor, thought a long while.

"There once were Romans here," she agreed. "But my people drove them out."

Mark could not tell if she was proud of the fact or very weary.

"Libyans?" he guessed.

"Yes," she said vacantly.

"Simon was a Libyan," he prodded. "Have you not heard of him?"

"I told you no," she emphasized. "Do you think I know every black man in Africa?"

Mark kicked at a clump of dust and sighed again. "What became of the dispossessed?" he asked.

"Most returned to Rome. Some went to Alexandria."

Suddenly Mark knew. Alexandria! Simon had once owned property there. Perhaps . . .

"Thank you," he cried, bowing again and again, as he ran toward the door. Stopping at the exit, he glanced again at the old house as if to imprint it forever in his memory, and then bowing once more, called, "Many thanks!"

As the woman and children watched him rush back down the street, the little ones snickered.

They could not know how intimately the stranger was a part of this dilapidated estate. For his connection was of the heart, not of rubble and stone.

CHAPTER

2

Although Mark had grown up in North Africa, he had never been to Egypt or its capital, Alexandria. One of the three largest cities in the world, along with Antioch and Rome, Alexandria was queen of the southern Mediterranean, famed for its vast libraries and magnificent temples.

If Simon or anyone who knew him lived here, Mark knew not how to locate them.

For three days he wandered the streets, asking over and over for a Cyrenian merchant, a black Libyan, named Simon. But he was met with shrugs and wagging heads.

Little by little he pieced together the story of what had happened in Cyrene. The restive Libyans, troublemakers since the insurgence there years ago, had gradually run the Romans out of town. Though Cyrene was still within a Roman province, the emperor had difficulty keeping the peace. Governor after governor had served the place, only to meet with hostility, if not death, just as Quintus had done.

True, informants agreed, many ousted Roman families had come to Alexandria along with others of Cyrene who were loyal to them.

"Simon would be such," Mark insisted.

But no one knew the man.

A searing sun beat down on the Egyptian street. Mark limped through the bazaar, favoring a foot whose sandal-latchet had just broken. He wanted to spare his sole contact with the oven-hot cobblestones as he looked for the shoemakers' stalls.

Rabid hawkers all, they spied him and his loose thong before he spied them. Seeing an obvious need for their services, they began shouting at him, vying with one another like a flock of vultures after their prey.

Except for one fellow. This man was intent on a project, working an awl on the heel of a sandal. Dark of face, his turbaned head bent over his workbench, he aimed the tip of the tool at a nailhead. But despite his expertise the awl slipped, spiking his finger.

"Heis ho Theos!" he cried, sucking his throbbing finger.

Mark stared at him incredulously, knowing that such a sentiment was alien to this place. "Simon!" he called. "Is that you?"

It did not occur to him that Simon would be much older. He remembered him only as he had looked three decades ago.

The cobbler glanced up in surprise, and gazing at the greeter, seemed slowly to recognize him.

"John Mark?" he gasped. "Can it be?"

He stood and looked the newcomer up and down.

"Simon!" Mark exclaimed.

"No—no! Rufus . . . I am Rufus."

As the realization set in, that those of one's generation are older with passing time, Mark found himself laughing aloud.

"Rufus! So I have found you! Where is your father?"

The cobbler left his bench to embrace Mark. Weeping like brothers, they stood for a long while amid the gawking marketers.

"Come this way," Rufus said. "You must be very hot and tired."

Forgetting his broken shoe, Mark followed the son of Simon into a fan-cooled teahouse, and there the two talked of the past.

"My father died peacefully several years ago," Rufus reported. "Many of his friends in Cyrene became Christians under his influence, and he founded a church there."

"I knew that you had returned to Africa for that purpose," Mark said sadly. "I am sure he is sorely missed."

"Because of political turmoil in Cyrenaica, the church never did well," Rufus continued, his expression wistful. "Did he not write to you or your mother about that?"

Mark shook his head. "We never heard from him after he left Jerusalem."

Rufus thought a moment, and then his brow furrowed. "The Libyans . . . ," he whispered. "They came to suspect my father of complicity with Rome, something he managed to avoid when he actively stood by your father. Ironic that only when he returned, caring nothing for politics, did his brethren begin to doubt his loyalty. If they had known how he tried to help your family . . ." Rufus shrugged. "That is likely why his letters never reached you. They were intercepting the correspondence of those not in league with their cause."

Mark wondered now what the content of those letters would have been—what word of the Pontis and of . . . Philea. But clearing his mind of such questions, he focused on his old friend.

"Alexander and I moved to this place," Rufus went on. "The Libyans never let up, pursuing even my brother and me with interrogations and taunting. As you can imagine, the entire church in Cyrene was under suspicion."

"Is there a church in Alexandria?" Mark inquired, having noted the lucrative stalls of the idolmakers.

"Isis maintains her hold in this city," Rufus replied, referring to the Egyptian goddess who, like Aphrodite of Cyprus and Diana of Ephesus, held firm sway in the hearts of the citizens. "Nevertheless, yes—there is a church. A small one. Alexander and I are deacons," he said with a broad grin. "The pastorate rotates among the men of the congregation."

Then growing very somber, he looked Mark in the eye. "We have heard of your fame in Rome, in Asia, and in Cyprus. You are a mighty evangelist."

Mark shook his head. "And have you heard what happened to our brothers, Peter and Paul?"

Rufus sat back with a sigh. "Indeed. These are fearsome times for the Roman church."

"Nero will not stop with Rome," Mark predicted. "His vengeance is only beginning. The church sent me away to save my life." Then pausing sadly, he reflected, "I had hoped to serve in Cyrene, to spread the gospel among my people."

Rufus clapped his hands. "So you shall!" he suddenly exclaimed. "Many of your people, both Romans and Jews of Cyrene, fled to Alexandria when the insurrection prevailed. You are meant to serve here!"

Mark had been blind to the obvious. Indeed, Alexandria should be his mission field.

"We need you," Rufus asserted. "We have made do among ourselves, but Christians here have prayed many years for a leader!"

CHAPTER

3

That very evening Mark followed his friend beyond the streets of the capital, down the beach of the narrow isthmus that lay between the sea and Lake Mareotis.

The church, Rufus explained, met secretly, for fear of the Isis worshipers. It had found that its meetings could proceed peacefully in an old farm house in Baucalis, a cattle-grazing region along the shore.

Tonight a service had been scheduled, and Mark could see for himself what a loving fellowship existed here.

The warmly lit cottage was first visible as they came over a grassy bluff. The sun was setting over the blue Mediterranean waters, and soft singing drifted on the salty air from the house's open windows.

"Good," Rufus observed, "there's a good crowd tonight."

Mark stayed close to his friend as he knocked on the low door. The hush of those who live with fear descended over the meeting place. But at last the door opened a crack, and the guide whispered, "It is I, Rufus, and I have a friend with me."

Quickly the door was pulled back, and the two men were ushered in.

Rufus was right. A sizable group, probably fifty or so, crammed together in the tiny parlor of the seaside home.

White faces and black mingled in a salt and pepper patchwork, and everyone wondered about Rufus's companion.

"Alexander," Rufus announced, calling to his brother, the leader of tonight's meeting, "I would like to introduce a visitor."

Mark was again taken aback by the appearance of his other childhood friend. Never would he have recognized the gray-haired pastor as a son of Simon.

"Jonah Marcus Quintus," Rufus said with a smile, "the evangelist, Mark, of whom we have heard so much."

The hum of whispers passed through the room, and Mark nodded to his new companions congenially.

Rufus began to speak to the congregation, declaring that God had sent Mark to minister to them, and that because of his experience with the apostles, they would be greatly strengthened.

As he elaborated, a woman appeared in the doorway of the kitchen, bearing the evening's refreshments on a tray. She had heard the newcomer's name and stood still, trying to control her trembling hands.

Instantly Mark knew her. Rufus's ramblings faded away as this lady drew his full focus.

While others had aged, she was only more winsome, her golden hair entwined with silver, her figure willowy though more fully developed than when she was a girl.

"Philea?" his lips formed the silent question.

They could not for the moment get close because of the people between them. But he could not put her from his mind as he was asked to address the crowd.

What he said he would never recall. His first sermon in Alexandria would be a blank spot in his memory.

His heart pounding, he scanned the room as he greeted the church, wondering if Brutus, too, were here. Perhaps he had never converted, he reasoned, when he did not see the big Roman. Perhaps . . .

Quickly he suppressed the thought that Philea might be a widow, shamed by the hope widowhood could give him.

Somehow he managed to present himself well. Telling of his work with Peter and Paul was helpful. People always enjoyed legends.

But he was relieved to conclude his talk. As he took a seat at the edge of the room, the audience applauding, his attention once again was drawn to Philea.

Self-consciously she began to serve, passing the tray from hand to hand. When she reached Mark, she again trembled.

As she handed him a goblet of cider, their fingers touched.

"Good to see you," was all he could say.

Philea could only smile, her lips parting a little.

After the meeting, Mark and Philea determined to be alone. When most of the others had departed and the dishes had been cleared, Rufus said he would wait awhile as the couple walked down to the beach.

A cool sea breeze was blowing up the shore. Philea drew her pale blue shawl close to her body, and her escort fought the urge to wrap her in his arms.

"Tell me," he began, "have you been happy all these years?"

Philea laughed gently. "Not all. There have been hard times as well as good."

"I must know," he inquired, "how you became a Christian. You were so set against it, last we talked."

"I did not understand," she explained. "And you had changed so. I resented what had taken you from me."

Mark's pulse was spurred by the revelation, but he said nothing.

"Nonetheless, you planted a seed with your witness that others watered in time. First Simon—who never left Cyrene—then other teachers came to us. When I moved to Alexandria, Apollos taught here for a while."

Mark had heard much of that Alexandrian, a great Christian, a convert of Pentecost. But he was most thrilled with her endorsement of himself.

"Then you mean it was not in vain . . . my testimony to you?"

"Oh, indeed not!" she assured him. "Nothing you have ever done for me has been in vain."

Mark remembered the night he had rushed to her villa, saving her from the Libyans, and as he studied her moonlit face, he knew she was remembering it as well.

She is still beautiful! he thought, noting the gentle toll time had taken on her. Somehow the years had made her more desirable, the little lines about her eyes a tender tribute to wisdom and to smiles.

"And your mother?" he inquired, recalling Sergius's elderly widow.

"She died shortly after we were forced out of Cyrene. The move to Alexandria broke her heart. But," Philea said brightly, "she died a Christian."

Mark's throat was tight. Though he had seen the growth of the church from its infancy to a world power, it struck him most profoundly to realize its impact on the lives of old friends.

The son of Quintus paused, seeking courage for his most burning question.

"So, has Brutus been good to you?" he managed.

"Brutus?" she repeated, as though the name were foreign.

"Your husband. Has life with him been happy?"

Philea stared at the questioner mutely, then giggled in a girlish way. "Oh . . . you thought . . . Why no—I never married Brutus!"

"But . . . you were betrothed . . . ," Mark stammered.

"Do you think because you saw him at my house, I belonged to him? Why, Marcus, you often came there yourself, but *we* never married!"

"Who then is your husband?" he asked hesitantly.

Philea laughed. "I have no husband," she assured him, "and never did have."

The one great sorrow of Mark's life suddenly lifted. So

often had he pictured Philea in another man's arms that the image was almost unshakable.

"My lady!" he cried. "You mean all these years I . . . we . . ."

"It was not God's plan that I hinder you," she said. "We could not have been together."

Mark objected but knew she was right. Would he have taken her to Cyprus, to Rome, into the heat of spiritual and physical distress? And could he have been a fit husband years ago?

"But, I am here now," he said softly. "Have you thought often of me?"

Philea's eyes misted as she gazed up at him. "You must know I have, my lord," she whispered. "How could I ever forget you?"

Mark looked into her beloved face again, tilting it tenderly upward with his fingertips.

Taking her in his arms, he held her close as he had done countless times in his dreams.

And as though they had never left his father's veranda, they shared their second kiss.

CHAPTER
4

As Nero's persecution escalated into a horror across the sea, the entire church on three continents faced oppression.

Christians at Rome were burned at the stake, beheaded by the hundreds, crucified, imprisoned, torn apart by dogs, covered with wax and set afire as torches at Nero's garden parties, sawn asunder, mutilated, exiled.

As the mania spread across the map, few outside the church associated with believers, not even with those of their own families. Christians became scapegoats for every social evil and natural disaster, blamed for everything from war to poverty, storm, fire, and flood.

In Alexandria, Antioch, and every other major center, Christians were suspect if the economy faltered. Rumor ran wildly, claiming Christians were cannibals, baby killers, that they plotted against kings and governors, and stored arsenals of weapons in their homes.

Mark and Philea were married shortly after his arrival in Egypt. The old farmhouse, willed to the church by its owner, was their parsonage, and the seashore the site of their honeymoon. Fulfillment was theirs such as most take a lifetime to achieve, as their days were filled with service, side by side, and their nights with love.

But their bliss would be brief.

A few months into Mark's rapidly expanding ministry, stories began to circulate that the Christians planned to ransack the Temple of Isis, to tear through Alexandria smashing idols and leveling shrines.

Though church leaders did their best to quell the rumors, to convince the citizens that they did not operate that way, the stories grew more preposterous each day until the relatively sheltered congregation feared for their lives.

Tonight they met without the benefit of lantern or firelight in Mark's home. They did not sing, and they kept the windows closed. Only the soft lowing of cattle in the fields beyond mixed with the sound of surf and wind, as they earnestly prayed together.

Mark, head bowed, sat beside his bride, her hand held tightly in his as the group prayed together. He knew that despite fervent prayer, persecution was inevitable. He cried out to God to blot out the visions that raced through his head—of Barnabas's burned body, of Peter's vile imprisonment, and of Paul's grisly death.

It was the season of the annual Festival of Isis called Serapis, and for the church it was Easter Sunday. Mark recalled the day Jesus had stood before him in the upper room. And he knew there was eternal life.

Such was the hope of the church through all its trials, the hope of resurrection, borne out in the story of their Lord. Few were left on earth who had seen the risen Savior. Their testimony was priceless, the memory they shared like manna in the wilderness of persecution.

"Tell us again what you saw," someone asked. And for the hundredth time since his conversion, Mark recounted the story.

"He called to Thomas," he replied, "saying, 'Put forth your finger and feel the print of the nails in my hands. Thrust here your hand and feel the place of the spear in my side. And be not unbelieving, but believing.' "

"Was it then that you believed?" another asked.

"I believed what I understood, and I understood that Jesus was divine," Mark confessed. "It was not until the day of Pentecost, however, that I knew he was God himself, and that I owed him everything."

"You *have* given everything," they confirmed. "You have lost much."

Mark shook his head. "I am just a fellow who went to Jerusalem for a visit," he said with a smile, "and ended up traveling on the skirts of history. I have gained everything and lost nothing," he asserted. "I have yet to give all."

Perhaps Mark sensed that the wolves were near the door, that the shepherd would be taken and the sheep confounded.

Suddenly the low entryway was pounded open, and glaring torchlight flooded the dark house.

Philea cried out, clinging to Mark as he was seized, as a rough cord was placed about his neck, and he was dragged from her.

Screams of fear and shouts of defiance filled the cottage, but no one could save the evangelist. The flock was restrained at spearpoint, until Mark, thrust stomach down over the back of a waiting horse, his hands bound behind him, was hauled away.

"Do not try to follow," the guards warned, mounting their chargers and heading for Alexandria.

The congregation moved quickly to the windows for a last glimpse of their pastor, but he had already disappeared over the Baucalis hills.

EPILOGUE

There is neither Jew nor (Gentile), slave nor free, male nor female, for you are all one in Christ Jesus. Galatians 3:28

It was Easter Sunday, five years after Mark's death. The Alexandrian church, rather than dwindle, had only increased as a result of his martyrdom.

He was, in fact, a legend in North Africa, and his wife, Philea, a deaconess of honored reputation.

The church, which had spread throughout Egypt, would one day be known as the Coptic or Egyptian church and would always count Mark its father. Easter, the day of his martyrdom, would be for them a more sacred day than it was for many others.

Philea, who now served the church from a gracious manse in the city, made a pilgrimage to her husband's tomb each Lord's day. Sometimes she went alone, sometimes in company, but always she went. Mark, whose body had been ravaged, dragged through Alexandria's cobbled streets until he died, had been laid to rest in a cave overlooking the Baucalis valley.

Whenever Philea visited the grave site, she scanned the old farmstead below, her gaze lingering fondly over the beach where they had walked together.

Today she was especially thoughtful as she came up the rise where Mark had been taken from her. Rufus and Alexander walked quietly at her side, each one bearing a small parcel in his hands.

"I have never left anything at his tomb," she said, "not flowers, not gifts. Somehow I always felt it would detract."

The men listened respectfully.

"But I found these yesterday, when going through old boxes."

Taking the bundles from her friends, she tenderly opened them. In one was Mark's Roman cape, wine red, a little worn and mildewed, never donned since his conversion but cherished as he cherished Quintus. In the other the Star of David on a tarnished chain, the one he had worn when he returned to Villa Ponti.

"Each was a gift," she said, "one from his father and one from his mother. Do you not think they say it all?"

The two men nodded, and Philea, turning toward the tomb's rock door, knelt in reverence, draping the cape across its stone step and placing the pendant upon it.

As the narrow chain nestled into a crimson fold, she rose, smiling, and glanced heavenward.

When Philea and her friends had departed, a coral sun settled over the mountain, glinting off the Star of David like a benediction.

People Making A Difference

Family Bookshelf offers the finest in good wholesome Christian literature, written by best-selling authors. All books are recommended by an Advisory Board of distinguished writers and editors.

We are also a vital part of a compassionate outreach called **Bowery Mission Ministries**. Our evangelical mission is devoted to helping the destitute of the inner city.

Our ministries date back more than a century and began by aiding homeless men lost in alcoholism. Now we also offer hope and Gospel strength to homeless, inner-city women and children. Our goal, in fact, is to end homelessness by teaching these deprived people how to be independent with the Lord by their side.

Downtrodden, homeless men are fed and clothed and may enter a discipleship program of one-on-one professional counseling, nutrition therapy and Bible study. This same Christian care is provided at our women and children's shelter.

We also welcome nearly 1,000 underprivileged children each summer at our Mont Lawn Camp located in Pennsylvania's beautiful Poconos. Here, impoverished youngsters enjoy the serenity of nature and an opportunity to receive the teachings of Jesus Christ. We also provide year-round assistance through teen activities, tutoring in reading and writing, Bible study, family counseling, college scholarships and vocational training.

During the spring, fall and winter months, our children's camp becomes a lovely retreat for religious gatherings of up to 200. Excellent accommodations include heated cabins, chapel, country-style meals and recreational facilities. Write to Paradise Lake Retreat Center, Box 252, Bushkill, PA 18324 or call: (717) 588-6067.

Still another vital part of our ministry is **Christian Herald magazine**. Our dynamic, bimonthly publication focuses on the true personal stories of men and women who, as "doers of the Word," are making a difference in their lives and the lives of others.

Bowery Mission Ministries are supported by voluntary contributions of individuals and bequests. Contributions are tax deductible. Checks should be made payable to Bowery Mission.

 Fully accredited Member of the Evangelical Council for Financial Accountability

Every Monday morning, our ministries staff joins together in prayer. If you have a prayer request for yourself or a loved one, simply write to us.

 Administrative Office: 40 Overlook Drive, Chappaqua, New York 10514 Telephone: (914) 769-9000